MORIAH

Rob Simpson

DEDICATION

To my mother and father, who didn't really start off knowing what to do with a kid like me, but figured it out. I ended up being a lot more like the both of them than any of us expected.

To my kids, who are no longer kids, who show me every day that love can appear in so many different ways.

And to Barb, who brought Sunshine – and all that followed – into my life.

WEEK 1 – SATURDAY NIGHT
December 18, 1999

In the workshop, in the dark, humming a lullaby, his large, rough hands rubbing the bar of soap across the bloody shirt. The pure, white soap darkened as the coagulated blood came off both shirt and hands. Clots of blood, hair, and flesh kept clogging the drain of the industrial sink. The lullaby continued, the words indistinct in the humming, until he reached the refrain.

"I can tell the wind is risin', the leaves keep tremblin' on the tree, tremblin' on the tree," he sang softly, as if rocking a baby to sleep, then chuckled to himself and went back to his humming.

He was washing the last of the blood out of his shirt when the phone rang. It was an older style ring, from an honest to goodness metal bell, and was muffled by the walls separating the workshop from the rest of the house. A half-second later a closer and more modern ring came from another phone, this one a cordless phone on the workbench next to the sink. The man stopped humming, turned off the water, and reached for the towel hanging beside the sink. Another set of rings from the two phones, this time synchronized. The man dried his hands thoroughly as he walked away from the sink.

A third set of rings.

He stopped near the workbench, staring at the cordless phone.

Fourth set of rings.

He started humming again and picked up the phone,

held it up to read the caller ID window, which told him that "B. Marty" was calling.

On the fifth set of rings, the answering machine in the house picked up. He couldn't make out the words from where he stood, but since it was his own message, he knew what it said. As he opened the door and walked into the next room, his greeting ended, the beep sounded, and Bob Marty's shaky voice said, "Hello? This is Chief..." – *a sob* – "this is Bob. Jesus Christ, I'm not even sure who I dialed. Is this...?"

At that, he touched the "On" button of the phone and said, "Bob? What is it? What's wrong?" As if.

"It's..."

"What's the matter?" He smiled into the receiver as he continued to dry his hand on the towel. He interrupted because he wanted to draw this out as long as possible. The more times poor old Bob had to stop and start again the worse it would be. God, it must be killing him. Well, ok, maybe not actually killing him. He had to stifle a snicker at that.

"It's Cissy. Somebody's killed her."

"Oh my god! Where are you?" *Al Pacino, eat your heart out.*

"Down at the school. It's bad. It's real bad." He was going to interrupt again, but he knew that he wouldn't have been able to keep from laughing.

Gagging sounds came through the earpiece. "Oh my god. They cut her all up and..." The sobs and gags stopped Bob from saying any more. The man on the phone wondered how many times poor Bob had retched tonight at the sight of the pieces of his wife on the cold, hard ground. The smell, too. Don't forget the smell.

He let Bob sob a little longer, savoring what the sharp edge of the cold air must be doing to the cop's gasping lungs, then, as if to cut off any more gruesome details, he said, "I'll be right there. You keep yourself together until I get there." There was no response, except for the pathetic noises from the other end.

"Are you there? Did you hear me? I'll be right there."

"Yeah. Yeah," was all Bob could croak out.

He had to hurriedly thumb the "off" button on the phone so Bob wouldn't hear the laughter he couldn't hold back any longer.

***

The three of them, now standing and talking in a small group, had arrived at short intervals, each getting to the school as fast as he could after Bob's call. Tom had been first, both because he lived the closest and because he had been the first to get the call. Billy and Ed had arrived at the same time. They had started in different places, one in Mineville and the other in Witherbee, but had converged in Moriah Center, and driven the rest of the way one after the other, Billy in front.

They couldn't park anywhere near the school. Just about everybody in the North Country owned a police scanner, so the road in front of the school was lined with cars and trucks. The State Troopers had beaten everyone there, setting up what Ed called the "Law and Order fence line" as well as ringing the immediate area with men in Smoky the Bear hats.

They knew that at some point, the TV vans would also finally arrive. The first crews from Plattsburgh and Burlington would be here soon, and the crews from Albany would likely be an hour behind them, adding the finishing touch to the picture that everyone had come to expect from a crime scene. Now that the three men had found each other, their next task was to locate Bob Marty in the crowd of blue, nylon windbreakers.

Eventually Billy stopped looking and started walking. "Shit. This is stupid. He's probably over at the ambulance being treated for shock." As he began to work his way through the crowd, Ed directly behind him, Tom stayed behind them both a step or two, marveling at how Billy could turn even a scene like this one into an opportunity to connect with people.

As they walked through the crowd, it made room for them as people recognized them. *Well,* thought Tom, *mostly recognized Billy and Ed.* Billy seemed to say something to every person on either side of him. Of course, it was an illusion. If he had said just one word to every person who nodded or smiled or held out a hand for a shake they would have stopped moving, which they did not do.

Tom never lost his fascination with watching Billy "visit," as he called it. "I'm just visiting," he would say. And the people who were the grateful recipients of each visit smiled as if he had said to each and every one of them the single thing that they most needed to hear. A personalized message for each. Tom noticed that even the ones who were skipped smiled as if that had been exactly what they'd needed.

The three of them reached the ambulance, which was outside of the yellow boundary. Another ambulance was inside the boundary and they could now see the crime scene specialists photographing... Sweet Jesus... they were photographing widely scattered body parts and measuring the distances between them. The police had done a shit job of setting the boundary back far enough and the three men could see nearly everything. The tall wall of the building, behind the covered walkway that connected the High School wing to the Elementary School wing, illuminated now by spotlights put up by the State Police, was defiled by two painted messages.

The Brute has spoken

AW was right

They saw that the frosted ground behind the covered walkway was darker than the white around it. The three of them knew instantly, two from past experience and the other because he had put the darkness there, that if they were here in the bright sunshine instead of this nearly moonless night they would have seen that the stain was a bright scarlet.

If only, thought the one, the one who had brought this evil to the Town of Moriah. If only there had been more snow this year, this would have looked that much more shocking. He wished he's had the foresight to think of what it would look like in the daylight. If it had to happen this way, he should have figured out how they could find her tomorrow morning.

Realizing he was clenching and unclenching his fists, he forced himself to relax, counting slowly to five. At five, as almost always, he regained control of himself with the flip of a switch. Oh well, he thought. Wish in one hand and shit in the other...

Bob was indeed at the nearer ambulance. He was sitting on the crash cart in the back, a cup of coffee in one hand, eyes open but empty.

As they approached the back doors, a young EMT stepped between them and Bob. "I'll have to ask you guys to back up please."

Tom could see what was coming as Billy started to puff himself up and kept walking until he was close, uncomfortably close, to the EMT. The kid was huge, maybe three or four inches taller than Billy's 6'2" but was now looking smaller and smaller as his confusion over the approaching man's palpable confidence began to overcome his training and experience.

"Look dude," Billy began, in a friendly but superior tone, "you're not from around here, so you may not know who I am..."

Not tonight, Tom thought. *I just don't have it in me to listen to him tonight.* "Shut up. He's doing exactly what he's supposed to be doing." He turned from his startled companion to the EMT. "We're friends of Chief Marty. He called us and asked to come down here."

The EMTs relieved face showed them that he hadn't had a clue how he was going to handle the confrontation. "Oh, not a problem. The chief could probably use some friends right now." As the EMT looked closely at them for the first time, a flash of recognition jumped to his face. "Hey. You're Coach McNamara."

Ed nodded and started doing a mental calculation of fifteen years of faces. "You... are... got it – Pete Martinez. Defensive end. You played for Plattsburgh, wait... Peru. You played for Peru." The kid's face brightened for a second, but then he remembered the situation and stopped himself from smiling. He barely noticed the other two men step up into the back of ambulance.

Tom sat down next to their friend without saying anything. Billy squatted down in front of Bob so that he was looking straight into his eyes.

"Hey?" Billy said quietly. When there was no answer he said it more insistently. "Hey." The cop blinked his eyes rapidly then focused on the face inches from his own.

"Thanks for coming, guys." His head dropped back down and he stared at the floor.

Billy said, "Take a drink of your coffee." He drank automatically. "Now look at me." He repeated it when Bob didn't look up, then a third time, raising his voice uncomfortably loud for the confined ambulance.

Now what is he trying to prove?

Billy's eyes narrowed as he looked at his friend. "What does the back of your jacket say?"

Tom now knew what he was getting at. "Save it, man."

Billy repeated himself, louder than the first time. "I asked you a question. What does your jacket say on the back?"

"For chrissakes. Knock it off." Tom could feel the sides of his face start to redden as the anger rose in him. He pushed it back down.

Billy hissed the question again, almost gritting his teeth. "What does your..."

"Town of Moriah Police. It says, 'Police.'"

"You're goddam right it does. Your badge says that too, doesn't it? And your paycheck?"

Tom started to rise from the cart, started to move towards Billy, who noticed the movement and instinctively rose to meet it.

"Hey!" It was Ed, looking in from the back door of the ambulance. "You two fucking idiots want to play your little game, go do it on your own goddam time."

Bob put a hand on Tom's leg. "It's okay. He's right." Everyone watched Bob as he drank the rest of his coffee in one long swallow. "I've got work to do."

No one spoke as he left the ambulance and walked back towards the crime scene. Billy looked at Tom, pointed at him, and began to say something. Tom's eyes narrowed as he looked straight back, but suddenly, surprisingly, Billy's face softened and he quietly said, "No," and shook his head, then turned and stepped out of the ambulance, walking towards the crowd.

Ed watched him leave then turned back to Tom. "You know what? You two are more than welcome to your little pissing contests over that... woman." Ed almost spat the last word in disgust. "But goddammit. Tonight? Tonight?"

"What? That's not what that was." Tom shook his head, tired to fucking death that everything in his life lately, whether he was happy or angry, whether he was excited or exhausted, glum or cheery, everything was attributed to a woman he wasn't even with. "It's got nothing to do with Kate."

Ed motored on. "For two friends to let..."

Tom put his hand up. "We haven't been friends since high school. And in case you hadn't noticed, high school was a very long time ago."

Ed sputtered, trying to find the words he wanted, then said, "You know what? Fuck you. Fuck you, fuck Billy, and fuck that Yoko Ono bitch."

Tom shook his head as Ed stomped away. *Yoko Ono was*

the best thing that ever happened to the Beatles, he thought. *Poor girl's spent the last forty years taking the heat so John and Paul never had to.* Tom looked over to where Bob was talking with the forensics experts. He looked remarkably composed now. More composed, in fact, than they did as they were clearly uncomfortable talking to the husband of the victim. Tom was surprised the State Police were letting him onto the crime scene at all.

He had always suspected that Bob's semi-rube persona had as much to do with playing to other people's expectations as it did to any real sense of who he was. Then he smiled slightly as he thought how one of his teachers would have termed it "the essential Bobness of Bob," then quickly swallowed the smile, not wanting to be misunderstood at a scene like this.

Tom looked around and found Billy talking with the Town Superintendent, Town Council members, and the Port Henry Mayor. Port Henry's insistence on maintaining its quaint semi-autonomy from the rest of the Town of Moriah was one of the quirks about his odd little village that Tom loved the most.

He found himself, as usual, alone, even in what was probably the largest gathering of the town since the high school football season had ended. It was ok, though. *Each of us has his place.* Bob was forcing himself to stay sane by focusing on the details of his wife's gruesome murder. Those details, if he could hold onto them, would let him depersonalize the "victim," as he might already be referring to her. Ed was in a group of guys, all smoking cigarettes, probably talking about the Knicks or the Habs. And Billy was in his element, dominating the discussion among the town's elected officials, though, as far as Tom knew, he had never run for a single office in his life, not even Student Council. Billy hated that people in town called him the Mayor of Mineville. They never did it to his face, of course, and almost none of them said it with a smirk, but it annoyed him anyway. Tom found a small, secret joy in that fact.

He looked back the way they'd come and saw that his car was now completely blocked in by other cars and the growing crowd, so he turned and walked out of the parking lot towards the main road. He would walk back up tomorrow and pick up his car.

He knew he could save time by going through the woods and across the golf course. It was one of his normal nighttime walks, especially on nights like tonight when you could hear the ice on the trees creak under its own weight. Sometimes, on nights with more moonlight, the smallest breeze would scatter a faint dust of snowflakes that would continue to sparkle all the way to the ground. On a night like this, a night of death and grief, it would be a perfect walk, even if the only moonlight came from the sliver of a slight crescent peeking out now and then from behind the clouds. But another part of Tom's brain reminded him that, no matter how unlikely it was that the killer *walked* away from that crime scene, the State Troopers would be combing the grounds all around the school at first light. The last thing they, or he, needed was to have his boot prints to investigate.

As he walked under the streetlights on the way home, the small ice crystals in the air glittered under them. It helped.

Tom was sitting at his desk in the small office at the store. It was officially the Port Henry Market, but everybody in town still called it the Grand Union. He was going over his thoughts of the previous night and drinking his first Yoo-Hoo of the day. Outside, Molly and Lisa were working the registers, talking about the murder. Tom put down his bottle when he heard Billy's voice.

"Mornin' Molly," Billy drawled in his loudest mock-flirting voice. "Lisa, how you doin'?" Tom took another drink of Yoo-Hoo as he heard Billy ask where "the boss" was. What did he want now? Hadn't he gotten enough antagonism out of his system the night before?

Molly apparently pointed at the office, because he heard Billy grunt his acknowledgement. Tom was forever amazed that people didn't realize he could hear them from an office that was only twelve feet away and bounded by seven-foot-tall temporary walls and no ceiling.

"My offer still stands, by the way," Billy said. Tom could practically hear the man's smile.

Molly answered, "Oh dear lord. Which offer? I have a hard time keeping track of them all."

"Yeah, Billy. Which offer?" Tom's face hardened as he heard the voice of Mike Rush, Molly's husband. He must have come in closely behind Billy. Tom hoped against all reason that Mike wouldn't do one of the two things he was virtually guaranteed to do; either get pissed off or try to join in on the joke. *Both probably*. Tom felt his chest and shoulders tightening up.

Billy laughed. "The offer to leave your dumbass of a husband and come stay with me for a little while."

That was bad enough, but when he heard Mike laugh at the joke, he started to stand up. What was he going to do? He knew what he *wanted* to do and he also knew that telling himself to find his center wasn't going to do any damn good at all.

Tom could dislike Billy at times, certainly, but he despised Mike Rush. Molly would never testify to it, but he knew, the whole town knew, that Mike had hit Molly more than once. At the very least, he was a physical bully who pushed and grabbed his wife. Tom had put himself into a complex situation when he had bought the boarded-up, out of business supermarket. Every one of his employees were either people he had grown up with or their parents or their kids. It didn't help that Tom had had a crush on Molly practically his whole life, though he doubted she had any idea how crazy he had been about her in high school. He smiled at the thought that, in a graduating class of 80 people, there had been different circles for them to move in, but it was true.

Molly's voice calmed Tom and made him sit back down. "Sorry Billy. I already have people lined up to shoot me if I ever get *that* desperate."

All of them laughed, but Billy's laugh sounded the most genuine. *Not sounded,* Tom scolded himself for judging so easily. It was the most genuine.

Mike stopped laughing first though and said, "I got a better idea, Billy. How about we trade? Molly for Kate?" Everyone else immediately stopped laughing. What Mike didn't get, what Mike never got, was that people like Billy had the gift of using exactly the right voice for each situation. Mike would never have this gift. He hadn't been born with it and he wouldn't ever develop it. You could argue that it was a virtue that Mike didn't adapt his voice or mood or personality to different situations. And Tom tried his hardest to find any kind of virtue to ascribe to Mike – *also unfair, if less so* – but Mike's problem was that he believed that he was just as funny as Billy, all evidence to the contrary. The current group's re-action, for example.

Tom was sure that Billy wasn't conscious about his gift. Pressed to explain it, he was also sure Billy would say something along the lines that it just "feels right." He also knew that feeling, in a different context, but his had taken years of training. Billy's was natural.

The situation had clearly changed, but to Billy's credit he tried to keep the mood light by saying, "I'm pretty sure Kate would kill me in my sleep if I ever brought that plan to her."

This time, everyone laughed except Molly and Mike. In his mind's eye, Tom could see Mike staring at his wife, his face reddening, daring her to join in the laughter.

"Afraid you won't measure up?" Mike drew out the words "measure up" to make sure no one missed his meaning. As if his words were too subtle for the audience. And then he said, "Why don't you tell them, Molly, exactly what he would be measuring up to?"

That was clearly enough for Billy and his voice showed it. It was lower, more serious. Disappointed. "Jesus, Mike. What the fuck? One step too far, dude."

Mike obviously felt like an idiot and he became a dangerous man when his pride was challenged. The awareness that he was no longer in on the joke was thick in his voice.

"Oh, so it's funny for you but not for me?"

"Yeah, Mike. It ain't fair, but it just always works out that way."

"Fuck you. I'm tired of your shit."

"Aw. Now that's a real shame, Mike."

"Yeah, you might think so when…"

Tom stood up quickly and walked towards the door of his office, loudly calling, "Hey, Lisa. Did you invoice those…?" He stopped as he pretended to be surprised by the small group.

"A party! What a treat! Thank the gods we don't have a store to run," he said. "Good morning, Mike. Billy? I thought you did all your shopping for cheap, foreign-made stuff at Walmart."

Billy flipped the switch on his voice back to charming. "I figured I would come in here for your good, old fashioned, proud to be an American, ramen noodles. What aisle are they in?"

Tom smiled in spite of himself. "Nice. Aisle five, smart ass." Then he turned to the others. "Hey Mike, you're on shift later today, right?" The question could have sounded accusatory – everybody knew that Mike was a hard worker, but one with promptness issues – but Tom made his best effort to sound as friendly as possible.

Mike's eyes narrowed suspiciously. "Yeah. I'm on seven to three this week. But I'm going in late because they have our shit shut down 'till ten."

"Great. Hey, would you mind bringing a coupla boxes of Freihofer's cookies in for Pete Garza?" Pete Garza, like Mike, was an electrician at the paper mill in Ticonderoga. Ti Mill, to the locals. "Today's his birthday and it would save me a trip."

"You're giving him Freihofer's cookies for his birthday?"

Tom did his best to ignore the sneer in Mike's voice. "Every year. It started out as kind of a joke. My grandmother used to baby-sit for him when he was a kid and she gave him homemade cookies for his birthday every year. He and I were talking a few years ago and he told me how much he hated those cookies – he hadn't quit drinking yet, which is probably why he was so honest – and how much he'd wished she'd just given him the little Freihofer's chocolate chip cookies instead. So, I've been giving them to him every year since then."

The sneer had softened some, but it was still there. "You're shitting me. So, what the hell does he give you for your birthday?"

Tom laughed. "Well, he may have quit drinking, but he still has that small-scale production facility back in the woods behind his place. Anyway, do you mind?"

Mike shrugged. "What the fuck. Why not."

"Thanks a lot, man. Just grab a coupla boxes off the shelf over in the bakery section. In fact, grab some extra boxes for the rest of your crew. Just let Molly know how many for inventory." Tom turned back to Billy, who was standing there quietly, a slight smile wrinkling the corners of his eyes. Lisa had moved in on him and was leaning against him with an arm draped over one shoulder. That girl just loved trouble, Tom thought, not without affection.

"So, you need help with those noodles there, Bill?"

"Actually, do you have a few minutes to talk? About last night?"

Tom was surprised. "That sounds like a good idea. Let's go out back." He looked at Lisa and added, "And maybe everybody else could actually go back to selling groceries. You know, keeping us in business?"

Lisa stuck her tongue out at Tom as she disentangled herself from Billy and sashayed back to her register.

As they walked through the back warehouse section of the store, Tom said, "Pretty thoughtful of you, you know. Driving all the way down here this morning just so I could apologize."

"That's not what I'm here for. As far as I'm concerned, that's over. Two grumpy, tired dumbasses stumbling onto the set of a fucking horror movie, pissing at each other because they can't come up with a better reaction. And I apologized to the poor kid in the ambulance after you disappeared last night. No, I'm actually here to talk you into helping me with something." He pulled a pack of cigarettes out of his coat pocket as they walked out the back door and the cold air hit them. "You mind if I smoke?"

Tom laughed, reached into a small drop box attached to the wall near the door, and pulled out his own pack. "Not if you can keep a secret."

Billy laughed too. "I didn't even know you smoked. You know, cigarettes." They both lit up.

"I picked it up in the Army when I was learning to blow stuff up and kill people with my bare hands."

"Please," Billy laughed, "You were a clerk in the Army."

"Yeah, but I was a scary-ass clerk. Anyway, I quit a little while before you came back."

Billy shot him and the cigarette in his mouth a questioning glance. "Quit?"

"Ish," Tom said. "I still sneak one once in a while."

For the first time, Billy noticed the pack Tom was holding. "You smoke Lucky Strikes? Those things are terrible for you. Like, really, really bad."

"I like them."

"Bullshit, nobody likes them. Nobody even liked them back in the day. The only way they could get people to smoke them was to send them to the troops for free."

"The troops? Who the hell says 'the troops'?"

"Roger Mudd does, asshole. On the History Channel. You know, that pack looks just like a Bob Seger Album. You think Lucky Strike did that on purpose?"

"What? No, you idiot, the album cover looks like the cigarette pack."

"Whatever. Potato. Tomato."

Both men were surprised at how quickly they were falling back into their old give and take. As if their four years during high school some 15 years ago represented the real them, not the more recent adults.

Then, as if he had replayed a tape in his head, something clicked for Billy. "Wait a minute. Did you say you sneak a cigarette once in a while?"

"Yeah. One or two a day. At the most."

"Dude," Billy said, shaking his head, "You're like thirty-five years old and single. Who are you sneaking them from?"

Tom looked down sheepishly at his feet. "Well, when I hired Molly she said she wouldn't come to work here unless I quit smoking."

"She negotiated with you? A thirty-something with no work experience? You drive a hard bargain."

Tom stammered, "Well, I mean I know I was doing her a favor by hiring her. At least at the time, although she's turned out to be the best worker I have." Billy hadn't changed the look on his face. "It's just the way we joke, that's all."

"You two sound more like an old married couple than me and Kate do." They both grimaced as he said Kate's name. "Yeah, next topic."

"You know what. Let's stay on this one for a minute."

"Your call."

Tom thought for a second. "You and I weren't doing all that great as friends when you first came back."

Billy nodded. "True. Very true."

"Even before Kate came to town."

"We're both a lot different than we were in high school. And was I ever going through some shit at the time."

"We are different, that's true. But the two people we are now, whatever that means, added to the history we have… We should be able to be friends, don't you think?"

Billy shrugged. "I'm here, ain't I?"

"Yeah, I'm glad. So, you said you needed help with something?"

He hesitated. "I think we should solve Bob's murder case for him."

Tom stared at Bill, unblinking. "Really."

"I know how condescending it sounds, but listen, Bob is a great guy and he's a good cop for a town like this. But even if it hadn't been his wife, he'd be punching way above his weight class on this one."

"Actually, I'm not a hundred percent sure you do know how condescending that sounds."

Billy's look was a challenge aimed squarely at Tom. "Then maybe it is condescending. But is it untrue?"

Tom looked away from Billy and down at the ground for a second. "No. Not really."

"Good, then we should get together sometime today or tomorrow to get started."

"Slow your roll. I haven't agreed with the plan, just the underlying premise. And even that part makes me feel like an asshole." He took a drag from his cigarette. "You know what you need to do?"

Billy laughed. "Now who's being condescending? Tell me, what do I need to do?"

"Ok, well, what you might want to consider doing is inviting me up to your place for dinner tonight."

Billy stopped and said, very carefully, "I might, might I?"

Tom smiled easily. "What you and Kate, as a couple, ought to do is invite me up for dinner tonight. Then we can talk about this astonishingly stupid idea of yours."

"That sounds good. Real good." The surprise in his voice was clearly a pleased kind of surprise. He dropped his cigarette and crushed it out with the toe of his boot. "I'll have to double check with the boss to see if she..." Billy noticed the scowl on Tom's face. "What? Seriously? Because I called her 'the boss'?"

Tom didn't say anything. He just looked down at the ground. Billy unconsciously followed the line of Tom's vision and his eyes fell on the cigarette butt.

"What?"

Tom still didn't say anything, but moved the target of his eyes to the red, metal ash can to Billy's left.

Billy scowled back at Tom and said, "Oh, for fuck's sake," but nonetheless picked up the cigarette butt, flipped the lid of the ash can with his foot, and dropped the butt into the can.

Sounding completely sincere, Tom said, "Oh, thanks for taking care of that, Billy. I would have gotten it for you." Tom's neutral look even seemed genuine for a second before a wide grin spread across his face.

"Douchebag," Billy muttered.

They both turned as the door behind them opened and Lisa walked out.

"Well, ain't this adorable?" she said. "You two gonna make out now?"

Billy smiled and said to Tom, "All right, I'm out. I have to go look Ed up this morning."

"That should be fun. All right, give me a call later about tonight."

Billy walked around the building towards the parking lot, followed closely by Lisa.

Tom walked back into the store, feeling as good as he could remember feeling in a long time. He felt as much as if he had made a new friend as he did that he had regained an old one. A man can never have too many friends and to gain just one is significant.

"Hey there, twinkly." Molly's voice startled him out of his thoughts.

"Did you just call me a Twinkie?"

"Twinkly," she said, enunciating. "When you smile like that, your eyes get all twinkly."

"Thanks." He could feel his ears start to go red and he changed the subject to the first thing that popped into his head. "So, I'm reading this book…"

"What about?"

"That's interesting."

"How so?"

Tom stacked a couple of cases of canned vegetables, then sat on the stack. "Most people, when you mention a book, ask the title. Or the author. You asked what it's about."

Molly started to make her own pile of boxes across from him. "So. What is it about?"

"Well, the title is *The Secret History* and the author is Donna Tartt." He smiled.

Molly looked around and found a dust rag, which she picked up and threw at him. "You're twinkling again, asshole."

They both started to laugh, then stopped as they saw Lisa walking towards them. She shook her head. "Hitting on the hired help again, Boss?" She could have said that sentence in a way that made it lightly joking. Instead, the disdain in her voice was thick.

Before Tom could speak, Molly said, "Nothing wrong with a little innocent flirting, Lisa."

"Really? Even if you're married?"

Tom spoke up before the two could start fighting. Again. "We weren't flirting any more than there was any hitting on going on."

Lisa looked at him and said, "Whatever helps you sleep at night, Boss. And there's no difference between hitting on and flirting."

"Single malt scotch helps me sleep at night, Lisa. And there is a huge difference between flirting and hitting on. Flirting has no ulterior motive. It's just fun. Hitting on has a definite goal in mind. And we were doing neither."

Molly shrugged and headed back towards the front of the store. "Don't know about you, Tom, but I was flirting."

Tom couldn't fail to hear Lisa's muttered "Bitch."

***

Billy drove down the road towards the school – *has it always been called Viking Lane? How did I not notice that when I was actually going to school here?* – smiling at his conversation with Tom. They had been a year apart in high school and Tom had not shared Billy's athletic abilities or interests – mostly because of Tom's own interest in smoking pot and reading weird shit like James Joyce and Thomas Pynchon – but they had been inseparable nonetheless. Tom, Billy, Ed, and Bob. A stoner, two jocks, and the Student Council President. A less likely set of friends would be hard to imagine.

Billy and Bob had graduated first, in 1983. Bob had commuted to SUNY Plattsburgh to get his Criminal Justice degree, then after graduating slid easily into the only job he had ever wanted. Town cop. When the Chief of the three-man police force unexpectedly died 5 years later, there was no question about who his replacement would be.

Billy had gone to SUNY Potsdam on a basketball scholarship, never cracked the starting lineup, but was the first guy off the bench during his senior year and became a fan favorite, as much for his refusal to finish a game without fully expending his arsenal of fouls as for his rebounding and defense. He was, in the words of his coach, a power forward's brain trapped in a shooting guard's body. He left with a large number of unassociated credits and no real prospects until a Potsdam alum and former basketball player offered him a security job in California, a job that had led to a life he had never imagined himself capable of.

Ed was the same age as Billy and Bob, but had been held back a year in 8th grade, graduating with Tom in '84. Ed was one of the best athletes to ever come out of the North Country and the extra year of growth hadn't hurt any. He could have excelled at every sport the school offered, but football consumed him. A full scholarship at Syracuse followed, but a career that showed some professional potential at middle linebacker was ended when a neck injury almost paralyzed him in the first game of his senior year. Surprising everyone,

Ed stayed at Syracuse, finished a physical education degree, and passed up an offer to stay with the football team as a graduate assistant to return to Moriah Central as Phys Ed teacher and head football coach.

And Tom. In a town like Moriah, a natural introvert like Tom could easily have been an outcast, could easily have never found close friends, could have slipped away after graduation and never looked back. But he did find friends. These friends.

His mother, Janey, moved to Port Henry after he was born out of wedlock in New York City. The father's parents did not approve of her, her parents did not approve of the child, and Janey was happy to be rid of the lot of them. Nobody, not even Tom, ever knew what led Janey to choose Moriah as her landing place, and she raised him alone, making close friends in town but never dating.

In junior high – which at Moriah Central was really just a state of mind, with 7th and 8th grade thrown into the deep end of the pool by sharing the same wing of the building with 9th through 12th grades – Tom had meandered into a group that spent every free moment playing *Dungeons and Dragons* and smoking pot. Somehow though, for no apparent reason, Ed had adopted him in the first week of their freshman year and Tom had grown past D&D and his previous friends, though not the appreciation for weed. From that time, the two of them and Ed's friends Bob and Billy had formed the unlikeliest set of friends.

Then, the summer before Tom's senior year of high school, Janey left. She just left. One night in August when Tom was camping alone to enjoy the last week of summer vacation, she packed a backpack full of clothes, got in her car, and drove away from her home and her son and into local legend. Janey's and Tom's lives became the primary source of gossip in a town that had little other than gossip to fuel its creative juices. The FBI and State Police were both initially interested in the disappearance until Tom noticed her missing backpack and clothes. To satisfy the authorities, Bob had moved in until Tom turned 18. Then, the day after graduation, Tom had left for boot camp.

Nobody had ever expected to see him again, so when he had returned after more than a decade away, everyone had been surprised. The surprise had turned to shock when it became apparent that he had brought back some money with him. Everyone assumed, though no one asked, that Tom had finally been able to have Janey declared dead, and had collected on a life insurance policy. The shock turned to questions about his sanity when he used that money to buy and re-open the boarded-up shell that had been the Grand Union in Port Henry.

As Billy drove into the school parking lot, he saw that the part of the lot closest to the school and the walkway that ran the length of the front of the school were still marked off as a crime scene. There were still news crews broadcasting from the accessible part of the parking lot. The crime scene crew was also still there, looking for God knew what.

Ed's old Chevy pickup was parked right where he knew it would be, the first spot in the parking lot. The longest possible walk to his office. No matter where he went, Ed would park as far away as reasonable so he could get his walking in. It was one of the reasons that he was still the strongest man Billy knew.

Ed had insisted on separate offices for his two positions – "In case you ever need to fire me from one and not the other," he had told the school board – and had carved out a space in the school bus garage for his football office. The garage was situated just below the practice field and the huge back wall of his corner of the building was a perfect screen for watching game film.

Billy, who considered himself a much smarter man than Ed, took full advantage of the nearly empty lot where the bus drivers, had they been at work on this day, would have parked their cars and trucks and he parked as close to the garage as possible.

The lights were out, as Billy knew they would be, and

Ed was watching a game from god only knew when. As Billy opened the door, Ed kept his attention focused on the gargantuan projections of football players running a play on the back wall of the garage. He stopped and started the play over and over again, watching it forwards and backwards, until he noticed whatever nuance it was that he had been looking for. Then he wrote something down in his notebook and turned around to see who had disturbed his studies.

"Seems weird to be working on a day like this, doesn't it?" Ed said this flatly, with no sense of guilt behind it. Just a statement of fact. Ed preferred to deal in facts. Football was like that for him. No matter how hard it might be to find out what had gone wrong or right on any given play, he believed it was there if you just worked hard enough to find it. This dogged sense of black and white logic was probably also the reason Ed was a lifelong bachelor. That and lines like, "You can't treat women like normal people."

"Not weird at all, dude. Tom's at work. Bob's at work. Life has to go on."

"Are you at work?" Flat tone again.

Ed had a way of sounding accusatory even when he wasn't. Or was he? Billy never could tell.

"Maybe I am."

Ed put his notebook down and turned around in his chair to face Billy, resting his big forearms on the back of the chair.

"You apologize to Tom yet?"

Here I am, reaching out… "What makes you think I have anything to apologize for?"

"Honestly, I don't think you do. But I don't even have to ask if he graciously accepted."

Billy pulled a folding chair from a stack near the wall, opened it, and turned it around backwards so he could sit straddling the back of the chair. "Not taking your bait. He and I will figure our shit out."

Ed shrugged. The two men sat facing each other, both with their chairs turned backwards. The way they sat was probably the only thing they still had in common, Billy thought.

"So? What's the plan?" Ed asked.

"Still not biting. Got a beer?"

"On school property? In the middle of a crime scene?" Ed got up from his chair and walked to the refrigerator. On the wall next to the refrigerator, there was a poster of a circus strongman holding up a barbell with men sitting in wicker baskets on either end.

"Regular, light, or gay?"

"Make it gay."

"Whatever, city boy." Ed came back with a Genny Light for himself and a Sam Adams for Billy. "Seriously, what's your plan?"

"You know I love Bob." He waited for a response and when none came, he went on. "And I genuinely respect..."

"Whenever you 'genuinely' anything, it usually means you don't."

Billy went on, undeterred. This was nothing he didn't expect or even, a part of him was telling himself, didn't deserve. "I genuinely respect Bob's abilities as town cop. He is exactly what this town needs in a cop."

"But..." Ed had finished his beer already and was getting up to get a second, though Billy had yet to take a drink of his.

"But, come on. This is way over his head. For fuck's sake, even if it wasn't his own wife, this would be over his head. But Jesus Christ, it's Cissy. To have to see her like that..." Ed looked away and Billy saw his shoulders tighten. That image would haunt them all for a very long time.

"To have to see her like that, then try to investigate something like this..."

"So, what's your point? Or what's your plan?"

"I think we should do some digging around. I think we should try to help figure this out."

Ed nodded. "So, we go to Bob and say, 'Hey buddy. The gym coach and the mysteriously unemployed guy don't think you're up to the task, so we want to jump in and solve this murder for you.' That about cover it?"

Billy smiled, but it was not an amused smile. "Close. You forgot to include the wimpy store keeper."

"You're seriously going to... you already asked him, didn't you? And of course, he said he would. That is so fucked up. Even for you." Ed was shaking his head side to side and had tightened his mouth to a straight line. He talked as he walked to the refrigerator to get his third beer.

"You know why he'll help you? You do know, right? To get closer to that goddam woman." He said the word as if it had a palpable taste. A palpable, bitter taste.

"You do realize he sees her a couple times a week at their little high school drama club, right?"

"Like that's enough for him."

"You've always underestimated Tom. Always." Ed started to speak, but Billy waved him off. "No, I'm not judging. I've always done it too. When I talked to him this morning I think he was already thinking the same thing. Are you telling me you haven't thought about it at all?"

"That's exactly what I'm telling you. What makes you think you – or you, Tom, and me – would be any better at this than Bob? Not to mention the fact that the State Troopers are the actual ones investigating and shit, who knows, this is probably the kind of thing they call the FBI in on."

"No, the FBI won't be called in unless they think it's part of a serial."

Ed took a long drink of his beer and set the empty next to the two that were already on his desk. "Listen to you, Mr. Cable TV. I watch ER, but that doesn't make me a fucking doctor. Look, some crazy from out of town was driving through and saw Cissy and made his move. Simple as that. They're probably never going to come close to finding him."

"Seriously? That's your theory? Somebody just wandered into town, into *Moriah,* where everybody knows everybody, and without being noticed hacked the wife of a cop to pieces? Then just waltzed out of town again, completely unnoticed?"

"Calling it a theory makes it sound like I put any thought into it at all. And I haven't. But, sometimes shit just happens to people and nobody ever figures it out."

Billy remembered the years before he'd moved back to Mineville and said a silent prayer that Ed was right.

Ed went on in a quieter voice. "Here's my question back to you. Is it a good idea for anybody, especially you, to be digging around in Cissy's past? Her recent past?"

"It sure sounds like you have a specific point you're trying to make."

Ed smiled an odd, uncomfortable smile. "I'm just saying, of all people who should maybe want to let sleeping dogs lie. You know, especially if the dogs weren't sleeping when they were lying."

Billy's face hardened. "Not what I expected."

"Well, maybe you should have. Or at least thought it through a little deeper, before you pulled Tom in. What happens when they figure out you were sleeping with her? Think maybe that makes you a suspect, dumbass?"

"Don't assume that everybody's rumors are true."

"Oh for chrissakes. You're the biggest whore I've ever met. Well, second biggest, after Bob's dearly departed bitch of a wife. Everybody knows what was going on before Kate got here."

Neither spoke for a moment. They both sat there, looking at each other.

After a while, Billy stood up, holding his beer by the

neck. "Nice visiting with you. Have a good one."

Ed nodded. "Thanks for coming by, Bill. Don't be a stranger."

***

One for two, Billy thought as he drove. His next move was going to be an even bigger mistake. He knew that for certain, but he drove on.

Bob was sitting on the back bumper of his police Tahoe when Billy pulled into the parking lot of the beautiful, old building that served as the Town Hall. Bob didn't look up as Billy's new Ram pulled in next to the white SUV, but continued to blankly stare out over the lake. The view across the lake, of the Green Mountains in Vermont, was spectacular but Bob was clearly seeing none of it.

"Cissy would be smoking a cigarette if she was here right now," he said, slowly looking up. "Every so often, she would come down and find me sitting here in my thinking chair... that's what she called it – my thinking chair... she'd pull in, not say a word, and just sit down and smoke while I thought." Then he turned his head back to the lake.

Billy changed his mind about the cigarette he'd started to reach for and leaned against the truck, waiting for Bob to say more. He watched Bob. At work, in uniform, on a Sunday. The day after the worst day of his life. Minutes passed and he tried as hard as he could to keep still, to keep from clearing his throat or moving from one foot to the other.

More minutes passed before Bob looked up again, with a faint, exhausted smile. "You and her are so much alike. She couldn't sit still longer than that one cigarette before she had to get up and start talking." He stopped. "*Were* so much alike, I mean. What can I do for you, Bill?"

Billy put a hand on Bob's shoulder. "I just came down to check on you, dude. See if there was anything I could do or if you just needed somebody to talk to."

"Maybe solve my case for me?"

Billy felt his face start to go red and dropped his hand. "That fucking son of a bitch. I'm sure he made it sound completely different than how I meant it."

Bob shook his head as he stood up. "I'm guessing the 'he' is either Ed or Tom. Most likely Ed because you wouldn't have talked to Tom about this. But nobody needed to tell me what you're thinking. I'm a cop. This is what I do." His voice sounded as though it was taking his very last reserve of energy to speak. He turned and started to walk to his office, then stopped. "You've always been able to cut deeper than any other friend I've ever had."

Billy silently watched him walk, shoulders stooped and heavy, to the door, open it, and go in. Then he turned back to the lake, and took out a cigarette.

Yeah. A big mistake.

***

Molly closed her cell phone, turned off the light over her register, and walked to Tom's office, shaking her head. She knocked before going in – she was the only employee who did. Tom looked up from his desk and raised his eyebrows in query.

"I hate to ask..."

He shook his head in mock disgust. "Oh my god, woman. What now?"

"Don't. I feel awful for asking, but I need some time off."

His look instantly changed to one of concern. "What's wrong?"

"The twins are with Erin because, you know..." She hesitated. "You know, because of school being out." Erin was Molly's older sister.

"Uh huh."

"She just got called in to work a double because some-body got sick, so I have to go get the kids."

"Oh, no problem. Is Mike bringing them to you?" Every-one knew that one of Mike's hard and fast rules was that Molly couldn't have her own car. There were rules Molly dared to challenge or bend, but this was not one of them.

"No." Her disgust was real. "He says he can't get out of work. I'll have to call the county taxi and work until it gets here. It's going to take forever."

Tom frowned. "That's nuts. I'll give you a ride and if you want, you can bring them back here to hang out." She started to respond, to tell him no, but he stopped her. "Seriously. Be-sides, that way I can get a full day of work out of you." She argued some, but halfheartedly, and they were on their way soon after.

They were laughing on the way to Erin's house in Eliza-bethtown. Molly had just told a story of a night of drinking with girlfriends that had happened while Tom was away in the Army.

"Ok," she said. "Now it's your turn. Most embarrassing moment of your life."

"Seriously? Narrow it down to just one?"

"Come on. Don't be a pansy."

"Pansy? Hard core. You going to cut me, jefe, if I don't answer?"

Molly folded her arms and made a determined face.

"Fine. Actually, I have a great one. When I first got back to town, I was driving around. It was a weekend, I guess it was a Sunday, and there was this yard sale. There wasn't much stuff, just a couple of pieces of furniture and some other things in the yard next to the driveway. I was determined to be more open and friendly than when I was a kid, so I pulled in and started looking through the stuff they had, and out comes this woman, a little snippy, and asks me what the hell

I'm doing. So I said, 'I'm just looking at the things in your yard sale,' and she looks at me with the most pissed off face I've ever seen and says, 'We're not having a yard sale, asshole. That's just our fucking yard!'"

Molly put a hand over her mouth, only minimally stifling her laugh as Tom continued.

"When I finished apologizing, I got back in my car, kinda thinking my stay back in town was going to be a pretty short one, and I thought to myself, you know, that's the kind of social faux pas that Billy never, ever makes."

Through her laughter, Molly said, "Oh I think you're wrong. I can completely see Billy doing the exact same thing. The only difference is, he would have talked her into selling him some of their stuff."

They drove on without talking, each in their own thoughts. As they drove on the bridge that cut Lincoln Pond in half, she glanced over and saw Tom looking at her. "What?' she asked.

"What... What do you mean?" he said.

"You were looking at me. Like you were going to say something."

He paused. "Nope, just looking out your window. When I was a kid, I was fascinated by that little island. Then, just as soon as I was old enough, I swam out to it."

"Disappointed in the reality versus the dream?"

He smiled. "Actually, no. Not at all. I mean, it didn't have a secret tunnel system or a portal to another world like I'd imagined, but it was still awesome. Reality doesn't always disappoint."

"Huh," was all she said, and they didn't talk the rest of the drive.

Once the two kids were picked up and safely buckled in the back seat of Tom's car – and once Tom had explained to Molly that actually no, the 1964 Dodge Dart didn't come standard with 3-point belts, front or back, but that he had put them in himself and yes, they were quite safe – they drove back to the store. They hadn't gotten far when the questions began.

"Mr. Tom?" asked Molly's seven-year-old daughter.

"Yes."

"How come you call me Katherine and not Kate?"

Molly started to interject, but Tom gently touched her arm and mouthed "Is it ok?" Molly nodded and he said," Because, Katherine, you are a very dignified young lady and should be treated as such."

"Mr. Tom?"

"Yes, Katherine?"

"You talk funny."

"Do I?"

"Yup. I like it."

"I'm glad."

"Mommy. Sean is grabbing his place again."

Sean, outraged, shouted, "I am not!"

"Am so," Katherine replied with no small amount of smugness.

Molly turned around in her seat. "Baby, don't tattle. Sean, do you have to go to the bathroom?"

Her son nodded with a serious look on his face as he whispered, "I also have to use my sphincter."

Tom stifled a snort and said, "That sounds like my call to speed it up a bit."

They made it back to the store in time and Tom took Sean to the bathroom in the back while Molly brought Katherine to Tom's office to find something to occupy her lively mind.

When Sean was settled in, Tom asked Grace if she would mind taking a break to stand guard until Molly came back. He understood that there probably wasn't a mother within 100 miles of Moriah who was leaving her children unattended, regardless of the number of locked doors between them and the outside world.

"Grace is watching the bathroom," he said to Molly as he walked into the office. Molly nodded and smiled her thanks and he saw that she and her daughter were looking at a picture on the wall of his office. As he walked in, Katherine looked up at him and asked, "What is this beautiful building, Mr. Tom?"

"That is the Taj Mahal, my lady. What kind of building do you think it is?"

She started to answer, then stopped herself and narrowed her eyes at him. On such a small face, the look could have been comical, but Tom knew from the girl's genetic donors that she was likely going to be beautiful as an adult and so he felt sympathy instead, sympathy for the generation of men who would have to try to keep up with this one.

She said, cautiously, "I was going to say it looks like a castle. But if it really was a castle, you wouldn't have asked me what it is."

Terrifying.

Molly stifled a chuckle and stood up, saying, "That's my cue. I'm going to leave you two to your talk and go check on Sean." As she passed him, Tom turned his face away from Katherine and, with a look of mock terror mouthed, "Save me."

She did chuckle at that and continued out of the office. She started to walk to the back to where the bathrooms were, but stopped when she heard Tom say, softly, "It is a grave, sweetheart. A grave and a testament to love." Unable to leave, she listened.

"What is a testament?" Molly shook her head at her daughter's raw brainpower. It was unlikely that Katherine had ever heard the word before, but she pronounced it perfectly, if slowly, back to Tom.

"Tell you what. Let me tell you the story and then if you

still don't know, we'll look it up." What an amazing teacher he would have been.

"Ok."

"So, once, many, many years ago, there was a king named Shah Jahan who was the ruler of India. Because he was the king, many women loved him and wanted to be his wife and because he was the king, he was obliged to have more than one wife…"

"What's 'obliged' mean?"

"Um, it's kind of a combination of 'he had to' and 'he was supposed to'. The rules were different because it was so long ago. Does that make sense?"

"Yup."

"Ok, so, even though he had many wives, he was in love with only one woman. The only woman who owned his heart was Mumtaz Mahal. He loved her from the moment he met her and she loved him too. And not just because he was the king. But because the stars weren't aligned…"

"The stars weren't…?"

"Aligned. It's just a fancier way of saying that the timing wasn't right."

"That's what I thought."

Molly could hear Tom's smile as he continued. "So, because the stars weren't aligned, Shah Jahan and Mumtaz Mahal had to wait for five whole years before they could get married. But the Shah didn't mind waiting because he knew that he could only be happy with his one true love. They finally did get married and they were married for 19 years, the happiest 19 years anyone on Earth has ever had."

Tom paused, then went on. "But, she died. And when she did, Shah Jahan was so sad that he hid for a whole year. When he came back from hiding, his hair had turned white from sadness.

"But, Shah Jahan and Mumtaz Mahal also had a daughter and she was able to help him understand that his wife, her mother, wouldn't want him to only think about the sadness of her being gone, but would want him to remember the happiness of their time together. So he stopped being so sad and he decided to build a building to celebrate the beauty of Mumtaz Mahal and the love they had shared.

"The Shah himself designed the building and it took 22 years to build, but when it was done it was the most beautiful building in the world. And it still is. Do you know why?"

"Why?" she asked.

Why? Molly echoed, silently.

"Because of love," Tom said, quietly. "Only with love can you build real beauty."

"And there's nothing better than love, is there, Mr. Tom?"

"No, sweetie. There is nothing better than love."

Tom sighed, then said, "Ok, young lady. I'm going to check on your Mom and your brother. Do you want me to find you a book to read?"

"No thank you. I'm going to keep looking at the picture."

"Good call. I'll have Miss Grace keep an eye on you until your Mom gets back."

Molly rushed ahead so that he wouldn't catch her, all the while unable to shake out of her mind the look on Tom's face that first day he had come back from talking to Kate. Tom's feelings for Kate were every word of that story.

"Mr. Tom. I'm still not sure what a testament is."

Lost in his jumble of feelings, he had completely forgotten the question. He looked again at this amazing little human, looking back at him with huge blue eyes of trust, and felt the pain of knowing that with every year that went by, he was less and less likely to ever have what Mike and other fathers have.

"Well, let's look at it again. I said that the Taj Mahal was a testament to his love. So, the building is a thing and love is a thing…"

Her eyes exploded with understanding. "Oh! Like the Christmas card I made for Mom in school! That's a testament to love too!"

Holy shit. "That is exactly right, Katherine. Exactly right." He leaned over and kissed her on top of the head and walked out of the office.

Tom stopped just outside the office on his way, unable to figure out for the life of him where that had come from. He was standing in the same spot Molly had stood as he was telling the story to her daughter.

He knew the story, had read many different versions of it over the years and had even been told the story by a tour guide at the Taj Mahal. But he didn't think he had ever told the story himself, and if he had, it certainly hadn't been told like that.

The thing that most rattled him was the face in his mind's eye every time he had said the name of the Shah's great love, the face of the woman he could never be with.

Ok. Get a grip, he told himself as he walked back, asking Grace to check in on Katherine as they passed. He saw Molly sitting outside the bathroom as he approached and he needed to find a new topic, something to clear his mind. "So, about that book from earlier…"

"I'm not going to ask again what it's about, so you'll just have to jump right into it." She was as happy as he was for the diversion.

"It's about this small circle of… friends, I guess is the closest word for what they are. Anyway, they are all clustered around a single professor. It is interesting, partly because it shows how unnatural a group can become when they separate themselves from the rest of the world. From the rest of life."

"Like you and your D&D buddies in junior high?"

He hesitated for a second, then answered, "Yeah, probably. But maybe no more than the football team in high school."

"I'll have to think about that. I may end up agreeing with you. Anyway, did you like Donna Tartt's book?"

He smiled at his own shock. "I'm surprised you know it."

"Because?"

"No shirtless pirate on the cover."

"Nice. Very nice. That wasn't sexist at all. But I have to admit that I saw you reading it and grabbed a copy from the library. It wasn't anywhere near as pretentious as I expected." She turned to the bathroom door and called through it, "Sean, honey? You almost done in there?"

A small voice answered, "I still have one more chunk to push out, Mom."

They each held a hand against their mouths and Molly replied, "Ok, hon." She turned back to Tom and invited him to continue.

"Anyway, this professor, their alleged center..."

"Alleged?"

"Yeah, alleged. I'll get back to that. He has a toast that he always does..."

"Live forever," she quoted.

He was past being surprised. "Ok. And I thought, as I was reading it, that is the stupidest toast I have ever heard."

"You don't go to many weddings, do you?"

"One point to you. It is stupid, though. If you want to live forever that desire will have you always looking to the future. What's next? What comes later? No thought for what is *now*. What comes *now*? 'Live *now*' is what it should be."

"Love the one you're with and all that?'

"That's not even close to what I'm saying."

Neither of them had heard Lisa walking towards them,

but they both now heard her deep sigh. "How did you two retards not end up going out in high school?"

Molly smiled and said, "Maybe because Tom never asked me." She stopped smiling when she saw his face redden. "Tom? What...?" Then she interrupted herself, looking horrified. "Oh my god. You asked me to prom. I completely forgot."

She was interrupted by the flushing toilet and the door to the bathroom opening. When she turned back, she saw Tom, walking away from them.

Lisa smirked at her, clearly pleased, and said, "Nice work, Mrs. Rush," and followed Tom to the front of the store.

***

Billy came home from his morning visits and found Kate on the back porch, sitting at his roll top desk, grading papers. "Good morning, Sunshine," he said, kissing her on the back of the neck.

"Good morning." He could tell from her voice that she was a little brittle this morning. *Tread lightly, brother.* "You got up early."

"Yeah, I went to talk to..."

"You don't have to justify yourself. I was just making conversation."

"Sweetie," he said slowly and softly, carefully measuring his tone, "I'm not justifying myself. I'm just talking about what I've been doing so far today. I went to see Bob to see how he's holding up."

Her tension dissipated. "I'm sorry, baby. I'm just on edge this morning. I didn't sleep at all last night."

"I completely get it. How long is school going to be out? Do they know yet?"

"No idea. They can't decide whether to wait until the State Troopers release the... I guess it's a crime scene, isn't it?"

"That's what it is, all right." *Thought I'd had my fill of them.* "So, what options are they considering?

"They are all over the place. There's talk of starting Christmas a few days early, or trying to get back into the school building through the back doors, or even trying to find alternate places to meet for classes."

"Well, that last plan certainly sounds ridiculous." He looked around absentmindedly and added, "So, what would you do?"

"There are only two days before vacation starts, so the only thing that makes sense is starting vacation early. We should put lesson packs together to send home with all the kids. Ungraded, obviously, but to give them something to work on if this goes on any length of time.

"I would also have the teachers start making daily calls to all their students. And then, when vacation is over, we can have the kids dropped off at the far end of the High School side if the front still isn't... cleaned." She looked at him and her face lit up when she saw him nodding in agreement. "And obviously, find every competent mental health professional in New York and Vermont willing to work pro bono with the kids."

He'd bet good money she'd already made up lesson packs and started those phone calls. "You should be the school Superintendent, babe." He kissed her on top of the head. "I'm going to make some coffee. You want some?"

She got up to walk to the kitchen with him. "Absolutely."

He stopped and turned back to her, taking her into his arms, and kissed her. She melted against him, pulled her mouth from his, and began to kiss his neck. "Mmm..." she murmured. She conquered their height difference by hopping up and wrapping her legs around his waist. "Or we could skip the coffee altogether."

"You are definitely the brains of this operation," he said as he strode up the stairs with her still clinging to him.

***

A red, digital number two was blinking on the answering machine when Tom walked into his house. Not an unusual thing for Tom, with calls from suppliers, employees, and happy and unhappy customers. There was no real separation between the store and Tom's life. The store, at least to the outside world, was Tom's life. *I've let myself think that way too.*

The first voice was Billy's. He sounded glum. "Dude, I'm sorry but we're going to have to rain check on dinner tonight. One of those days."

The second was Kate's. She sounded serious. All business. "Tom, I called the kids and we're going to have drama practice tonight as originally planned. We'll be rehearsing in the movie theater. The back door will be unlocked, so you can let yourself in. See you there."

Well, I'm no genius, but those two calls may be related.

***

The shower water was running so hot that every mirror and window in the bathroom and bedroom was completely steamed over. All around the bathroom – on the floor, on the toilet seat and toilet back, on the sink and on the counter – were porn magazines, each folded open. He stood in the shower as the near-scalding water ran down his back, slowly swaying, eyes darting around the room from page to page, masturbating. A constantly mumbled stream of filth poured from his mouth – anger, hatred, jealousy, rage.

It hadn't started for him with hurting things. It often

does, but not always. He was a watcher. An observer.

He was cataloguer of plant and animal, of sky and clouds, earth and water. Of the natural and unnatural. He loved fire, which he knew was a cliché. But he loved to create fire and to watch the dance that science told him was from air currents and the varied temperatures as different parts of his fuel burned at but that his heart, his soul, told him came from the mysteries of the universe. Mysteries that science could label and count, but couldn't really understand. Not the way he understood.

The universe spoke to him. It sang to him. Which was why his love of fire never grew into pyromania. There was no tension or stress that needed release through fire and there was no need for a huge fire if the song was already in a small one. The movement, the dance – it was as much there on the head of a match or a fireplace log as it would have been in a gratuitous forest fire. In fact, the intimacy of the match or the fireplace would have been lost in a huge conflagration. It would be like listening to a Bach solo cello suite too loud. The music would still be there, but you wouldn't be able to hear it.

The ability to control some things — the size of your fire, where a tree would fall if you notched it just right, a perfectly controlled rifle shot — and the inability to have any sway whatsoever over others — the rising of the sun, the freezing of the lake in winter, and love, either your own or theirs — made life beautiful and infuriating all at the same time. Sometimes, the beauty of it, the beauty of the control or the beauty of the chaos, overwhelmed him with joy. Other times the weakness of people who allowed him to control them or the stupidity of people who couldn't see what he had to offer brought forth a nearly limitless fury. The dark, angry, dangerous times had always been with him and from an early age he had learned to recognize their approach, to either swallow the bile or hide himself away so nobody else could see the monster he hid.

But not always. There are times when Chaconne just wouldn't cut it, times when you need Toccata and Fugue turned up to 11. He had only allowed himself to completely surrender to the fury five times in his 34 years, and only twice in town. The first time, both the first time in his life and the first time in town, had been when he was in high school and the ramifications of that act had forever changed the lives of everyone close to him. No one else knew, even to this day, that it had happened at all. It was that act, and the ease with which he had covered it, that showed him what kind of man he was. That he could bring himself back under control in the most pressure-filled and dangerous situations. This knowledge served him well, he thought, in his chosen life. It also, and he smiled with great joy as he thought this, had led to a partnership purer and more holy than he had thought possible.

***

Tom got out of his shower and cleaned up the things he'd left lying around the bathroom. He'd walked home from the store a little earlier than usual to get ready for dinner, but after listening to the message from Billy, he'd decided that instead of going back to the store, he would take the opportunity to do what he called Screw You Vikram Yoga out on his deck overlooking the frozen expanse of the lake. Maybe the sting of the cold would overwhelm some of the sting of Molly's forgetting that he'd asked her to the prom.

Doing yoga in such cold weather forced Tom to focus on breathing and on the precision of movements and holds. Any loss of focus could lead to speeded up, imprecise movements, which in this cold would likely mean injury. That threat of injury — the momentary threat of pain and the much worse threat of lasting limits on speed and strength — brought a sort of focus that Tom thought was probably as close to Nirvana as he would ever see in this life.

He had discovered this in an entirely different environment, when he had found that extreme pain could bring the same focus. The first beatings of his captivity had startled him, because no matter the mental or physical training, no man is prepared for the power and variety of pain that can be inflicted by one both gifted and experienced in its application. There are places on the human body, large and small, that are doorways for pain. They act as if designed specifically as pain's entry point into the body.

What no man can know, until placed in such a position, is how his training will imprint itself upon his character and manifest itself in reactions to torture. Most men never have cause to find this out, and society is the better for it. Tom did not feel that his reactions to torture, later declared heroic in still-classified reports, were to his credit. He was born with his character, he had unintentionally honed his ability to focus inward through his high school years of drug use and reading, and he had received the best training in the world.

Faced with previously unimaginable pain, Tom's focus sharpened to as fine a point as the soul can create. Until the rescue three days after his capture, when left alone by his captors for random amounts of time and at random intervals, Tom would meditate and would draw himself up into what few poses he assumed would do no further harm to his body, not ignoring the pain, but using it to tighten that focus even further.

So, sitting in the snow for an hour doing yoga, after that, was no real biggie.

Tom had smiled while toweling off after the yoga. He was looking forward to his shower. No matter how tight the focus, a hot shower after snow yoga was damned sweet. He'd need one before drama practice tonight anyway. A shower and an ice cream sandwich. Bliss.

***

Billy got out of the shower and cleaned up the things

he'd left lying around the bathroom. Some were his and some were hers. Billy had learned from far too many instances of letting women move in with him that no matter how well put together a woman appeared on the outside, the true character of her soul was shown in how much crap she kept in the bathroom. And whether or not she ever put it away.

Ok, that wasn't all that true or all that fair, he admitted. They were all fucking slobs when it came to the bathroom.

How goddam hard is it... He stopped, opened the bathroom door, and listened. His old reflexes and senses had faded some as he'd let himself get soft the past few years, but he could still, when necessary, focus out all the white noise and listen for — hear — his target. She hadn't come back.

The sex had been fantastic. It nearly always was. Kate might look and sound uptight — ok, she was pretty uptight — but in the bedroom (and plenty of other places around the house and even around town) she let herself go with an abandon that had initially startled him and continued to thrill the hell out of him. And mid-morning sex was his favorite. Neither of them was sleepy or grumpy or anything but alert and engaged. Which also usually meant that neither fell asleep afterwards, so there was the chance of multiple laps around her amazing body.

Not today.

As they'd lay there in the afterglow, she'd looked at him with those eyes of promise. "What's on tap for the rest of the day, sexy?"

He kissed her, hard. "What do you think?"

"Mmm... Sounds like a plan. As soon as you think you're able again."

"It won't be long, baby."

"God, I hope that's not the case."

"Funny girl."

She sat up a little, resting on one elbow. She was stunning. "No seriously, what are you going to do today?"

Oh, well. There goes the rest of the sex. He wouldn't lie to her. Lying made a man less of a man, he believed. Billy was many things, but a coward wasn't one of them.

"I have to head down to Glens Falls today to check on some investment properties." Ok, that actually was a lie. But one made for reasons other than cowardice. A lie that he knew would make things worse, not better. But there were also things in his life, past and present, that Billy wouldn't share. Couldn't share. Not yet.

She had the power — who was he kidding; they all had the power — to not only change her mood in an instant but to change the mood of an entire room. Now, for example.

"Seriously? Seriously!" She pulled the sheet over herself as she sat the rest of the way up. "Of all fucking days?"

She didn't swear often, never in public, so when she did she sounded a little silly. Awkward. Like a child trying those words out for the first time, still looking over her shoulder for adult correction and disappointment. She would do things in bed outlawed in some states, but Billy couldn't help but smile the smallest of smiles whenever she swore. His barely discernable smile right then pretty much clinched the end of sex for the day.

Talking, too. If there was one thing Billy appreciated about her anger, it was that it was like a man's. She got out of bed, silently, pulled on the nearest clothes, and stormed down the stairs and out the door.

As she left, he thought about Cissy, lying in that very bed before Kate had arrived in town. Kate, who got his heart where the others, Cissy included, had only gotten his body. The others had all quickly recognized that they had lost Billy to this girl. All of the others had, except Cissy.

How fucking low do you have to be to sleep with your friend's wife? The first time was his first week back in town. He wasn't even formally back in town yet. He'd come back and arranged some purchases with a realtor in Plattsburgh, so he was staying in Plattsburgh waiting for the title company to finish the papers and schedule closing.

Billy had also been stalling. He'd had to leave California with no warning, no preparations, and he'd stayed on the road for months, waiting to see if the people who wanted him dead believed he was. That world knew him by a different name – by multiple different names – and had no reason to connect him to the name Billy Ridge or to a tiny hamlet in the Adirondacks, but he had to be certain.

And eventually he was. He used fresh identities that he'd saved for an emergency to plumb the communications channels of his past life and every bit of news about him told of the story of him going down in a gun battle with the cops. The fire that swept the fields he'd been hired to protect was so fierce, there was never any certainty of how many bodies had been burned. And there was no way for his former employers to know that, when faced with the most important moment of his life, Billy had turned on them and on his own security team and tried to save the two cops who stumbled on them. That failure, the failure to save the two cops, would never leave him, but the identity known as Billy Ridge had been nowhere near California during the shootout and he had a carefully cultivated backstory and records to prove it. But he had been stalling, staying in Plattsburgh, because he knew that once he moved back to Mineville he was done moving. He was going home, to make his stand if necessary.

It had seemed like he was the only one over 25 that night in the Monopole Bar and was going to leave after his first beer when she sat down beside him. She wasn't really pretty any more, not like in high school, and her body wasn't what it had been, but she still knew how to carry herself in a way that made men look twice.

"Billy Ridge. Holy shit," she'd said, nodding.

"Cissy Marty. Holy shit, yourself."

She wagged a finger at him. "Just Cissy. The Marty part is on hiatus."

He could have asked more questions. Fuck, he could have asked any questions. Later, he'd used every rationalization that was available to him, but when it came right down to it, he took her back to his hotel room without a second thought as to what hiatus meant.

Three straight nights they'd ended up in his room. The next day, his childhood home and hometown were finally back to being his and he'd moved to Mineville. Moved back to town and found out that Bob wasn't aware his marriage was on hiatus.

And to his shame, a shame nearly as deep as that which he felt for the death of the two cops, the first night he spent in what had been his parents' bedroom, it had happened one more time. The next morning, he felt as dirty as a man could feel and she had turned his revulsion into anger.

For the next... well, for the rest of her life, she hadn't forgiven Billy for rejecting her. Cissy was used to being the one who ended things, goddamn it. Even after Kate had arrived, after Billy was entirely off the market for the first time in his life, she had made innuendoes that led some circles in the town to believe that she and Billy still had occasional hookups.

The shame that he couldn't escape kept him from doing anything about it, from coming to his own defense. Because he knew that even though she was lying about the details, she wasn't lying about the essential truth – he had knowingly slept with the wife of his friend.

He looked at the bed again, at the impression on Kate's pillow and shook his head. Nothing is ever really clean, he thought. Nothing.

"I guess I'd better call Tom and cancel dinner," he said to the room as he headed to the shower.

***

Ed got out of the shower and cleaned up the things he'd left lying around the bathroom. The workout at the school weight room had been a good one and Ed's muscles still twitched. His legs would be dead tomorrow. It was a great feeling.

He lived alone, rarely had visitors, but he kept his trailer as organized as one would expect a man who used an amplified metronome in football practice. There was no woman's touch in this bathroom, or anywhere else in the house, but it in no way resembled a frat house.

Much like his office in the school bus garage at Moriah Central, Ed's house was entirely functional. In fact, both were focused on the same function – football coach. The lone personal extravagance in Ed's life was the screening room he had created by combining the dining and living rooms of his trailer to give his 35mm projector enough length to cover the entire end wall with scenes of his frequent triumphs and occasional defeats. The canisters of film were organized chronologically in pristine rows on shelves along the walls of the room and the only furniture in the room was a leather recliner, sat alongside the table that held the projector. This room encapsulated Ed's entire adult life, up to a moment the previous year that had changed so much about him. The moment Ed had found a lover.

Or, rather, the moment a lover had found Ed. They never met at his place. Her place either. Ed's sense of organization, of order and of structure, made him easy to manipulate when she'd told him they had to keep their relationship a secret. And when the relationship had first begun, he'd been happy to keep the secret because he still held out hope that he could seduce Cissy. He never understood why she'd resisted him when she had resisted so few other men. Which had made his rejection of her on the previous night, the night of her death, all the sweeter.

***

Bob got out of the shower and cleaned up the things he'd left lying around the bathroom. This was his third shower in the 12 hours since first seeing his wife's remains. He had taken one when he'd gotten home the night before. The second had been on waking after four hours of sleep. And he had left work soon after Billy's visit to come home, punch the living shit out of the heavy bag hanging in his garage, and shower again.

He didn't know what else to do. The images of the night wouldn't leave him. And the sense that he didn't know how to go forward. Billy had no idea how right he was, how unequipped Bob knew that he was for what had happened the previous night. The entire night, before and after his wife's butchering.

"You're already a suspect," he could almost hear her mock. He knew that, of course. Partly because that's the path of least resistance in a homicide investigation and partly because her affairs and the open knowledge of them throughout the county gave him motive. Like he'd told Billy, he was a cop. This is what he did. Bob found thieves. He stopped drunks from beating on their wives, when the wives would let him. He stopped the kids from racing on Decker's Flats and the Rock Cuts because for too goddam many of them it was their last ride. And he knew a lie when he saw one. Cissy had been a good liar when they'd first dated, a mediocre one during their early years together, and an indifferent one as time went along.

Bob, better than many men, knew his strengths and he knew his weaknesses. Quick, intuitive leaps were not his strength. A slow, methodical, tenacious approach to a problem, an entirely internal analytic process — that was his strength.

The fight with Cissy the previous night had played to her strengths, not his. He hadn't been ready for it, hadn't been expecting it. She'd gone out and had announced she'd be staying out most of the night. On nights like that, she wouldn't come home at all. She would half pretend to have stayed with friends in Plattsburgh and he would half pretend to believe her.

So, he'd had a couple of quick beers watching the news, which had slowed his reflexes by the time she got home. Reflexes that middle age was already slowing. Reflexes that shouldn't be slowed around such an abusive woman. He would probably never know why she'd come home so early. Or so angry. He didn't even remember her excuse for swinging at him. She had a variety of favorites she drew from. But this was the first time she had ever gotten through his reflexive defenses, the first time she had ever actually hit him in the face. The first time she had ever drawn blood. And the first time he had ever raised a hand to her in return.

That was it then. He had hit his own wife. He had hit a woman, something a true man could never do. You couldn't come back from that, Bob believed. You either hit women or you didn't. And if you were the kind of man who would hit a woman, people would be justified in wondering if you would stop there?

***

One of the first things Billy had done when he'd returned to town had been to buy out Richie's Newsstand and return the building back to what had been its original purpose, a movie theater.

Tom had walked the third of a mile from his house to the theater, then let himself in the back door. It was unlocked, just as Kate had said it would be. He sat in the theater, alone, in the dark.

There hadn't been a theater program when Tom had gone to Moriah Central School. No drama club, no school plays, no community theater. Tom had never even been to a live show before he joined the military. On his first tour, a two-year hitch in Germany, when he had still actually been a clerk — a Financial Management Technician in Army-speak — he had discovered the vibrant network of Army community theaters across Europe. Several of the other soldiers in his unit were active in the theater and the first week he was in country, they dragged him along to the show they were performing. The show was *Who's Afraid of Virginia Woolf*. He had never seen the movie, so the story was fresh for him, the revelations were stunning. The slow, downward spiral of the night's festivities chez George and Martha carried him deeper and deeper into the utterly convincing world these amateurs had created in spare time carved out on nights and weekends. By the end of the night, he was hooked.

When the next production started, he was building sets. The next show, he built sets and ran the lights during the performances. He stage-managed the following show and he directed the one after that. Work, the gym, and the theater. The setting of his life was limited to only those three places, but his world was still immeasurably larger than it had been just the year before in Moriah.

Just as quickly as it started, it was over. One conversation at the gym led to an informal interview, which led to a briefing, which led to a series of mental and physical tests that sometimes even now he couldn't believe he'd passed. With no plan or forethought and almost without realizing it, one day he'd looked up and found himself in North Carolina, in a training program that would distill him down to the very best parts of himself.

For the next decade, his only connection to the theater was in the audience of an occasional show, maybe two or three a year. Then, just as surprisingly and with just as little planning, he was out of the Army and back home and there was still no drama club, no school plays, no community theater.

So Tom had started a community theater company. He hadn't been sure what to expect, but there had been immediate and fervent interest and within a few months, he had built a theater company of twenty people. They were an inverted bell curve in age. His youngest member was 13 and his oldest was 79 and the ages were clustered in high school and retirement. They had put on two shows in their brief existence — a night of one acts and *The Odd Couple*, both great successes.

Less than a month after *The Odd Couple*, Kate was hired by Moriah Central as the new 11th Grade English teacher and one of her first acts had been to get permission to add an elective Drama class that could be repeated all of a student's four years of high school.

Tom had known his high schoolers wouldn't have the time to belong to both groups, but to ask them to choose between the two would be unfair. He hadn't been able to decide how to solve the problem, but Kate had solved it for him.

He had been sitting in his office on a Friday evening, plotting — there was no other word for it — how next to irritate Billy. It was beyond childish, he knew, but he figured that if he could better the town and annoy Billy with the same actions... Nah, it was still childish. He knew that besting his last effort was going to be nearly impossible, though it had also caused him the most guilt. Billy, in an increasingly rare moment of reaching out, had stopped by the store and had mentioned to Tom his plan to buy the Lee House, a stately, red brick hotel built in the latter half of the 19th century that was now subsidized housing for seniors.

Billy had planned on maintaining the facade of the building, but would convert it to a mixed-use property with both retail and residential units. It was one of the most important steps in his plan to revitalize Port Henry as a tourist destination, the first step in beginning to rebuild the whole town. He had a plan to initially compete with towns like Vergennes in Vermont and Westport, the next town up the lake on the New York side, then eventually take up a spot somewhere between those towns and others like Shelburne, Vermont, that were the gold standards of quaint tourism.

Tom's problem with the plan was that Billy intended

on emptying out the current residents. Billy planned to find new places for them to live, but Tom believed that most of them wouldn't have wanted to find new places.

He'd had barely had enough time to get his offer, through proxies, in ahead of Billy's. Nobody in town had the remotest idea how much money Tom had brought back with him. Any guesses would have likely been off by a full comma. He surmised, through his research and friends in the financial world, that they also would have been just as low in estimating Billy's wealth. The odds that two friends from a town the size of Moriah would both come back secretly wealthy... It was a wildly unlikely scenario, which Tom understood made it easier for both men to conceal their wealth.

Through different proxies, he had already started the renovation of the building and had been able to plan the changes without moving out a single resident. As soon as a floor was finished, all the residents from the next un-renovated floor would move into the new apartments, right up to the top of the building. The restaurant he planned for the ground floor would give the residents a healthy place to eat, with their meals subsidized by grants from the county Housing Assistance Program. Once the building was complete, he would transfer ownership of it to The Friends of Lee House, a non-profit foundation he'd gotten an out-of-town friend to establish. Tom's name wouldn't be on any of the documents related to the building or services. And if the grants that the Foundation had already identified ever proved too little to keep it running, he'd just anonymously donate the difference.

The renovations to the exterior of the building were right in line with Billy's aesthetic view of what the main street of Port Henry should look like. Which helped soften his guilt. Soften it enough, in fact, that he was looking for his next project.

"I'm looking for Tom Hudson," she had said.

He sat up at the unrecognized voice, a voice with just the slightest hint of Alabama. No, Georgia. One or the other, anyway.

Lisa answered in her charmingly prickly way. "Why?"

Matching prickle for prickle, the voice responded. "Excuse me?" Oh, this could be good.

Molly ruined the potential fun. "He's in that office over there. You must be Miss Colburn."

Colburn? Not...

"Oh please, call me Kate." Oh, my... But he knew there was no way the look matched the voice. Life just didn't work like that.

"Kate, it is. I'm Molly and you've already been charmed by Lisa. Just knock on that door right there."

Tom leaned forward to stand up from his chair, then leaned back, then repeated both moves again. Stand up and be ready to open the door? No, then they'd know he was listening. Crap, but if he was behind the desk, it would take too long to get to the door. He could stay seated and just tell her to come in. No, that would be rude.

Her knock stopped his twitching. "Uh, just a sec." He was able to get up from the desk without banging his knee, which was good. He opened the door and found himself looking over the top of a very blonde head. When he looked down, he was looking into the bluest eyes he had ever seen and he was lost.

"Are you Tom Hudson?"

He nodded, stupidly. "Mm hmm." Even knowing he was nodding stupidly, he had no ability to stop. She was short, no more than 5'2" and simply the most beautiful woman he had ever seen up close.

And she was that. Close. So close, she had to look straight up to look at him. She didn't waver though. Didn't flinch under his dumfounded look. She just looked right back at him until he finally came back to himself. The entire moment had only been a few seconds, but it seemed to him to have lasted much longer than that.

He shook his head and quickly regained himself. "I'm sorry," he said laughing a small laugh at his own expense. "Long day." She probably wouldn't buy it, but it was worth a shot. He stepped slightly back, putting a small amount of distance between them, as he extended his hand.

"Tom Hudson. Nice to meet you, Miss...?"

She took his hand and shook it firmly. "Kate. Kate Colburn. You have a problem, Mr. Tom Hudson. And I am here to solve it for you."

"Are you indeed? And I assume you are the Kate Colburn of the 11th Grade English Colburns? The infamous, actor-stealing Colburns?"

She laughed and he was lost again, though he was better able to hide it this time. "Why yes, sir. I do believe my reputation precedes me."

"Not all of it, Miss Colburn. Not all of it. I'm tempted to sign up for 11th Grade English again. I'm sure there's something I missed." *Where the hell did that come from?*

She smiled, playfully. "Clearly, I was not appropriately warned about you, Mr. Hudson."

"As I alluded to a moment ago, Miss Colburn, likewise. Please, come in." He looked back into the tiny, crowded office. "On second thought, why don't we sit outside? There's a very nice bench under the trees out front."

He motioned for her to lead and followed her past the cash registers towards the door. As he passed Molly and Lisa, he gave them a goofy, conspiratorial grin. The kind of grin teenage boys share when the gorgeous girl isn't looking. Neither Molly nor Lisa were teenage boys, though, and both glared back at him, then snapped their heads away from him in synchronization. *Oops.*

Mr. Hudson and Ms. Colburn sat on the bench at the corner of the store parking lot, under trees that shaded them from the setting sun.

"So, Miss Problem Solver, what next?"

"I have asked the superintendent to create a new volunteer position as School Theatre Director and she has agreed, with one stipulation." She paused, offering him a chance to interject, but Tom just raised an eyebrow and waited.

"Her one stipulation was that you had to be the one to fill the position."

"And is this acceptable to you?" he asked, eyebrow still raised.

"Why Mr. Hudson, it's the very reason I wanted the position created. Instead of competing for a limited talent base, we can work together."

"I accept, Miss Colburn, but I will tell you that you can expect to be surprised at how unlimited the talent base is in this little burgh."

"Touché."

He looked over at her, at the contrast of her hands placed so primly on her lap with the adorable, little girl way her ankles were crossed. One foot was unconsciously bouncing against the other. Should he? He hoped he wasn't staring, but her next words told him he was.

"Were you just checking yourself out in my sunglasses, Mr. Hudson?"

He chuckled and shook his head, but didn't answer. They both sat quietly, looking at each other without looking directly at each other.

"I'd like..." He started.

"Yes?" she said, looking over at him, chin raised.

"I'd like, if you think it appropriate between colleagues, to take you to dinner sometime, Miss Colburn." He laughed. "I'd also like to stop calling you Miss Colburn."

"Tom and Kate, it is. That part I can answer you now. As for the first part, I will think about it and I promise to get back to you. Soon."

But she never did. She was introduced to someone new the next day and in what Tom assumed was the universe's unwitting payback for his real estate shenanigans, Billy swept her off her feet at their first meeting.

Tom's memories were interrupted by the lights coming on with a loud *thunk*. He stretched and looked back over his shoulder, turning to the back of the theater to see Kate walking in. She looked tired.

"Kate. Over here." He waved an arm over his head. She didn't answer, just walked over to where he sat, dropped her bag onto the floor, and held out her arms.

"Aw, don't say a word, kiddo." Tom rose from his chair and encircled Kate in his arms.

The second time Tom had even seen Kate he had been at Moriah Central, meeting the school superintendent to formalize the volunteer arrangement. It was two days after their first meeting and Tom had already heard the news about Kate and Billy. He had seen her in the hall, had said, "Hi," and had known instantly he was too late. That all of her thoughts and feelings were now with someone else. She had been wary, unsure of how he'd react, but Tom had immediately fallen easily into a role to which he had become accustomed in high school and had perfected in the years since, the platonic best friend. It sucked. It sucked hard. But he was good at it.

In the two years since, their relationship had settled into a comfortable pattern. Tom didn't go to Billy's and Kate's house, Kate didn't go to his, but they saw each other at rehearsals a few times a week and had lunch at the Miss Port Henry Diner every Wednesday. The relationship had led to a nickname for Tom, one he'd first heard when Mike had come into the store one Saturday morning, hung over and angry, and had called him "GBF." Neither Tom nor anyone else had ever seen Molly raise her voice to her husband before, and for her to do it when he was hung over, a time he was always at his most dangerous, meant that the nickname must be an ugly one. Molly refused to tell him what it meant, but Lisa was only too happy to let him know that a significant percentage of the town now called him Gay Best Friend.

That sucked too, but here he was nonetheless, consoling this beautiful woman who would, as soon as rehearsal was over, go back to the bed of his friend. The friend who, he assumed, was the reason she needed consoling in the first place.

The smell of her, the texture of her hair against his cheek, was not what he needed right now. He set his chin on top of her head and asked, "You all right?"

"I will be. I always am." She knew he wanted to disengage from the hug, and she knew it was at least partly because he didn't want his body to react to her and embarrass them both, but she still needed a little bit more.

Tom's arms were her safe place. Whenever she and Billy fought, she invariably went to Tom, who never failed to pick her back up. She also didn't mind how solid he felt when she hugged him. Emotionally, yes, but physically solid too. She couldn't help but imagine what was under the long sleeved, button-down shirts he always wore.

It probably wasn't fair to him. No, it definitely wasn't fair to him and she recognized that, but she still came to him every time.

Without lifting her head from his shoulder, she said into his neck, "Choices. Do you ever want to go back and change yours? There are certainly times when I do."

He hugged her tightly one more time — though she could tell he was holding back from his full strength and she wondered how much more there was — then he stepped back. She did too, pretending with him that it was mutual.

"A favorite philosopher of mine said, 'When we know better, we do better.' Maybe it's true, maybe it's not."

"Maya Angelou. Very nice."

"I thought it was Oprah."

She laughed and punched him on the arm. "You suck."

They were both surprised to see the entire cast and

crew that night, just twenty-four hours after the discovery of Cissy's body. Some of the parents even sat in the audience and watched the rehearsal. There were a lot of people in town, it seemed, who needed to feel normal.

Bob had started to stand up from his desk as he saw Billy walking towards the door of his office. He took a slow, deep breath. Just to fill his lungs and clear his head. Billy saw him blink two times, slowly. He looked exhausted.

Which makes me that much more of a dick, thought Billy, realizing that the previous night he'd probably gotten double the sleep Bob had. *This office is all he has right now.*

"I suck, huh?" he asked as he held out the large coffee he'd brought as a peace offering.

A weary smile softened the cop's edges. He said "Oh, every once in a while," as he took the offered drink.

"I'm sorry about yesterday. I just hate to feel like… like there's nothing I can do to help."

Bob shrugged. "You're the only one honest enough to admit what everybody else is thinking."

"Still. A friend isn't supposed to be just like everybody else."

"Hold that thought while I go take a leak." He held up the coffee and said, "I've had a few of these already today and it's not gonna wait any more." Bob set the coffee down and left his office with that tight emergency walk that every man knows.

Billy reached to move Bob's coffee off the papers on the desk so they wouldn't get stained and saw the note. The corner, at least, sticking out of a manila folder. It was easy to spot — the paper was heavy stock and a soft blue and the page was encased in a plastic sleeve. The printing on it was an elaborate, Victorian font.

Billy looked back over his shoulder and silently cursed Kate for putting phrases like "elaborate, Victorian font" in his head. There was no movement in the hall outside of the room. He pulled a pencil out of the old Lake Champlain Bridge coffee cup Bob used as a pen and pencil holder and, looking back over his shoulder again, reached down and used the eraser end to pull the sheet out of the folder, then tried to scan it quickly.

Dammit. The bullshit, steampunk font was impossible to read upside down. He stopped for a moment and, hearing no steps in the hall, moved to the other side of the desk. For a large man, tall and broad and still muscular despite his quieter life, Billy moved with the assurance of an athlete. He read quickly.

> *She wore pants.*
>
> *She worked.*
>
> *She had no children.*
>
> *She broke the compact and*
>
> *met the brute.*

"What the fuck?" Billy said aloud. Then he heard steps in the hall. Using the pencil, he slid the note back into the envelope. Halfway in, the folded edge where the envelope was sealed stuck against the papers on the desk and instead of sliding the note into the folder he was sliding the entire stack of papers across the desk. He pushed the mass back into the center of the table, set the pencil back into the cup, and by the time Bob re-entered the room, was sitting in Bob's chair with his feet up on the desk.

"This is all there is to being a cop? Seems easy."

Bob shook his head and smiled unguardedly for the first time is three days. "Get your feet off my desk, punk."

Billy got up from the desk, quickly scanning the papers. The note was clearly in a different position, both on the desk and in the folder, than it had been when he'd arrived. With all that was going on — and the mess of papers on the desk on a good day — Bob likely wouldn't notice. "So, like I was saying before your potty emergency, I get all stupid when I feel like there's nothing I can do to help my friends.

"There's plenty you can do to help, just not my job. And hell, I don't know, at some point, if we don't get lucky and this... thing... takes a while, I probably will be looking for somebody to bounce ideas off. I'm sure you had some encounters with the cops when you were working out in California."

Billy suppressed his fight or flight reaction and tried to look quizzical instead of suspicious. He was able to produce a smile and a laugh as he asked, "Encounters?"

Bob didn't seem to notice the reaction. "Sure. Didn't you do private security out there?"

"Ahhh... Actually, we did help LAPD on some break-ins at one of our warehouses. But I'm not going to pretend that was anything like your training."

Bob's watch started beeping and he looked at it quickly, then silenced the alarm. "Crap, I have a conference call with the Staties in like 10 minutes and I'm not ready for it."

"No problem, dude. So, we're good, right?

"Yeah. We're good."

"Ok. That's why I came down. The last thing you need right now is your friends not having your back." He unconsciously stole one last glance at the desk, then turned and left.

Bob watched him leave, pondering the odd reaction to his comment about Billy's security work in California. *As tired as I am, I'm probably seeing things that aren't there.*

He sat down at his desk.

No.

The note from the killer, the note that had been left under his windshield wiper sometime the night before, the note that was the subject of his upcoming conference call with the State Police and FBI, had been moved.

***

The call went badly. The FBI was furious Bob hadn't turned over the note as soon as he'd found it, that he'd instead set up the conference call with them and the State Police and announced the find during the call. It was clear to Bob that, even if it hadn't been his wife cut to pieces in the snow, they'd still have been offended at his presumption by acting as their peer. He sure as hell wasn't going to cement their opinion by telling them that a friend of his had read the note while he'd left it unattended to go make a pee-pee, so he'd left that little gem out of the call.

The night of the murder, out of professional courtesy and genuine sympathy, the FBI and State Police had only informally asked him to avoid the appearance that he was involved in the investigation. The note gave the FBI the leverage they needed to push the State Police in the direction they were already leaning and Bob had been ordered to secure it for pickup and to stand down on anything remotely related to the murder.

Minutes after the conference call had ended, he'd gotten a call from Ed, who was insistent that they talk about "the trouble that asshole was stirring up." Bob was happy for an excuse not to be in the office when the cavalry rode in to clean up his mess, so he left the note in his office safe. Marcy, the town clerk, was also in the office and had the combination to the safe. Bob figured she was as capable as he was of humbly handing over the note to the real professionals.

Bob hadn't been to Ed's place in a while. A few years, probably. Funny, the turns life takes. Bob probably drove past several times a week and even had to pass by on the way to Ed's hunting camp. Despite the previous tension between Tom and Billy, the four of them had managed to spend at least one weekend a year at the camp the past few years. *Iner-*

tia, Bob figured.

Ed lived in a well maintained, older trailer on the twisting, isolated road — the Tracy Road — that connected Mineville and Witherbee with I-87, the Adirondack Northway. The workshop door was open and he was washing his motorcycle, a gleaming, Moriah Viking red Harley Fat Boy, ever present Genny Light at hand and old blues playing in the background. Laughing to himself about his own belly, Bob looked at the expanse of Ed's t-shirt and noted that the Genny was much more effective than the Light.

As he approached, Ed looked up from where he sat on a small stool. "You look like hell."

"Thanks."

"Just saying. You want a beer? Wait, on duty. Never mind."

Bob sighed. "You know what? Give me a beer. According to the State Police and the FBI, there's not much difference between me being on duty and not."

Ed got up and walked to the fridge, returning with the familiar blue can. "Fuck them, man."

"Yeah," Bob said, as he popped the can open. "Fuck them."

Ed cocked an eyebrow at the out of character F-bomb and watched as Bob took a drink, a long, cold drink that visibly relaxed his shoulders and forehead.

"Have I ever told you how much I appreciate you leaving the stock mufflers on your motorcycle?"

Ed's reaction wasn't one of appreciation, but instead one of anger and disgust. "I can't stand those douchebags who pull the baffles out of their pipes just because they have a small dick." He paused a moment, then looked a little sheepish.

"Not your first beer of the day?"

"Nope. Plus, you struck a nerve. There's a lot of reasons people don't like bikes. And assholes on loud ones is the biggest."

"Don't those guys argue that louder is safer?" Bob knew the arguments to this question, but Ed's reaction intrigued him and he wondered how much thought had gone into it. He got his answer.

"Shit no. You can't tell directionality from low frequency sounds, so cars know there's a bike around someplace, but they have no fucking idea where it is. And since nearly every motorcycle accident involves a bike in the back and a car in the front, the last thing you want is some fuck knuckle in a car slowing down and looking around to see where the noise is coming from."

Bob nodded, but Ed wasn't done. "Ninety percent of all traffic information comes to drivers from sight and only 10% from sound, but how many guys with loud pipes have a helmet that's not black." Bob nodded again in agreement. Ed was pretty much describing Mike Rush and his Vulcan 1500 to a "T".

Just as abruptly as he had spun up, Ed spun back down and without saying a word, he finished his beer and got another from the refrigerator, then opened it and sat back down by his bike.

They both drank in silence for a few minutes. If there was one thing that Bob appreciated about Ed it was his ability to not talk, in stark contrast to Billy and even Tom. His appreciation for simple quiet. Tom could force himself into quiet, had clearly worked on himself to get to that point, but it wasn't born to him. Not like it was with Bob and Ed. And Billy couldn't not talk if there was a gun to his head.

After a while, Bob started. "So, about Billy..."

Ed shook his head. "I don't know why he's got to be like this. And I hate to be the one to tell you, but you need to know."

Bob drank his beer and let Ed go on. It was odd, but so like Ed, that he wasn't nearly as animated about this as he had been about motorcycle exhausts.

"Billy came to visit me yesterday morning. At the school." He emphasized that last word, as if to make sure it stuck in Bob's mind. "He's decided you're not up to the task of investigating something this serious and he wanted me to help him solve the crime for you."

Bob nodded and spoke carefully. "What time? What time did he talk to you?"

"Why's that matter?"

"It matters."

Ed shrugged. "Around ten or so. Why?"

"Just gathering data. He must have come to see me right after he talked to you."

Ed looked startled. "He came to see you?"

"He did. Billy's a lot of things, but he's not a sneak. He came to openly offer his help."

Ed looked instantly furious and jammed his hands into his pockets. Bob watched his jaw rhythmically clench, something he'd done since he was a kid when he got angry. Bob just couldn't figure out what it was about this information that made the big man react so strongly, so he filed it away and waited it out.

Then, just as quickly, Ed's entire body un-tensed and his eyes refocused on Bob. "Come in the house. I have more to tell you, but I want to make some coffee."

"I got time."

Ed put a kettle on the stove and asked Bob if he minded instant.

As he sat down, Bob said, "No, that's what I drink too. After this many years, my taste buds can't tell the difference between Walmart instant and Starbucks' finest."

"Same here. At least it's real coffee and not that goddam Postum. My parents drank that shit when I was a kid."

They sat there at the kitchen table, Bob looking out the window and Ed looking at Bob.

"Cissy struggled living in such a small town, didn't she?" Ed began.

Bob nodded. "She always figured she was meant for bigger things, bigger places."

"I never really could figure out why she took so long to run for office. I'd bet the school board was going to be just a start."

"I guess you don't get to be as good as you are at leading teenage boys without being able to read people."

Both men took drinks of their coffee and Bob said, "After she got elected, she started to joke that I'd have to quit when she was the…"

"Town Superintendent? I bet she did."

Bob laughed. "No, she said Governor." Ed laughed too, not a warm laugh, but a brittle one. One with thoughts behind it. They both looked out through the kitchen window. There wasn't any real snow yet this year, but the icy crust on the pines around Ed's house made them look like a Christmas card.

Bob saw that Ed didn't look at him when he looked back at the window, didn't even look past him, but looked… near him. Ed had never been comfortable with eye contact and always wore sunglasses when he was coaching. Bob assumed this was so the kids didn't know he wasn't staring straight at them when he was talking to them.

Ed didn't say anything, so Bob asked, "This is about Cissy, then?"

He nodded. "When you know something about your friend, something you know you ought to tell him, but that you know will hurt him…" He trailed off, took a drink of coffee, then started speaking again. Slowly, clearly. "You tell yourself that if everybody else knows, then he probably knows too. And by bringing it up, you'll just be bringing something into the open that he clearly doesn't want in the open. It's the worst kind of rationalization a man can do."

Bob's shoulders slumped and he stared into his coffee cup, as if there was an answer there, a solution, something, anything that would wipe away the last two and a half days of his life. He was still staring into the cup as he spoke.

"Of course I knew. She didn't really bother that much to hide it the past couple years."

Ed waited. He hoped that once Bob started talking, he'd keep going, leading himself to the logical conclusion without prodding. Later, when Bob remembered this thought entering his mind, Ed wanted it — needed it — to have been the result of Bob's own thought process and not of Ed's prompting. He waited.

"Of course the Troopers are going to find out about the affairs. It won't take much digging." Bob looked up from his coffee and, though he still looked tired as hell, Ed realized he also looked different. More comfortable talking about the crime, almost as if it had happened to somebody else. "They'll go in two directions. First, they'll look for evidence of me knowing about the affairs. For motive."

Even talking about himself, Bob was able to sound as if he was describing a normal investigation. Ed had never really seen him this way before. He didn't like it.

"The second path they'll take, hopefully in parallel to the husband angle, will be to try to find out if a former or current lover had motive. Jealousy or some sort of blackmail gone wrong." He paused. "No, blackmail's no good. The crime was too..." He stopped and Ed saw the memory of the scene at the school flash across Bob's eyes.

To get Bob back on track, he asked, "So, a jealous former lover?'

Bob's eyes refocused. "Yeah, or a jealous husband. That'll be the primary focus of the investigation until they can eliminate him. Me."

"Well, I'm ok eliminating him-slash-you now. Here's my thing. Do we understand everybody's agenda here?"

"Back to Billy?"

Ed held his arms out and shrugged. Then he pointed at Bob's coffee cup. "Refill?"

Bob stood up and shook his head. "No, I'm ducking a responsibility I have back at the office. Thanks for the talk. It helped a lot to put these things into words. Now I know there are two… well, I guess, three working theories to expect from the Troopers and I'll see what I can do to help them."

"Three? We got husband and jealous lover."

"Yeah, I just thought of another one. Rejected lover. I have to be honest with myself about Cissy. She not only cheated, she was outright promiscuous. So, imagine if somebody who was known to, you know, fool around with a lot of men… Imagine if they rejected somebody. That would hurt. That could explain the violence of the crime if it was the right guy. Or the wrong guy."

Ed nodded as he walked Bob out of the trailer and to his Tahoe. "I can see that."

When Bob's truck had passed out of sight around the corner, Ed, who had been tightly holding himself together since that one trigger phrase, and had nearly lost hold with Bob's third theory, erupted.

"A sneak?" he screamed to the sky. "A sneak?" He imitated Bob's tone in a voice that drowned in mockery and hatred. "Billy's a lot of things, but he's no sneak… Fuck you!"

He staggered to the back of the trailer, barely aware of his surroundings but with enough of a glimmer of consciousness to know he couldn't be seen like this. All the while he was balling and unballing his hands and raging "Sneaky fuck! Sneaky fuck!" over and over again.

It took long minutes for the fury to pass. When Ed calmed enough to see clearly again, his breath was coming in gasps. He stood, leaned over, hands on his knees, a cloud of steam erupting from his face with every ragged, sobbing breath. He lifted his head and looked around. The yard looked like a tornado had touched down in the center of it and, in a fashion, one had. Centered on where Ed stood, there was a circle of thrown and broken lawn chairs. One had broken through the picket fence encircling his small garden plot. Broken pieces of chair and fence lay on the dead, frozen ground that earlier in the fall had yielded corn, beans, and squash.

Ed put his head back down, then slowly crouched lower and lower, eventually sitting in the snow, then lying back with his arms stretched back over his head. He embraced the cold, then the wet, as the frost beneath him melted and soaked through the seat of his jeans. He sat up when he heard his phone ring. It was an older style ring, coming from a real bell, and was muffled by the walls of the trailer. A half-second later a more modern, digital phone rang from inside the garage.

***

Ridiculous. Tom knew he was being ridiculous. To be embarrassed about the high school prom, after all these years. And still thinking about it, a day after Molly's unintentional hurt. His teacher had told him once that he had the power to control his mind, just as he controlled his hands or his legs. In this moment, he felt his teacher was full of shit.

He was driving to Billy's to repay the visit of the previous morning. That was probably ridiculous too, because he knew full well that part of his motivation for the visit — in addition, of course, to wanting to keep the reconciliation on track — was to make sure Billy didn't keep the higher ground to himself.

Different circles. Hell, he and Molly had been on different planes of existence. The cheerleader didn't go to the same parties as the druggie who played Dungeons and Dragons and walked around with a worn, paperback copy of *Gravity's Rainbow.*

The thought of different planes of existence made him

smile. He'd been on a few of those during high school.

He had been high as shit that morning, Christmas vacation, junior year, writing a terribly romantic ghost story about two kids who die together in a snowmobile accident. He still had it somewhere.

Out of the blue, with no forethought, he'd gotten her number out of the phonebook and dialed. As soon as it rang, he started praying that they would have an answering machine, that the machine would pick up.

"Hello."

Crap it was her. And oh my god, she sounded just the way a voice on the other end of the phone should sound.

"Helloooooooo?"

"Oh, hey. Uh, Molly?" *Good start. Glib even.*

"This is she."

"Uh, her." *Really? Correcting her grammar? Really?*

"Excuse me?'

He was committed now. "Her. It should be, 'This is her.'" The rock he had started rolling when he dialed was headed downhill and no matter how hard he grabbed at it, he couldn't stop it.

Without a pause, she came back with, "Ok. Who is he?'

Unlike her, he did pause. "Who... Who is who?" Just out of reach, that rock was picking up speed, rolling faster and faster. He'd given it the initial push, but he had no control of it now. Not it's speed, and certainly not it's direction.

"He," she repeated. "I'm her. Who's he?"

"What he?"

"The he on the phone."

"The he on the... Oh shit. Uh, this is Tom... Tom Hudson."

She laughed and the rock... just... stopped. To his 17-year-old ears, angels should weep that their voices were so thin in comparison. "You didn't have to say 'Hudson' once you said 'Tom,' you goofball."

And then, as quickly as it had stopped, the rock started again, careening downhill, laying waste to everything in its path. He blurted out asking her to the prom. She was startled and paused, so he repeated himself, speaking even faster and less steady than the first time. She started to talk over him and the words would not stop pouring from his mouth, so he speed-talked the rest of it, just to get to the end. Then she said something about not being able to commit yet, because she didn't know if she'd be dating anybody when the prom came around, but he only half heard her because the roaring noise in his head overwhelmed her quieter and quieter voice. He wished her a happy New Year, she did the same, and it was over.

At least it was for her. Of that, he was certain. It had stayed with him for a long time.

He turned right, off Joyce Road onto Sherman Street, and realized his face was as red now as it had been when he'd hung up the phone that day. And his plan to sit in the car for a minute after he'd pulled into Billy's driveway wasn't going to work. The garage door was wide open and as Billy heard Tom's Dart make the turn into the driveway, he looked up from the motorcycle he was working on.

Billy wished he was glad to see Tom. He really did. But not today. Kate had stayed at the motel in Ti the previous night, just to make sure he fully understood the error of his ways. That and the knot in his stomach from the certainty that Bob had seen his handiwork on the desk this morning made Billy pretty certain he would be piss-poor company. He looked over at the tall glass on the workshop bench, guessing the vodka he'd started drinking as soon as he'd gotten home from his visit to Bob probably wouldn't help either.

Oh well. He stood, picking up a rag to wipe the oil from his hands, and pasted a fake smile on his face.

Shit, Tom thought, when he saw Billy's initial reaction, then the fake smile he replaced it with.

He got out of the car and faked a smile of his own, knowing that his face still hadn't faded to a normal color.

"Good morning, man. Hey, if you're in the middle of something..."

"Nah, dude. Come in the garage and grab a beer. I was just changing my oil."

Tom looked towards the house. "Is Kate...?"

The corners of Billy mouth got tight for a second, just a second, but enough time for Tom to see. *Goddammit. Of course. He's going to think I'm here hoping to see her.*

Billy knew he'd lost his poker face at the mention of Kate and he also noticed Tom's reaction. He could practically hear the gears in Tom's head turning. Was he thinking that Billy would assume he was here to see Kate? Was he only here to see Kate?

"No. She's out this morning."

Tom nodded, then looked to the motorcycle, knowing the topic could be a place of safety. "Have I ever told you how much I love this bike?"

Billy smiled, not with pride at his motorcycle, but at the transparency. All of the hopeful feelings he'd had after talking to Tom the previous day seemed to be evaporating. Billy wanted to find a way to hold onto them, but he just wasn't getting that same vibe from Tom.

Fuck it. "She's beautiful, all right. A lot of people are jealous of her." The bike was a brand new Harley, a Heritage Springer. Tom knew Billy wasn't talking about the motor-cycle.

Tom nodded. Humor would work. "I bet they are. But I didn't come up here to lust after your... bike."

Billy's face hardened again, but this time he didn't try to disguise it. "Oh, that's pretty fucking funny."

Ok, humor wouldn't work. It didn't matter, because anger was taking its place anyway. "Seriously? I'm making an effort here."

"Fuck you and your half-assed effort. We both know why you're here."

If there was one thing that moved Tom off his center, it was everyone's sincere belief that he had one and only one motivation for every action in his life. "Man, we just had a rehearsal last night. If I wanted so desperately to see her, wouldn't I want it to be when you're not around?"

Billy continued as if he hadn't heard Tom. "You look at my life, my friends, the way people looked at me and talked to me at the school the other night."

"Where the hell did that come from?"

"Hey, you said it the other day. We weren't friends even before Kate came to town."

Tom was fighting the anger. Fighting and losing. "Yeah, and I'm remembering why."

"Are you? Are you remembering the way I took all the attention from you when I came back? I came back with a shit ton of money and all you have is the fucking Grand Union. Pretty shitty and unfair, the way life turns out, but that's just the way it goes, dude."

Tom was shaking his head and smiling gently. "After all these years, you still don't have the faintest idea what I'm about, do you?"

"Oh, give me some credit. The money I made, the so-called 'adventures' you always sound so jealous of. None of that is what really eats you up."

"Meaning?"

"Meaning those are the things you can bitch about as your way of not bitching about what I have that you really want." The look on Tom's face told Billy that he had caught Tom off guard, maybe for the first time since they were in high school.

"Oh ok, so we are back to this shit."

"Yeah, this shit. I come back with a bunch of money, nobody quite believes me that I made it in stocks. I buy up a bunch of old shitty properties, pump some dough into the town, and suddenly everybody has a new attitude about the place. And about me. Suddenly nobody cares where Billy Ridge got his money and everybody loves what he's doing for the town."

He realized he was out of breath, but he didn't want Tom to interrupt him; not just yet. As Tom started to say something, Billy put up a hand. "And you, Tom. Mr. Hero, serving your country in the Army, coming back to take over the Grand Union when everybody was driving to Ti to spend their money at Walmart. I read what you said in the paper. About the people who needed a grocery store within walking distance. About the people who needed the jobs to stay in the town. How Walmart was going to suck the town dry, then leave. Well, they're still here. And nobody treated you like a hero, did they? Not like me. All you got for your trouble was a crappy store to run in a town that doesn't fucking care." He was ready to be interrupted now.

Tom, thinking that they had dodged the Kate bullet, utterly misjudged where Billy was going. "Nice speech, Billy. Somebody like you, with such a desperate need to be loved, probably can't get this, but I really don't begrudge you any of the attention."

"Ah, but Tommy, I know that." Billy's smile was cold now. He called it his "Old Days" smile and it had indeed been useful in its time. "See, after all these years, I do know you. I know you aren't jealous of my money or the attention these goobers give me."

"Then what the hell was that whole stupid speech about?" Billy's smile was making him uneasy. It made Billy's eyes look so empty. Cold and empty. He'd looked into eyes like those before and he knew what they meant about what the man behind them was capable of.

"Oh, it's about what I have that you want all right. All of the external stuff is just the frosting. It just gives you something to fixate your jealousy on. Maybe you've even convinced yourself that those are the things you hate me for, but I know better. The thing that I have that you want has nothing to do with money, does it Tommy?"

"You… Fuck this. I'm done." He threw his hands up in surrender and turned to walk away. Billy grabbed his arm to stop him. Both stopped and stood still. Rock still.

Neither of them had heard Kate's car pull into the driveway, neither had heard her engine stop, neither had heard her car door open. It was the closing of the car door they had finally both heard.

Kate was the reason for their continued stillness, but she hadn't caused the initial stop. Tom had been stopped by his reflexes, dangerous reflexes that Billy had activated by grabbing him. Billy had no idea of the extent of the danger he had put himself in, but he was quite aware that his grabbing Tom's arm had nothing to do with Tom's stopping. Billy outweighed Tom by at least twenty-five pounds and he also knew that the work he had been doing with weights over the past year, work that had a lot to do with how he wanted to look for Kate, had made him stronger than he had been in years. He now knew, by the ease with which Tom had continued to move for the short second after Billy had grabbed his arm, that Tom was powerful in a way that he had not expected.

Kate look puzzled and wary. "What are you boys doing?"

Billy was frozen and Tom's voice sounded as if it were coming from far away. "Billy was feeling my muscles. You telling me you didn't notice I've been working out?" Billy came back to himself in time to see, and appreciate, Tom's completely natural-looking goofy wink at Kate. "You're not jealous of his attention toward me, are you?"

Kate burst out laughing and missed Tom's squinted look at Billy as he smoothly detached Billy's hand from his arm.

Billy mentally shook himself. "Yeah, Sweetie. I swear that our relationship is totally platonic. Isn't it, Tommy?" He jokingly punched Tom in the arm and Tom bounced almost a foot. Billy understood in a way he wouldn't have before how much of that reaction was for show.

"Actually, Kate," Tom said, "we were arguing about some of the things Billy here has, um, acquired since he came back to town."

"Oh were you?" She walked towards the front door of the house, completely unaware of the tension between the two most important people in her life.

"Oh yeah," Tom continued, as they both walked with her. "Isn't that right?"

"Yeah, where were we?"

"The Newsstand. I can't believe you took away my newsstand."

Billy was having enough trouble detaching his focus from the feeling of Tom's strength against his. Tom's apparent ease with the transition was making it even harder. More surreal. "The Newsstand?"

"Yeah, before you turned the Newsstand into a movie theater, I used to go there every morning on the way to work. Grab a cup of coffee, argue with Richie about the Knicks or the Jets."

Billy shook his head. "Wait, what? You're fucking nuts. It was a movie theater when we were kids. The building looked stupid as a newsstand, plus Richie was just wasting all that space in the back that used to be the theater. I can't believe *that's* the thing that bothers you."

"Who knows," Tom said. "Maybe it's just a symbol for some other thing that bothers me."

Kate was distracted by something and continued to be oblivious to the tension below the surface. "Come on, Tom. A town's got to have a movie theater. He even put in the soft ice cream place next door."

"Yeah," Billy was able to get out through a suddenly dry throat. "Just like when we were kids."

"Please. You played that shitty, racist *Star Wars* movie

for like four months. You should show some Hitchcock or Billy Wilder movies."

"Hey, they kept coming to see it, so we kept running it. I'm surprised you're not bitching at me for playing *Toy Story* for Christmas instead of *Eyes Wide Shut* or some fucking Italian movie about a sad clown."

"Plus, the Newsstand was the first place I ever had Orangina. It holds a special place in my heart."

"Seriously, Orangina? I never could believe you drank that wussy shit. Mountain Dew, now that's a manly drink."

"Wussy? What are you, eight?"

Kate's violent inhalation of air stopped them both as they turned to look at her. "A manly drink," she said. "Manly."

Billy and Tom both had that same puzzled look, the one that men get on the frequent occasions women go away, far away from where the men thought they were going. "Kate?" they asked in unison.

"The notes. Your bickering made me forget about the notes, but then you made me realize…"

Billy caught on before Tom, but he had the context to key in on what she said. "Notes? What notes?'

"The *Plattsburgh Press* is posting notes from the killer. They showed up on their web page today. It's all over the news."

"Son of a bitch!" Billy ran into the house, leaving Tom and Kate looking blankly at each other. When they went in, he was already at the kitchen table, fingers flying on the trackpad of his laptop. He quickly navigated to the web page. The normal photo ticker of several stories rotating in succession was replaced by a single headline.

"The Killer Speaks," it read and Billy couldn't stop his brain from thinking about Kate's inevitable critique, once it occurred to her that the paper was equating writing with speaking. And there the words were, just as he feared they would be.

She wore pants.

She worked.

She had no children.

She broke the compact and met the brute.

"Fuckety fuck fuck fuck."

Kate looked at him as if he'd just gone insane. "What is wrong with you?"

Billy looked from Kate to Tom. He knew that people don't usually have clarity like this at the pivot points in our lives. Those moments usually come to us unannounced, we make a reactive decision, and only in retrospect do we say, "Oh, shit. I screwed that all up."

Or sometimes we get to say, "Sweet. I nailed that one." Billy firmly believed, at least based on his experience, that a retrospective "Sweet" was far less frequent than an "Oh shit," and in this moment, he realized why. Even in a moment like this, when the difference between the two was clarity itself, everything in him was screaming for him to choose "Oh shit" over "Sweet." He nearly always had in the past, so why stop now?

You know what? Fuck it. Let's try it the other way and see what happens. "Bob is going to think I gave the notes to the paper."

Tom started to say, "Why," but Kate was quicker and more definitive.

"What did you do?"

Billy sighed. Sometimes she just made him so tired.

He explained his morning visit to Bob, the notes, the fact that Bob was certain to have seen the change in their position on the desk. Billy had a running joke with Kate that he could see the future. By that, he meant he could predict with some consistency how she would react to any given mistake of his, much as her anger the previous morning was written in the stars for him to read. He could have seen this disappointment coming a mile away.

"Well, anyway," she said through pursed lips, "the manly stuff that the killer wrote in his notes. I figured it out."

"What's to figure out?" Billy asked.

Tom added, "Yeah, he's overcompensating. Like Billy always does."

She missed Billy's glare and kept talking. "No, there's more to it than that. There's genuine literary and historical analysis in his work."

"*His work?*" the two men thought at the same time. Tom added a silent prayer that she was talking about the notes and not the killing.

"His notes—*thank you, God*—reminded me of something I've read. It's been nagging at me since that first night when I saw the messages on the school wall and I just figured it out. He thinks he's… that guy." She waved her hands in the air, trying to remember. "The one in that book."

"Aha! You've solved it!" Billy smilingly mocked.

Tom's voice was gentler, but pressing. "What guy, Kate? What book?"

Kate looked at Billy with unveiled anger. "I assumed you would know what I meant because it's the only book I've ever asked you to read that you actually picked up."

Billy's mouth opened and closed once, then his eyes opened wide. "Oh my god. Oh my god. You're right. It is that guy. The one from the book."

"What book? What are you two talking about?"

Billy stared up at the corner of the ceiling. He looked as if he was counting very long numbers. "Hang on. Hang on." He snapped his fingers once. "Got it. Almoth Wright was this fruit pie of a British biologist in the early 1900s who cooked up a social compact theory to explain why it was ok for men to rape feminists."

Tom's jaw dropped. "What?"

"No, no, really. His thing was that being on the receiving

end of chivalry wasn't so much a right for women as much as it was their half of the deal. The *compact*. Like in the note. Women acted like women and in return men treated them with chivalry. If women stopped acting like women, then the compact was broken."

Kate nodded, impressed, almost stunned, and said, "Right. He said that civilization was built on the gender differences, and when those differences were lessened, as the early feminists..."

Billy cut her off. "Actually, that was Sedgwick, the American who picked up on Wright's book. Bederman uses them both in the chapter on Charlotte Perkins Gilman, so I can see how you could mix them up..." He trailed off and popped the "p" at the end of "up" as Kate turned and stalked out of the room. "What? What's the matter?"

He turned to Tom, who was starting for the door. "What crawled up her ass?"

"You did, stupid. Now go and tell her you're sorry and fix it."

Billy wished he was a better man than to slip one last jab in, but it had been an extraordinarily shitty morning. Oh yeah, and the vodka. As if that made it ok. "You sure you want me to do that? Wouldn't it work better for you if she stayed mad at me?"

Tom slowly shook his head, then sighed. "Fuck me running. Look, obviously I was interested when she first came to town. Everybody knows that. But she picked you, I got over it, and now she and I are friends. Why can't you or anybody else figure that fucking part out?"

"Just friends."

"Yeah. It's pretty cool. And you know what would be even cooler? If you and I were friends, too." He turned and left.

Billy stood there for long moments after Tom left. Then he sighed, said "Fuck," under his breath, and went to find Kate.

She was on the back porch, sitting in the rocking chair, reading a book. The Bederman book. The one he'd bought her to replace the school library's copy after she'd extended it twice. He remembered the title now, *Manliness and Civilization*. "Yet another book on the crisis of masculinity," he remembered Kate saying. But he also remembered her reading it more than once and knew she'd made copious notes in the margins. Not enough books have nice, wide margins anymore.

"You just going to stand there?" She startled him out of his internal, vodka-lubricated tangent. "Or are you going to make one of those famously insincere Billy-with-the-big-eyes apologies and make everything all better?"

There goes that plan. "Kate, I can't apologize if I don't know what I did."

"Really? So you've never apologized to me when you had no idea why I was angry?"

Humor might work. "Define never," he said.

She started to smile, in spite of herself, but it didn't last long and she slowly shook her head. "If you weren't so damned charming, somebody probably would have killed you years ago."

You have no idea, sweetheart.

"You never actually apologize anyway."

Billy looked at her incredulously. "What does that mean? I apologize."

"That is not even close to true. How many times have you looked at me and in complete sincerity said, 'I'm sorry'?"

"Look, not every apology has to have the words 'I'm sorry' in it."

"Not every apology... Ok, give me an example of an apology without an 'I'm sorry' in it. Wait — an apology that *you* have used that doesn't have an 'I'm sorry' in it."

He didn't hesitate. "Absolutely. When I say "Huh," that means 'I was completely wrong and I am so, so sorry.'"

"Oh, that is complete bullshit. So every time you say, 'Huh,' you're saying you were wrong and are sorry?"

"Well, clearly not every time. It's based on context. Sometimes it means, 'This chick is crazy and I need to be careful not to say anything that will make her even more crazy.'"

"You are such an asshole."

"Huh."

She threw the book down on the floor beside her chair, got up, and stalked past him back to the front door of the house. He waited for her to walk out, slam the door, then get in her car and drive away before he moved. Up the stairs, to take a shower, sober up, and plan his actual apology.

OK, Tom thought. *Here goes nothing.* He could hardly believe what he was doing, so the look on Billy's face when he pulled into the driveway the next morning did not surprise him one bit. He saw that Kate's car was also in the side driveway next to Billy's truck. *Might as well rip the whole damn band aid off all at once.*

Billy was in nearly the same position he had been the previous morning, sitting on a small, folding chair next to his beloved Harley. He hadn't been drinking this morning though, so when the powder blue Dodge Dart rolled into the driveway towards him, his mind worked quicker than it had the previous day. His first thought — a fleeting thought, but a conscious one — was that Tom was going to floor the gas and run him down. In those short, short moments a man gets the craziest ideas. Billy's next coherent thought was that he and Kate shouldn't have parked in the side driveway, leaving him vulnerable to this sort of attack. Then, in the split second he thought he was going to die, his instinct was to curse the fact that he was going to die chewing this bullshit nicotine gum as a way of making amends to Kate.

But, once the crazy went away and he was making more logical assessments, the car rolled to a stop as he now expected it to and Tom got out. He was carrying a paper grocery bag. This had potential.

He got up and put his hands in his pockets. "Of all the things I expected to see this morning, this ain't it."

"Well, it's complicated."

"Keep going."

"Ok, it's actually simple. You came to my turf and things went great. I came to yours and things went to shit. I think that left you with the moral high ground and that is an unacceptable state of affairs."

Billy laughed. "You're a fucking idiot, but I am too. I was figuring *you* had the moral high ground because you were the better host."

"I'm good with both of us being idiots."

Billy eyed the bag. "And so..."

"Just wait." Tom walked past him and into the garage, looking up and down the workbench. "Ok, no vodka. I just want to be positive where we stand."

"See? You're starting again already."

"Hush, I brought Freihofer's."

"Oh, Jesus. Gimme." His eyes darted to the house. "For chrissakes, hurry up before she comes out."

"She doesn't let you have cookies? Seriously?"

"No, I don't want to share."

They were too late. The door opened and Kate walked out. She looked back and forth between Billy and Tom, judging the mood and finding it good.

Billy spoke first, grabbing the bag from Tom's hands. "Look, baby. I had Tom bring us some cookies." He glared back at Tom, daring him to disagree.

"There's some soda in there too. Just for you."

"Awesome. This is a great day." Billy pulled the six pack of cans out then said, "What the fuck?" with disgust. "This is DIET Mountain Dew."

"I thought you were starting to look a little... I don't know... puffy."

"Oh that's funny. Very, very funny. Guess who's got the moral high ground back."

Kate was holding her hand over her mouth, shaking silently in laughter.

Billy said, "All right. You might as well come in. For real this time."

Tom started to walk towards the door of the house, then caught himself and turned back towards his car. "Oh, wait. I brought something else we're going to want to talk about." He opened the car door, reached in, and brought out a stack of newspapers, holding them in the air. "Guess we're finally on the map for something other than Mario Cuomo's abject poverty. The murder made the national news."

"Fantastic," Billy said flatly, sarcastically. "I'll catch up in a sec. I gotta piss like a race horse."

"What? On all fours?" Tom asked. Then he cocked his head at Billy, caught off guard by his own words, searching for whatever implanted memory had caused the blurt. Billy looked back at him and they looked quizzically at each other a few more beats. It clicked for both of them at the same time and they started laughing together.

"Oh my god. I haven't heard that in a million years." Billy said. "Wait, wait. What were the other ones? What was that one Ed always said?"

Tom held his hands together in front of his face, then pressed them to his lips, bouncing them slightly while he thought. "Aha. I have to shit like a madman."

Together they said, "And rub it all over the walls?" then burst out laughing.

Suddenly Billy made a panicked face, hurriedly but quietly said, "Oh god," and ran into the house.

Kate, who had silently watched the entire routine, asked, "What in the world was that?"

Tom held the door open for her as they followed Billy into the house. "It's from high school. It started with us trying to come up with the most ridiculous similes for... you know... bodily functions. We had the same wildebeests and wookies that everybody else had. Russian racehorses were quite popular for a while. Then it got boring, making the same jokes that everybody else was making. So whenever one of us said something like, I don't know, 'I have to…" He stopped and censored himself. "I have to poop… like a fruit bat," the others would have to come up with an answer, like…"

She interrupted. "I'm still listening, but two things first… One, coffee?" He nodded and she went to the freezer for the coffee beans. "And two, thank you for using simile correctly. I'm certain Billy would have called them metaphors."

Billy had opened the door to the room, then remembered he hadn't flushed and had started to go back in when he caught their conversation. He looked down at the floor, hurt by Kate's insult.

Tom's firm response surprised him. "Oh, Billy may have called it a metaphor or he may have called it a Metamucil, but don't be confused, Kate. He would have been doing it on purpose, partly to amuse himself and partly to give you the chance to show that you see through the act."

Kate waved him off, unconvinced, and went back to making coffee.

Jesus Christ, Dr. Phil. Had he always been that transparent to Tom? And that opaque to Kate? He went back into the bathroom, silently chuckling about the word opaque and the myriad of different ways to misuse it. Myriad nearly made him laugh out loud. He flushed, then came back out with a big smile on his face.

"What are we talking about?" he asked.

Tom smiled as well. "Analogies."

"Gesundheit."

Later, they sat over coffee, re-reading the articles in the *Plattsburgh Press-Republican*, the *Times of Ti,* and the *New York Times.*

Tom looked up — he had moved on to the *Times Book Review* — and said, "Hey, I got a call from Kevin the other day that you'll think is funny." At Kate's questioning look, he said, "Kevin Gilman. Friend of ours in high school. He graduated with Billy and Bob."

"Wait. You guys didn't all graduate together?"

Billy said, "Nope. Squirt here is a year younger than me and Bob. We graduated in '83 with Lisa, Kevin…"

"Which year did Ed graduate?" she asked. She knew the four of them had been close friends in high school, though she hadn't been able to get many details from Billy, who in the past hadn't been willing to indulge her curiosity about his history. Especially his history with Tom.

Tom said, "Ed's the same age as Billy and Bob, but he was held back a year in junior high and graduated with me."

"And Molly…?"

"She graduated with Tom," Billy said.

"Which brings me back to my story," Tom said. "Kevin was the first person I hired when I got the loan for the store."

Tom had actually paid cash for the store, through a fictional loan, twice removed, but he saw no need to give up his "barely hanging on to the store" persona until there was a strategic purpose behind it. Or an emotional one.

"That's right," Billy said. "I forget he was working for you."

"As micromanaging as I am now, I was so much worse when I first started. Kevin was ready to operate on his own early on. Hell, we practically learned the business together as we went along. And it wasn't so much ego — at least that's what I like to think — as much as it was that I just didn't want to share. I opened every morning. I closed every night. I made every decision, big or small. So, when Walmart recruited him, well, I would have left me too. But I was really happy for him and we've stayed friends."

Billy got up for another cup of coffee. "Ok, funny call. Focus."

"Right. Well, apparently he's moving up the corporate

ladder at the Great Satan and they want him to start a management intern program, so he called to ask me if there was anybody else I was overlooking who he could poach from me."

Billy turned back from the coffee pot and started to say something, but Kate spoke first.

"Lisa? She's probably the closest you have."

Billy shook his head. "Oh god. I can't imagine Lisa with the power to hire and fire. But Molly could completely run the place better than you do."

Billy could see that Tom had started to nod, but before he could say anything Kate laughed a sharp laugh. "Molly? She can't even run her own home." She might have gone on, but she stopped short when she saw the reaction from Tom first, then Billy.

"I'm sorry. I'm sorry," she said, in an insincere, little girl, oopsie tone. "That was a little mean."

If they'd been alone, Billy might have reacted strongly to Kate's harshness, but he stopped himself, waiting to see Tom's reaction.

It only lasted a split second, but was there long enough for both of them to see it pass across his face. His eyes narrowed, hardened, and the muscles in his jaw clenched once, reflecting some internal struggle that they each wondered whether or not they would see more of.

They didn't see more. As quickly as it had begun, it ended and Tom's eyes softened.

When he spoke, his voice was as light as it had been before Kate had mentioned Molly.

"So anyway, I told Kevin I didn't have anybody I could lose, but I did know somebody who'd been in town a while and still hadn't been able to find any work." He smirked at Billy.

Billy laughed and, a beat later, Kate realized she was being let off the hook and laughed too. The tension evaporated as each pretended it had never been there.

Tom stayed and chatted, mostly about the evils of Walmart, waiting just the right amount of time to minimize the awkwardness Kate had created, then told them he had to get back to micromanage the store.

Kate looked up from the table where she was re-reading the details of the crime scene.

"Hey. You were supposed to come up for dinner Sunday night," she said, as if remembering something from a long time ago.

Billy flinched internally, though nothing showed on his face.

"I was indeed. But I ended up stuck at the store receiving a shipment late, so it sounds like it wouldn't have worked for any of us."

"Stupid store," she pouted.

Billy marveled at Kate's ability to act as if she was realizing for the first time that something had happened that she had been present at, even when the thing that had happened had been her doing. It was an unsettling coping mechanism for what he assumed was her need to avoid responsibility for anything unpleasant.

Her face brightened. "How about tonight?" She turned to Billy. "Tonight would work, right?"

"It sure would. I don't even think there are any games on tonight that I'd have to miss."

Tom asked, "Are you guys sure?"

They both nodded, and Kate said, "Christmas vacation officially starts tomorrow, so regardless of what they decide to do with the school today, I'll be off for the next week and a half. And there's a bottle of wine with my name on it tonight."

Tom asked, "Red or white?"

"It's an old vine zin that I have been dying to open."

"Mmm, sassy... Sounds great. I'll bring some steaks from the store."

As Tom drove away, Kate got a call from school to let

her know that the teachers were being allowed into their classrooms to gather what they needed to work on over the vacation, so she left not long after Tom did.

Billy went back out to the garage, thinking how different the three of them were, but also honing in on how similar they were in one fundamental way. Each of the three of them, each for their own reason, had been only too happy to ignore the tension of Kate's commentary on Molly's life. To submerge it, pretend it wasn't there. Billy knew that when Tom came back that night, none of them would bring it up.

Their dynamic wasn't settled yet. There was no way to know when it would be or for how long it would hold once it had settled, but none of them wanted to be the one to force it off the tracks before its direction was established.

Billy also knew that if Bob had been there this morning, he'd have stayed on the topic, he'd have stood up for Molly. He felt guilty for not doing it himself. And of course if Ed had been there, he too would have stayed on the topic, pretending innocence at the subtexts, making sure that everybody twisted uncomfortably as long as he needed them to. For his own amusement.

***

Molly hated getting stock from the far back corners of the store. The light never quite seemed to reach all the way to the edges of the walls, the vague sense of dampness with no visible water creeped her out, and she was certain she had never once made it out of there without walking face first into a spider web.

It was probably the noise she was making, loading cases of cans onto the dolly, that let him slip up so close behind her before she, startled, sensed his presence and spun around with a soft cry.

Her husband's only response to her frightened reaction

was a short, unpleasant burst of a laugh.

"Jesus, Mike. You scared me," she blurted. He'd surprised her, which had caused her to speak to him in a sharpness that she was usually careful not to use. She was normally much more wary than this with him. This was a wariness earned from years with a man whose moods were ever changing.

Actually, that wasn't true anymore. His mood with her had consistently been pissed off for at least the past year. When they'd first met, first dated in high school, his moods were more good than bad — far more good than bad. In the grip of young love, she was able to convince herself, like women have always done when in love with an angry man, that Mike just needed a calming influence and some growing up. As the years and the hits piled up, that ratio of bad mood to good mood worsened until now she could hardly remember the last time he'd smiled at her, the last time they'd laughed together, the last time he'd touched her with tenderness.

He wasn't smiling at her now. "Why didn't you tell me Tom was the one who drove you to pick up the kids?"

***

A knock on the door brought Billy out of his thoughts. After finishing with his motorcycle, Billy had cleaned up and was sitting in the kitchen, looking at the articles in the newspapers without really reading them.

"Yeah. Just a second." He threw on a t-shirt and opened the door. It was Bob.

Oh shit. Here it comes. Billy mentally glanced back at the articles in the paper.

Bob waited for a moment for Billy to say something, then when he didn't, said, "Hey. Mind if I come in for a minute?"

"Oh, sorry man. I was sitting around daydreaming and I guess I haven't come out of it yet." Billy stepped back and let him into the kitchen.

As Bob sat at the table he said, "I know what that's like." He said it in a way that didn't invite a response — *or is that the way I want to hear it?* — so Billy let it go.

"Coffee?"

"Yeah, that sounds good. Black."

As Billy got the cup and poured the coffee, he waited in vain for Bob to say something else, anything else, until the quiet in the kitchen was too uncomfortable for him to let it stay. "How's the uh, you know, the investigation going? Anything?"

Bob took the offered coffee with a "thanks" mumble and blew on its surface. He shook his head slowly. "It's tough. You know, just tough."

Whenever Billy talked to Bob, whenever he actually *listened* to him, he had to constantly stifle the urge to reach into his mouth and grab the words that he knew were in there and get them out. Processing what Bob was saying, at least those times he tried to process it, was almost painful.

As Bob was saying, "Tough," a few more times and slowly shaking his head back and forth, Billy inwardly shook his head at himself. *Imagine yourself in his place, trying to talk to a smug fuck like you.*

He forced himself to pay attention to Bob, to take in the man's pain. In doing this he realized that Bob didn't look as pained as he expected him to. He looked like hell, no doubt, but there was more going on in there. Much more than the catatonic zombie he'd expected.

"You know what's probably the toughest thing?" Bob never asked rhetorical questions, so he didn't go on until Billy had raised his eyebrows quizzically. "Realizing, or at least not pretending otherwise anymore... realizing how many people did not like Cissy. She wasn't nice to many people."

Billy's expression was genuinely quizzical now. Of course, people didn't like the bitch. She was fucking evil. Even the sex with her had been angry and abusive. But Billy was surprised to hear Bob openly say anything negative about her, even as mildly as he had phrased it. This must be his lead-in to the notes.

"Well..." Having started the sentence, he felt lucky that Bob interrupted, because he had no idea where he was going to go with it.

"What about you? You didn't like her very much, did you?"

Billy stopped feeling lucky and started feeling cold. That detached cold he'd used to feel in the old days. Back when he'd needed it. He stopped and forced himself to remember who he was talking to, what the man had gone through, and what the man faced in the days and weeks ahead. Finding his wife's killer. No, his wife's butcher. If he ever did find him.

He spoke slowly. Carefully. "People sometimes just don't go well together, you know? Cissy and I were very different people. Listen, man, it won't help you feel any better bringing up old hurts like this. Trust me."

"Oh, I don't know. It might help. Somebody didn't like Cissy enough, hated her enough, to... to... well, to do what they did."

"And?" Billy could feel the cold creeping in around the edges again.

"And I need to talk to the people who hated Cissy. All of them." Bob paused and took a deep drink of the black coffee. "So, tell me about you and Cissy. What kinds of problems did you two have?"

The cold was back in charge of him now and Billy did nothing to chase it away this time. "Are *you* asking me, Bob? Or is Chief Marty?"

"Same guy, Billy. Same guy."

"Then ask me the question. It's already out there. Just ask it."

Bob paused, then, in an entirely different, conversational tone asked, "What time do you have?"

As the misdirection of Bob's question hit Billy, he realized he had been leaning far forward in his chair. He wondered if he ever did that in the old days. And if it was a good thing or a bad thing. "What did you say?" he asked, mostly to gain time to think.

"I was just asking what time it is." Then Bob abruptly stood up. Billy didn't flinch – he rarely flinched – but his senses were as alert as they could be. "Oh, hell, there's a clock right there on the wall," he said. He drank the last of his coffee, then walked across the kitchen to the sink, rinsed out the cup, and set it in the basin. Billy said nothing.

"I gotta head out," Bob said. "Got some stuff to do." Still Billy sat, refusing to play his game. As Bob started out the door, he stopped and turned back around. *Here it comes. Cop 101. The man's been watching too goddamned much TV.*

"Hey, was Kate here that night? The night Cissy was killed."

"No," Billy answered evenly. "I was here alone all night. Until you called, that is."

"Watching TV when I called?"

"Nope. Reading. I was reading a book."

Bob nodded. Billy wondered if he was nodding to acknowledge the answer or the mutual understanding of the change, the probably permanent change, between them. "Ok. Thanks. I'll see you," Bob said in the same friendly, conversational tone.

"See ya." And he was gone. As Billy listened to the thud of the Tahoe door and the sound of the engine starting, it occurred to him that, as Bob had asked his final, hokey, Columbo question, standing there framed in the doorway, he hadn't fumbled over saying that Cissy had been killed. For the first time in Billy's presence, he had simply stated it as fact.

***

When he arrived, Tom handed the ribeyes over to Billy as though making an offering to the high priest of an ancient god. Billy accepted the steaks, then used his secret, magical coffee and cayenne dry rub on them before grilling them — outside, in the cold, with a cloud of frozen breath around his head — to medium rare perfection.

Tom had also brought along a few side dishes that Kate heated up while Billy grilled the steaks and Tom opened the wine.

The steaks were amazing, the wine was fantastic, and as Billy had expected, there were no visible wounds from the morning.

"Ok," he said. "These are not regular mashed potatoes." He held up a forkful of what certainly looked like mashed potatoes, but a yellow-orange in color.

"I know!" Kate said. "I was going to ask what that flavor is? What did you mash them with?"

"So...?" Tom wasn't sure if the reactions were positive or negative. "Do you like them?"

Kate answered first. "They're amazing. But I can't place the flavor. And the texture is different. Like... like... woody?"

Billy snorted into his glass of wine. "You said woody."

Kate hit him with a condescending glare, but said nothing, probably because the comment had made Tom laugh too.

Billy winked at Tom as he said, "Well, to use an analgesic, like this morning, these are to regular mashed potatoes as venison is to beef. The same ballpark, but... wilder."

Tom hid his amusement at Kate's reaction to Billy

malapropism, then stopped himself when he realized that Billy hadn't been in the room for the conversation with Kate.

He filed the thought away for later and said, "They're not potatoes. They're rutabagas."

Billy's eyes sparkled. "Rutabaga? I thought that was a bad back."

"No, that's lumbago."

"Lumbago's an RV, dumbass."

"Nope, that's Winnebago."

"I thought that was a rash."

"Impetigo."

Billy paused, then said, "No wait, I thought that was the guy who was crucified."

Oh, good dig, Tom thought. "That would be the impenitent thief." He was having serious trouble keeping a straight face.

Billy smirked. "I will fight no more forever."

"What the... Chief Joseph?"

"Oh, I'm sorry. The right answer is Nez Percé. Tell the man what he's won, Johnny." Billy pronounced the tribe's name, with an extravagant flourish of his hand, as "nay per-say."

"Bullshit! Impenitent thief is nowhere close to Nez Percé," Tom said, indignant but also into the joke enough to mockingly echo Billy's pronunciation and hand flourish. Tom turned to Kate, hoping for a judgment call in a game he and Billy had played as long as they'd known each other, but he saw from the open mouth and look of utter astonishment that she was in no position to help.

"What the hell was that?" she asked.

Billy looked at Tom questioningly. "Does it even have a name?"

"Uh, no. We just call it 'the game'."

Kate threw up her hands in mock indignation. "Oh great. You just made me lose."

Billy and Tom looked at each other, neither understanding what she meant.

"The game," she insisted. "You just made me lose the game."

Billy asked, "What game? Our game?"

"No, *the* game. You know, the one where you lose the game by thinking of the game..."

Tom had no earthly idea what she was talking about and when he looked at Billy, he saw that he was not alone.

Kate beamed with triumph. "I know something from pop culture that neither of you know?"

Billy pouted and said, "I think you're making it up," which made her beam even brighter.

Tom laughed and picked up their second bottle of wine, pouring enough in each of their glasses to finish it off. "So anyway, rutabagas, butter, goat cheese, and some seasoning."

Billy took the bottle from Tom and got up to open another. "Let's move out to the back porch," he said.

Billy still called it the back porch, which it had been when he'd grown up in the house, but since moving back he'd expanded the room into a cozy, windowed sunroom with a large, stone fireplace on one end.

He came back out with another bottle of wine, which he set on the table at the center of the u-shaped couch, and started to make a fire in the fireplace.

"Hey," he said over his shoulder. "I don't think I know what play you guys are working on. How do I not know that?"

Kate answered. "We're doing *The Man Who Came to Dinner* and the reason you don't know is because you never asked."

Billy grinned with one side of his mouth. "That sounds

like an awful lot of hooey."

"Hooey? When have you ever said...? Wait, that's a line from the play." She looked amazed.

Billy slouched over and flicked an imaginary cigar. "Come to my room in half an hour and bring some rye bread."

Tom started to correct Billy's impression, as well as his paraphrase of the line, then stopped when he realized how fantastic Groucho Marx would have been as Banjo. This entire train of thought also made him realize how much wine he'd had.

Kate's mouth was set. "Why did you ask, if you already knew?"

Billy looked surprised. "I didn't know. That's why I asked."

"Oh, you just happened to have lines memorized from a play written in the 1930s?"

"No, my dear, I just happen to have lines memorized from a movie made in 1942 by Warner Brothers. Neener. Neener." Tom smiled at how much wine Billy had also apparently had. He wondered if the year and studio of the movie were right or if Billy was bullshitting Kate.

Kate looked like she was close to anger, then suddenly she burst out laughing. The wine was apparently working on her too.

"I need to start staying up and watching your old movies with you."

Billy looked at both of them. "So how in the hell did you two convince the school to do such an old play?"

Tom answered, "That was a piece of cake. Big cast, clean humor, only one set to build..."

"And, weirdly enough," Kate added, "Cissy Marty loved the play."

Tom looked surprised and started to say something, then thought better of it. Billy noticed the look on his face, but didn't press when he saw that Tom had decided not to say anything.

Not that I'm not going to find out later, Billy thought.

Kate missed Tom's look and went on. "She had never said a word to me, not once, from my first day teaching here, and then out of the blue she pulled me aside one day to talk about Drama Club. She asked what play we were doing and when I told her, she said she loved the movie. Then she said something weird about Tom usually making the wrong choices and maybe this is a sign that he's getting smarter, but then she went back to how much she loved the movie. I remember her saying, 'It's a story about finding your one true love in the most unexpected of places.'"

Tom said, half to himself, "Prometheus."

Kate looked stunned, then looked down and shook her head. "Of course you would know that. Why wouldn't you?"

Billy cocked his head to one side. "Know what?"

"The Greeks believed that Prometheus, a Titan who had fought with Zeus against the other Titans, made man out of clay. There are different versions of this myth."

Kate, seemingly unconsciously, had switched from her normal conversational voice to what Tom thought of as her Lecture Voice. Tom had heard the voice before, at rehearsals, and didn't much like it. Unlike her natural smile and twinkle, the softness he could hear in her normal speaking voice, this one was clearer, crisper, and just a little condescending.

"In one version, the Titan made man last after he and his brother, Epimetheus, had made all the rest of the mortal creatures. They had given all the positive characteristics away by the time they made man, having forgotten to save any for him. Because of this, they convinced Gaia to breathe a soul into man, making him alone among the creatures of Earth the possessor of a sense of self and of love and of knowledge of mortality and of immortality. Prometheus' love for his creation also caused him to steal fire from the gods to give to man, for which he suffered a famously terrible punishment.

"The Titan first made man in only one sex and with four arms and four legs. Zeus, seeing this creature, decided that it was too grand and feared its pride, so he cut all men into two halves, a male and a female, each with two arms and two legs. From that time on, the two halves of each original man have sought each other out, trying to re-tie the knot that Zeus cut. Sometimes they succeed, and the two halves are reunited into one complete whole. Sometimes a man and a woman try to convince themselves that they have found their Other Halves, even when it is not so. For many, perhaps for most, the true Other Half is never found."

She stopped, then looked around as if she was just realizing she had been speaking. Her face reddened and she swallowed a large drink of wine.

Tom looked at her. "You know, as you were telling that story, it sure sounded like something you had told many times." Kate looked down, almost shyly and Tom figured it out. "Oh, you wrote that version of the story, didn't you? It was beautiful."

She smiled widely. "Thank you. I wrote that, actually a much longer version of it, in grad school."

Billy grinned evilly. "For a boyfriend?"

"For a class," she scowled.

Billy's evil grin expanded. "For a professor boyfriend?"

She slapped his arm, then turned back to Tom with a look of revelation on her face. "You write, don't you?" When Tom just looked back at her quizzically, she pressed. "Oh come on. You have 'secret author' written all you."

"Really?" Tom smiled as suavely as he could muster two bottles in and cocked one eyebrow. "Not secret superhero?"

"Actually, maybe that too, but you're not getting off that easy."

Tom shrugged. "Come on. Who hasn't started a novel at least once?"

Billy's hand shot into the air and waved back and forth.

"I meant, who, among those of us who can read, hasn't started a novel at least once?"

Billy, with a fake, sheepish pout that made Tom laugh, slowly lowered his hand and looked away.

Kate beamed. "I knew it. Come on, I showed you mine..."

Billy was less tipsy than he appeared. He hadn't seen Kate with her flirt on since they'd met and it was interesting to watch from the outside. Tom, to him, seemed oblivious to the signals she was sending. But was she really sending them, or was Billy's macho jealousy seeing phantom signals that weren't really there? And if she was sending them, was Tom missing them or ignoring them. He thought about the previous morning, owning that none of his anger had really been directed at Tom about Kate. Those goddam notes...

Tom surrendered. "Fine, I write. But just for myself. I've never published anything. I've never even submitted anything.

"Before you say anything else," she said, pointing at him, "I won't take no for an answer. You have to let us read something."

"I promise... to think about it."

She pointed once more, emphatically, then waved her empty wine glass at Billy. "Oh, baaaaaaaaby..."

"Nice," he said, but still got up and took the glass from her.

Tom got up too. "Potty break," he announced and followed Billy into the kitchen. He continued following Billy all the way to the wine rack.

Billy looked back over his shoulder. "Dude, you know there's zero chance she's going to forget your promise, right?"

"I only promised to think about it."

Billy laughed. "That's adorable. Listen, I have an idea,

but I need you to do half of it."

"I'm listening with a vague sense of suspicion and unease."

"You have good instincts. Anyway, last week Ed asked me to help him button up his hunting camp now that musket season's over. I'm going to call him and see if he wants to stay up there tomorrow night and do it the next day."

"Okay, and my half… you cannot be serious."

"Will you do it?"

"There's no way he'll say yes."

Any residual humor was gone from Billy's eyes. "He will if you ask him to."

"I won't lie to him."

"I don't think you'll need to. He came here today."

Tom stood more upright, sobering. "What?"

"Yeah. And he was asking about problems between Cissy and me."

"Oh, man…"

"It's ok. I think he'll jump at the chance to have us all in one place."

Tom shook his head. "Do you think he really thinks you did it?"

"Sweetie pie," Kate called from the other room. "Are you *making* the wine?"

Billy looked past Tom to the porch to make sure Kate was staying in place. "Slow your roll, hotfoot. I'm coming." He turned back to Tom. "I'm hoping he's just flailing, so maybe both of us can work on him. Kinda reset him."

Tom sighed and said, simply, "Ed."

"I know. But I'll work on him tomorrow." He looked back to the porch. "You in?"

"For no sensible reason, yes. Now move before I piss my pants."

"Ok, but hurry up. I have to go see a man about taking a shit."

Kate and Tom each had one more glass of wine and they talked about Kate's Prometheus story. Kate insisted that it was completely true, that there really was only one true love for each of us. Billy was also insistent, though less aggressively so, that loving someone was a choice. That is was work, "sometimes very hard work," he said as he smiled at Kate. The fact that you choose to love someone and the fact that you each have to work at it make it real. Not a romance novel.

Tom could tell that Billy had made this argument before, even if just to himself. For Tom's part, he refused to be pinned down, partly to stay out of the middle and partly because he felt that there must be a way to reconcile the two sides. That there might certainly be a special person for each of us, but that without choosing every day to do the hard work of love, that special bond couldn't hold.

Abruptly, Kate called Billy a "big stud" and told him to take her to bed or lose her forever. Tom had no intention of driving in his condition — he had already created the scene in his head of being pulled over by Bob and using the opportunity to mention the hunting camp — so he had started to put his boots on for the five and a half mile walk home. Billy stopped him and gently steered both Tom and Kate up the stairs, then scooted Tom towards the guest room. Kate was asleep as soon as she hit the bed. As he tucked her in, Billy heard snoring coming from the guest room.

He shook his head and softly said, "Good night, John Boy."

Kate laughed and shook her head. "Wow, this is really bad."

"It can't be that bad," Billy replied.

She laughed again. "It's worse."

They were sitting in bed, both naked, both reading from laptops. The morning had been a relaxing one. Billy had only been out of bed long enough to make a pot of coffee and bring it and their computers up to the bedroom. They'd both had e-mails waiting for them from Tom, who was gone by the time Billy had gotten up. He had emailed writing samples.

Kate had started reading them immediately and had been chuckling to herself — and to Billy — ever since. Billy had started to open the file, then stopped himself. He wanted to read the pages, badly, but he also wanted to read them when he had the time and the peace to give them a fair reading. He was reading *The New York Times* website instead, but he had also found Almoth Wright's *The Unexpurgated Case Against Woman Suffrage* on gutenburg.net and downloaded it for later. He knew he was being childish, but he didn't want Kate to see him reading it.

"Wait, wait. Listen to this."

He looked over at her, amazed at himself for having the capacity to be perturbed by the inhabitant of such a glorious body. But he was perturbed. Twice so far he had stopped her from reading aloud, telling her that he wanted to read Tom's work later when he was alone.

"Seriously, listen to this." She looked directly at him with eyes that sparked so bright you could almost hear them.

He wondered how long it had been since he'd found her insistent self-absorption to be cute. "I surrender. Go ahead."

"Ok, are you listening? Really focus."

"Kate..."

"Ok, here goes. The title is... I'm not joking... the title is Slugs...

> *We know we're not cute*
>
> *like puppies or kittens*
>
> *we're ugly as hell*
>
> *and leave snot on the lawn*
>
> *it's not our fault*
>
> *that you think we are gross*
>
> *but what about that little Holocaust thing of yours?*

Billy did listen; he really focused, just like she'd asked.

"Oh my god," she said for what must have been the 20th time since starting. "It's like somebody writing a spoof of what an O Henry poem would be like."

"Read it again."

"Seriously? We haven't been punished enough."

"Yeah," he said quietly. "Read it again."

So she did, still chuckling, but quieter. When she finished, she asked, "What are you thinking?"

"Two things. The first is I may end up liking the poem, the more I think about it. But the other thing is... I don't know... It's not cool making fun of him for this."

"Billy, relax. We were just having a little fun. You guys always pick on each other."

Billy sat up straighter. "That's not the point, Kate. And this is different. He didn't even want to tell us... well, he certainly didn't want to tell *you* that he had written anything."

She smiled. "Me, most of all?'

"Of course you most of all. He went out on a skinny ass limb letting you see it."

Kate looked at Billy with a devilish glint in her eye. "Maybe that's why you pick on him when it is just you and me – because you feel threatened by the way he feels?"

It was Billy's turn to smile. "Listen to you, trouble maker. I think you like it."

"I don't hate it."

"No, I don't imagine you do. This is interesting, though."

She said, "The fact that this is the first time we're openly talking about the way Tom feels about me? It is interesting."

"Yeah. I have to tell you, the Tom in high school might not have been able to get past this. He'd have mooned over you, left little notes in your locker."

"In high school, that's terribly romantic. Or at least flattering."

"But as an adult..."

"Seriously. Stalker."

Billy closed his laptop and held his chin with his hand. "Have you ever worried? You know, that being friends with him, doing the theater thing and being as close to him as you are... That it... That it would be hard for him?"

She looked at Billy, hurt. "I'm not completely heartless. It's something I've thought about, sure, but like you said, we're all adults. This isn't high school anymore. There's no reason we can't all be friends."

She paused, then continued, "I do love being around him. But honestly, I love even more being around the two of you. There's a link between you two, a... I don't know... a yin and a yang that's somehow... just right. And not right, all at the same time." She laughed. "Sometimes I wonder if I'm the third wheel, not Tom."

"What about me?"

She was puzzled. "What do you mean?"

"The third wheel. What about me feeling like the third wheel?"

Her face became as serious as he'd ever seen it. "Billy, never, not once, in your entire life have you known what it feels like to be the third wheel."

He wasn't sure how to respond to that. He should know how to respond to it by now. Billy had spent his entire life being looked at as the one who has everything figured out. To the outside world, he was always the center of a group, un-plagued by self-doubt. He was always the one you came to if you needed help, never the one who actually needed the help.

A good part of the blame lay with himself; this Billy knew. People saw him as invulnerable because he projected invulnerability. Well, maybe it was time to put himself out there to someone. To her.

But, of course, at that moment the phone rang.

He laughed at himself, silently. He knew damn well that phone or no phone, he would have let the moment pass without saying a thing. He could feel his defenses going back up, the belligerence setting in. He was always there for the people in his life without being asked, sometimes before they even knew they needed him. So why should he have to ask her to be there for him? Shouldn't she be able to see inside him or at least make the effort to see inside him without him having to beg for it?

It was Tom on the phone. "It's on. Pick me up at like 5."

***

Awkward didn't begin to describe the moment when

all four men met at the front door of the hunting camp.

Billy had hoped that the two of them would have gotten to the cabin first, had pictured himself and Tom in the very place that they were now seeing Ed and Bob. Billy and Tom welcoming the other two men would have been less awkward for him and might have put Ed on the defensive from the beginning. He needed to find a way to make some space, some distance between Ed and Bob or he knew he'd never get Bob's trust back.

He'd been uncharacteristically early to pick Tom up, but Tom had been running just as uncharacteristically late. He had arrived at Tom's house a little before 5 PM and had waited 15 minutes before calling Tom's cell.

"Oh shit!" had been Tom's answer when he'd finally picked up the call. "I'll be there in 10 minutes."

It had been twenty.

"Man, I am so sorry," Tom said to Billy, who was feeling less and less composed. Rocking in the chair on Tom's front porch hadn't been the least bit soothing. "Let me just grab my go bag."

Billy got back into his truck and Tom was in and out of the house in seconds, now carrying a black backpack, black parka, and black boots (*Ninja much?* Billy thought) but still wearing his standard work uniform of khakis and untucked blue button-down dress shirt.

"You want to change?" Billy asked.

"I'm good."

"You're going into the woods in khakis?"

"Warm khakis. They're flannel lined. Look," he said, and crossing one leg over the other, rolled the bottom of the pants leg up to reveal plaid flannel. "It's really soft. Here. Feel it."

"What the fuck is wrong with you? I'm not feeling your pants."

"Come on, touch it." He lowered his voice to a deep bass and said it again. "Touch it."

Billy pointed a finger at Tom's face. "Stop it."

Then he broke. Shaking his head, he said, "Oh for fuck's sake," and he reached over and felt the thick flannel between his fingers. Still shaking his head, he said, "Yes, I'm sure they're very comfortable. Happy?"

Tom nodded. "I think we've really turned a corner here, Bill."

He pointed his finger at Tom's face again, then turned his head forward, put the truck in gear, and pulled out of the driveway.

As Billy turned right on Main Street and drove past the Market, he asked, "So what the hell happened, dude? You're never late."

Tom started changing from his shoes to his boots and sighed. "What a day... Just a bunch of shit. Two — not one, but two wrong deliveries. Water pipe out back froze and burst because Lisa forgot to turn off the goddam water after she used it."

"Oh, fuck."

"Oh wait, it gets better. After she used it to wash her truck during her shift."

"Oh, super fuck. Who ratted her out?"

"Seriously? It's Lisa. She told me herself. In fact, she told me while she was yelling at me for not having an insulated water line."

Billy burst into laughter. Gales of huge, body shaking, unapologetic laughter. When he saw that Tom was not sharing in his little moment, Billy stifled himself as best he could.

Tom threw up his hands. "The worst part of the whole day was Molly calling in sick this morning. I had to friggin' take care of everything. All day. No matter what happened. No matter how big or how small. Important or fucking stupid. It's going to be a miracle if the store gets closed up right tonight and opened up right tomorrow."

"Sick?"

"Yeah, she said she was coming down with something and might be out a few days. I mean, I hope she's not, but she was coughing pretty good on the phone."

"So, Lisa is running the place tonight and tomorrow?"

Tom shook his head. "Tell me about it. I blame Kate for putting the idea out there to the universe last night." He finished lacing and tying his boots, then took off his shirt, opened his backpack, and fished out a black turtleneck and dark gray commando sweater. "But seriously. I'm overreacting. Right? It's only 24 hours." He looked pleadingly to Billy. "Tell me I'm overreacting. Please?"

"Ok. A — you're not overreacting. You're completely fucked."

Tom leaned back against the headrest and sighed again. "I know. Shit." Then he looked back. "That was A. What's B?"

"What... the... fuck... are you wearing? We're going to the hunting camp, not Navarone."

"Ha, ha. Don't bitch to me when you're freezing to death."

"Just as long as you understand, I'm not going to be the one to drop the last grenades into the air shafts."

"Grenades? Air shaft? What the hell are you...? Jesus Christ, that's not even the right movie!"

Billy shrugged. "I'm just saying."

***

As the truck rounded the last bend in the dirt road, they could see through the front window to Ed and Bob sitting at the kitchen table. There was a plume of smoke rising out of the chimney and the two looked relaxed.

Well, let's go right in and fuck that all up, Billy thought.

The two men in the cabin must have heard the truck, because both got up from the table and walked out the door and onto the front porch.

Ed walked out first, of course. He had a broad smile, as if this was the most natural situation in the world. Four old buddies spending the night in the woods. He was carrying an open beer.

Bob came out behind Ed. The death grip he had on his coffee cup belied the sense of calm he was clearly trying to project.

As Billy turned off the truck, Tom quietly said, "I got this." Billy was still getting the key out of the ignition when Tom exited the truck, his backpack already over his shoulder.

Fuck! This just keeps getting better. At least they could have been walking up to the porch together, but now Billy would be walking up to the three of them instead. As he got out of the truck his eyes med Ed's, who smiled and winked one twinkling eye. Billy went to the truck bed and grabbed his duffel. As he turned back to the cabin, he saw Tom walking back towards him with the palm of one hand on his face.

"What a dumbass," he said loudly. "I forgot my phone." He jerked a thumb back towards the cabin. "Go back inside, you guys. It's friggin cold out here." As he passed Billy he winked.

Billy looked back to the cabin. Ed's twinkle was gone. The men made their awkward hellos and Tom and Billy followed Bob and Ed into the cabin.

The front wall of the cabin, on either side of the door, was dominated by two huge windows Ed had salvaged from an out-of-business bar. Billy always felt a mixture of fondness and loss when he saw those windows. Ed had scraped off the painted name of the bar, but had left the two large painted ovals that had framed the bar's name, so they were immediately recognizable. All four of them had spent countless hours in the bar but the other three had followed Billy there. Billy considered it his church. Practically every Sunday of the year, from the time he was 10 or 11, Billy's father would take him fishing or hunting or ice fishing on Sunday morning, then they would spend the rest of the day at the bar, Billy's father drinking Genny Light after Genny Light and Billy keeping pace with Royal Palm Orange Soda and, once he outgrew that, Mountain Dew.

As the four of them walked through the door, both of the newcomers stopped and stared at the interior of the cabin. They were stunned at the improvements that had been made since they'd last been there at this same time the previous year. The basic structure of the cabin was the same as it had been since Ed had built it ten years earlier, but beyond that skeleton the interior was entirely new.

They walked directly into the cooking, eating, bullshitting, card playing room from the porch. To their right, along the adjacent wall was the kitchen — sink, stove and fridge — with the sink under a window on that wall. The layout was all the same, but the appliances were new and the configuration of the cabinets, as well as the cabinets themselves, was entirely new. This area didn't hold their attention, though.

Previously, the wall to the left had hosted a pellet-fired box stove, effective but modest. Now, a substantial portion of this wall was covered with a massive, stone fireplace. These were real stones, not molded concrete, and the mantle was made from a single, thick, plank that was polished and finished to a glasslike shine. The work, though solid and imposing, had a beauty to it that amazed both Billy and Tom. Hanging on the wall above the fireplace was a mirror framed with a thick, rusted length of steel cable that had been welded together to form an oval. Centered on the mantelpiece was a huge, gray stone, probably a foot across. There was a fire roaring in the hearth and each of the two men thought to himself, in disappointment, that he should have noticed that the smoke coming from the chimney was from an open fire, not a pellet stove.

At the back of the first floor on the side walls were the bunks, four to a side. Eight bunks for the most alone man in town. The pellet stove had been relocated to the back wall, centered between the bunks.

Above the half of the room that held the bunks was the original loft, reached by a metal spiral staircase centered at the front of the loft. The loft held the most astonishing change of all. Where for the past ten years had been storage, Billy and Tom now saw a fully finished master bedroom, with closets, a bed, and a desk. Because of the angle of their view, they couldn't see the fireplace on the back wall of the bedroom, but the stone chimney that was a smaller version of the one downstairs gave it away.

Ed watched them marvel at the change in the cabin, unable, unwilling to hide the pride he felt in their reactions. Bob had reacted in much the same way when he'd first walked into the cabin, though without the oohing, aahing, and pointing.

Someone had come into Ed's life at this same time last year. Someone who had motivated him to feel and think and, most important, act in ways he'd never done before. All of this work had been for her. Most of all the bedroom, where she'd shown a lonely, middle aged bachelor things he'd never believed real women did for free.

Tom walked to the kitchen, paused a moment while he considered the new cabinets, then without hesitating he opened the cabinet that held the coffee cups and poured himself a cup of coffee. Ed had still been watching Billy, so he hadn't seen this, but Bob had.

Tom walked back to the table and sat down across from Bob. "This…" he said, holding his hands out as if trying to grab hold of the entire cabin, "This is… well, it's two things."

Prepared for the effusive praise that Tom normally gave even the smallest accomplishments, Ed felt his stomach clench. There should be no qualifiers for this. No shades of gray in his triumph.

Billy spoke up. "Yeah, it is. Fucking and amazing."

Ed barely heard him but continued to stare at Tom

through half-closed eyes. "Two things?"

"Yeah. One, obviously, is that it's gorgeous. If a hunting camp can be gorgeous, this is it. It's astonishing."

Ed didn't care about "one." "Okay. And two?"

"Two is — it's the perfect metaphor for what has happened to the four of us. And the fault is mostly mine."

Billy, playing his role, asked, "You made us beautiful and rustic? Thanks."

Tom fought his smile. It was entirely possible that the next few exchanges would determine the success or failure of this mission. And it was a mission. He hoped Billy would see where he was going.

"No. That he did all of this work over the past year and we weren't here to help. We didn't even know he was doing it."

He looked directly at Billy, talking as if they were the only two in the room. "He didn't want to listen to you and me bitching at each other. Pretending to find mundane things to argue about as our way of not talking about what was really between us. Why else wouldn't he tell us?"

Exactly, Billy thought, and he knew that he and Tom were on the same wavelength. *Why else, indeed?*

"It's not all you. Hell, it's probably not even mostly you."

He turned to face Ed squarely. "Dude, I'm sorry too. I wasn't here to help you and because of me, Tom wasn't either. We're not in high school anymore and me acting like we are has gone on way too long."

Ed was seething and when he snuck a look at Bob — he tried not to, but he couldn't stop himself — he saw the cop's face softening at this fucking bullshit act.

It didn't feel rehearsed and the emotion in their voices couldn't have sounded more real, but he knew. He fucking knew. They were manipulating Bob into believing what the dumbass wanted to believe, what he needed to believe.

He was afraid that they had even more bullshit scenes of fraternal good will up their sleeves, but Ed also knew he had to get out. It was a calculated risk, leaving the three of them alone, but an eruption from him was a bigger risk, so he put on his best look of disdain, and said, "Jesus Christ, what a pair of fags. You two lovebirds can have the upstairs tonight. Me, I gotta shit," and walked out the door and headed to the outhouse.

The three of them watched him leave, then looked back at each other. Billy was the first to speak.

"Do you really think he'd let us sleep up there?"

Despite himself, Bob laughed and shook his head, but he didn't say anything more and went back to nursing his cup of coffee and looking out the window.

Billy went to the kitchen for a coffee cup. Pretending he hadn't seen Tom get his, he fumbled through the cabinets as if he wasn't sure where the cups were.

"Wait, board games?"

Tom said, "Maybe he got them in case we didn't want to play spades."

"What do we have here?" Billy let his fingers run across the boxes as he read out the titles. "Backgammon... surprising. Quarto... very brainy and even more surprising. Blokus... I love Blokus!"

Tom asked, "What's Blokus?"

"My colon, a tiny bit. I need more fiber."

Tom shook his head and refused to engage. Billy got his coffee and sat at the table, smiling expectantly at Bob, who only nodded at him and went back to looking out the window. The three of them sat silently — horribly, awkwardly, silently — until Ed came back.

Tom engaged him before he was completely through the door. "Ok, what is it?"

Ed was startled, as were Billy and Bob, and Ed felt the calm he had fought so hard to grip onto start to slip away so much faster than it had been gained. "What the fuck? What is what?"

"Next year's offense, knucklehead. Don't tell me you haven't started already."

Bob and Billy both exhaled more loudly than each intended, then smiled at each other.

Ed was famous throughout the state, well beyond the small schools of New York State's Class D, for his innovative football mind. He understood that the kids he had were the kids he had. Nobody was moving their kid to Moriah to play football, so Ed essentially built a new offense every few years, rebuilding the playbook to match the skills of the players he had available to him. The previous two years had been more stable than ever before because of Mike Rush's nephew, Paul, who ran Ed's version of the West Coast offense like a miniature Joe Montana.

Ed smiled, wickedly. "I have two words for you. 'Cloud' and 'Dust'. My quarterback may not even have to warm up before the games."

Tom said, "You passed over 60% of the time this year."

"Sixty-three," said Ed. "But on over 70% of the passes, the ball was thrown fewer than 10 yards. We were still playing ball control. The last two years I had the second coming of Joe Montana and now I have the second coming of Maurice Carthon."

"Maurice," Billy said to himself, laughing quietly. "Hey, you guys know pompatus isn't even a real word, right?"

All three looked at him and Tom started to ask him what the hell he was talking about, but Bob surprised them all by interrupting. "New Jersey Generals."

Ed looked impressed. "That's right. That cat was the best blocking fullback I've ever seen."

"New Jersey Generals?" Tom asked.

Bob was just warming up. "Yeah, he was a great blocker, and that's pretty much all he did when he went to the Giants, but don't forget he also ran for over a thousand yards in '84. He and Herschel Walker both went over a thousand that year. That was the Walt Michaels, Brian Sipe year."

Billy said, "Holy blast from the past. Dig you with the mad USFL knowledge."

Bob nodded. "He was a beast. The year the USFL folded, he went straight to the Giants and played a second full season. He played like 40 some games that year." He shook his head. "I loved the USFL and I'll never forgive the idiot owners for following a pied piper right into a toilet." He turned to Tom and said, "I can't believe an 80s sports nut like you doesn't have an encyclopedic knowledge of the USFL."

"Mmm..." Tom thought for a sec, then asked, "You're talking '83, '84, right?"

"Exactly," Bob answered.

"Yeah, I was pretty much baked every day those years."

Bob's laugh, a genuine, affectionate laugh, affected Tom and Billy very differently than it did Ed.

Ed had hoped for more from Bob. He had known the cop would see through whatever Billy came with, but he had hoped Bob would just as easily see through Tom's new man crush on Billy. He had visualized, over and over, Bob's anger, Billy's smartass remarks, and Tom's defensiveness making things worse and worse, until they boiled over... He felt his hands clenching and unclenching at his sides and forced himself to do his count.

His primary scenario wasn't materializing, at least on its own, but he wouldn't have lasted very long as a coach if he wasn't prepared for his initial plan to meet resistance. He believed, along with Mike Tyson, that everybody has a plan until they get punched in the face. Ed smiled to himself at the thought of filling Billy's gaping mouth with his huge fist.

Ed had contingency plans for his contingency plans. He would have already been derailed if he hadn't, because neither he nor his friend had believed for a second that Tom would sign on to Billy's plan to solve the crime.

He walked over to the counter by the sink and picked up the newspapers he'd placed there before any of the other three had arrived. He forced himself to wait as he thumbed through the pages, ostensibly looking for the sports section.

Wait for it... Wait for it...

The paper rustled in Ed's hands.

Tom looked up.

Billy saw exactly what was happening and was powerless to stop it.

Tom asked Ed, "What are you looking at?"

Ed was still facing the counter, so none of them saw the huge grin that engulfed his face.

"I'm just looking at the sports page. Here's the rest if you want it," Ed said, as he walked towards them and tossed the paper on the table in front of Tom.

It was that morning's *Plattsburgh Press Republican*. The headline read, "Killer Speaks!" and below that was a subhead that read, "Moriah's Top Cop Taunted by Wife's Killer."

All three of them flinched at the paper. Billy and Tom because they had each seen it already, Bob because he hadn't. Billy and Tom had discussed the article, but hadn't been able to come up with a strategy with how to handle it if it came up. Well, here it was.

"Well, that's just perfect," Bob said, looking directly at Billy. Ed was silent, knowing he had done enough and understanding the danger of over-stoking the fire.

Tom tried to defuse the new mood, but he only got as far as, "We thought you had already..." before Bob stopped him.

"Shut up. This isn't about you." He turned back to Billy. "This is about you and me." He said it slowly, but with an intensity that had pushed away his tiredness. "When *The Times of Ti* put the first notes online, you and me were the only ones who had seen them."

Billy started to say something, stopped himself, then started again. "You know, just now, I was going to pretend I hadn't seen the notes on your desk. But I've dicked this up enough already. I've been dicking it up right from the beginning." Out of the corner of his eye, he saw Tom twitching like the know-it-all kid in class when he wants to be the first one with the answer. He knew that if he and Bob paused, Tom would jump in and he also knew what Tom would jump in with. But Billy not only had to be the one to say it, he needed the time to say it in the right order.

Hoping Tom would get it, Billy shot him a quick glance out of the corner of his eye. Bob saw it and understood that Billy wanted Tom to stay out of the exchange.

Ed also saw it, but concluded that Tom and Billy were ready for this line of conversation. They were ready for it and had already planned how to attack it, how to attack him.

How? How the fuck had they been able to anticipate every move he was making tonight? His fists started to ball and un-ball, but he was self-aware enough to notice, to start his counts. He had started them down this path and he would just have to ride it out and redirect things if Billy and Tom started to make any headway with Bob. So far, he had been able to keep things on edge, and he knew that he had one card left to play. A card that wouldn't fail.

Billy went on. "So, that's what you think? That I gave the notes to the papers? Man, I wouldn't do that. I didn't say anything to anybody."

Bob looked down at the table, then looked back up at Billy. "That seems pretty unlikely. You might not have told Kate, but there's no way you wouldn't have told Tom."

Busted, thought Ed. It took all of his willpower to hide his smile. He had been thinking that exact thought and had been trying with everything he had to will the thought into Bob's head.

Billy again looked at Tom, this time inviting him to speak up.

He did. "Bob," Tom said, slowly and deliberately. "I have no idea whether or not Billy would have told me or Kate about the notes if he'd had time, but he didn't. Kate saw them online before either of us did. After they were posted, Billy about shit his pants and told us that he had looked at the note on your desk and that you were probably going to think he told the paper."

Bob turned to Billy, but said nothing. Billy said, "I probably… no, I definitely would have told Tom. I probably wouldn't have told Kate, just because I wouldn't have wanted to get scolded. But I never would have told the press. Never."

All the tension that had been holding Bob so stiff in his chair released and he leaned back and took a drink of coffee.

"I'm glad," he said. "Really glad."

"Well, that was a touching moment," Ed said. "Sounded a little scripted to me, though." *What are we at? Plan F? G?* he thought, as he went to pour another cup of coffee. The other three stayed silent. He clearly had more to say, so they waited.

He filled his cup, brought it up to his lips, and blew across the surface of the coffee to gather his thoughts.

"Ok," he said, "Let's say we believe Billy didn't give the notes to the papers. Bob didn't, obviously. That leaves two possibilities."

"Two?" Billy asked, ignoring Ed's implication that the question of his innocence in the matter wasn't fully settled.

Bob nodded. "I see where you're going. I absolutely see where you're going, but I guess that would be three."

"Good point," Ed said.

"A little help over here?" Tom said "I got the easy one. The killer."

A light went off for Billy. "Oh fuck. No way." He raised his hand.

Ed smiled and said, "Yes, you in the back."

"The cops, man. The Staties and the FBI."

"That's right," Ed said. "The fuckers."

"Sons of bitches," Billy agreed.

"The part that gets me so pissed..." Ed started. "I mean, yeah, I get it. The fact that she's your wife complicates it, but the part that pisses me off is they have completely cut you out."

The hairs on the back of Tom's neck started to stand up. Ed had been steering every conversation with aggression so far. Force, not flow. He had been pushing Tom and Billy apart from Bob. His tactics had changed from football to judo, but his goal certainly hadn't.

"We talked about this," Bob said to Ed. "It's protocol."

More warning lights, with sirens this time. *What had they talked about?*

"Fuck protocol," Billy said. "You're the town cop. You know the people in this town better than anyone. Nobody is better placed than you to figure this out."

Oh shit...

Bob didn't need Ed's prompting, though it was there for the asking. All four of them realized at the same time what Billy had said, though only Tom and Ed knew that Billy had been pulled into the trap.

"Based on the look on your face, I'm thinking you wish you could unsay that," Bob said.

"A little bit." Billy sighed. "The thing is, if I hadn't been such a dick, if I hadn't looked at that fucking note on your desk, what we talked about that day..."

Bob said, "I haven't forgotten what we talked about."

Ed saw his opening and hit it. Aggressively. "About how you're over your head? You guys talked about that?"

Billy's face tightened. "Dude, you do not want to..."

"Even if it wasn't his own wife, he'd be over his head," Ed continued. "That's pretty close to verbatim, right?"

"You're gonna want to stop."

"Oh, just one more. Because we all know why you need this case solved so quick."

The short exchange had started out of nowhere and had changed in tone so quickly that Tom and Bob had both stayed silent, trying to keep up. This last comment showed up on both their faces like a slap.

Billy didn't see it coming either. "What the fuck?"

Ed smiled that same odd, uncomfortable smile Billy had seen at the school the morning after the murder. "Why, we talked about it that morning. How your activities... and Cissy's activities... might line up and make you a suspect." He said the word "activities" slow and hard each time, then accelerated through the end of the sentence.

Billy went after him. Fast. Faster than Tom had ever seen him move. Only the distance between them and the arrangement of the men around the table gave Tom enough time to get in front of Billy and slow him down long enough for Bob to step in and help.

Ed was silent, waiting, as the three men struggled. He made no effort to hide the look of triumph on his face. The night had been tough, a real struggle. The most satisfying wins always are. It hadn't looked good for him a few times, he thought, but there's a reason people only watch the last quarter of a basketball game. That's when the winner is decided.

The struggle only lasted a few seconds because Billy quickly stopped trying to push past. He put up his hands and stepped back, staring into Ed's eyes. Billy shook his head once, then turned and walked out the door. They heard the truck start up, heard it being thrown into gear, heard the rear end slide out on the frozen dirt road as he drove away.

Ed hadn't moved, and hadn't been able — hadn't tried — to relax the victorious look on his face. "There goes your ride, Tom," he said quietly.

Bob looked around, scratching the side of his neck. "I'll give you a ride, Tom. I think I need to call it a night."

The victorious look left Ed's face, but he didn't say anything. All his work, the entire thing, had gotten him nowhere and he just stood there as Bob and Tom gathered their bags and Billy's. Stood there as Bob said good night and thanked him for the invite. Stood there as Tom said nothing when he walked out the door. He didn't know it, couldn't know it because he couldn't see it, but he was standing under the winter solstice full moon, a moon that would have been the biggest and brightest of the millennium if the solid cloud cover hadn't completely and utterly shrouded its light.

Ed was still standing there when his friend came. His friend who had been waiting in a truck on a logging road, who had seen the others leave, who had been planning on killing three of the four men that night as they slept. He was still standing there when his friend came in through the front door of the hunting camp, took him by the hand, and led him up the spiral staircase to their bed.

Tom was at work even earlier than usual the next morning. He had been at the store an hour before Molly arrived, also earlier than usual. It was still an hour before opening and as he saw her approaching the front door on the security camera, he reached over and tapped the power button on his fancy new Keurig coffee maker.

He watched her closely. She was holding her left elbow tight against her side as she unlocked the door. Shoulder? No, ribs it looked like.

He had just made a cup of coffee, so the water was already hot and he had a fresh cup of hot chocolate waiting for her when she reached the office.

"Oh sweet jesus, that smells good," she said as she took off her coat and hung it on the coat rack in the office. "You spoil me."

"I'm just terrified you'll leave me for another man."

"Good. That's the right attitude to have. You keep that thought in mind and you'll stay on the straight..." She stopped, grimaced, and pushed her left elbow tight to her side again. Her face was white.

Tom jumped up and helped her sit. She saw the combination of concern and nascent anger on his face and knew she had to do something to change directions. She held out one hand in front of her, held the other pressed across her abdomen, and pushed the most genuine cough she could out through tightened lips.

"I had the worst cough Sunday night. I think I sprained a muscle in my side." She coughed again. "Son of a bitch, that hurts."

Tom sat back down and before he could talk, she cut him off. "I know what you're going to say and I promise if it still hurts tomorrow or Saturday, I'll run down to Ti."

"Is that what I was going to say?" Tom asked.

"It was if you don't want me running into the arms of Kevin Gillman and the Great Satan."

"That fucker! I knew he was going to call you."

She laughed, gasped from the pain, held her ribs, then laughed again. She had to laugh at the contortions Tom's face was going through because if she didn't, she'd cry. Looking at the concern on his face, trying to remember the last time someone had looked at her like that. Or if anyone else ever had. She had to laugh. She had no choice.

Tom knew the topic they were both avoiding, knew that she hadn't hurt herself coughing, and understood that she probably knew she wasn't fooling him. But she wanted him to pretend she was fooling him and he didn't know how to not. Didn't know if he should or if he even could bring up the topic she didn't want to address.

He reached down to his desk drawer and pulled out a small, gift wrapped box with a red bow. He had to give it to her today, because he wouldn't be able to on Christmas. And what better way to change the topic?

"So, I may have gotten you a present." He paused, waiting for her reaction. What small reaction there was didn't give him any hints as to what she was thinking.

"It's not that big a deal and…"

"Shush, dummy, and hand it over. You're going to screw this all up."

"Shushing," he said, handing her the box. She took it and moved her hand up and down to test its weight.

"It's heavier than it looks." She rotated the box several

times. "Ok, it's a cube. The wrapping job is too precise to be done at a store." She smiled at his inability to hide his pleasure at the last observation.

She rotated it a few more times, just to vex him and he nearly said something, but she stopped him with a glance. She un-taped the paper with one nail, carefully, not tearing any of the paper, until the box was completely unwrapped. She carefully folded the paper, shooting him another glance when he sighed dramatically, then set the paper on his desk and pulled the top off the plain, white box.

Her breath caught in her chest when she saw the white dandelion puff encased in a perfectly clear ball of glass about the size of a tennis ball. She carefully pulled it from the box and held it up so she could see the sunlight through it.

Blinking away tears, she put it back in its box and looked at Tom. He was so adorably unsure of himself in this moment.

"It's so beautiful. It's perfect. Where in the world did you get it?"

He beamed as he said, "I made it."

"You what?"

"I made it. For you. I made it for you."

She couldn't stay in the room with him any longer. She set the box down and walked closer to him, right to where he was sitting in his desk chair, then took his face in her hands, and slowly leaned in. At the last instant, she turned his face and pressed her lips against his cheek. She held them there for several seconds, then stepped back, picked up her present, and walked out.

As everyone began to arrive and start their work, he stayed in the office trying to distract himself by double checking inventories. He figured the best way to process Molly's reaction to his gift was to not actively think about it. It was failing as a plan, utterly and miserably, but he hadn't yet come up with an alternative.

Lisa walked to the doorway and leaned back against the doorframe, watching him work. He sensed her presence, but kept working, hoping she would give up and go back to work. She had more patience than he did, or at least less interest in work, so he eventually looked up. They looked at each other for a few seconds, then she walked into his office, sat in the chair opposite him, leaned back and put her feet — in pink and black cowboy boots — up on his desk.

"How come nobody ever knew you asked Molls to the prom?"

Tom shrugged. "She was probably as embarrassed about it as I was. Honestly, I always half expected it to come up at some point. I assumed she'd tell one of her friends and pretty soon everybody would be laughing about it."

"Well, then. You should have asked me to go."

"Sure," he said with a big smile. "Ask the most popular senior to my junior Prom. That definitely would have had the whole school laughing."

"Did you spend every day of high school waiting to be laughed at?"

He looked at Lisa. Really looked at her. Her high school good looks had aged into an even deeper beauty. She rode horses as often as she could — she had friends at every farm and stable in the North Country — and the sun and wind had given her face a vibrant, outdoors look that only emphasized its classic lines. Impossibly, her figure was even better than it had been in her youth.

But her eyes… Those windows showed a soul that had always been angry. At her parents, at her friends, at the world. At life.

They weren't angry now, though. Tom thought he saw, maybe sympathy? Or pity. Fine line.

"Be honest, Lisa. Did you even know who I was in high school?"

"Oh, for fuck's sake. Yes, Invisi-Boy, I knew who you

were. We had less than 250 kids in the entire high school." She grinned. "I promise you, I knew the name of every boy in the class ahead of me and the class behind me. A girl's got to do her research."

Tom couldn't help but chuckle. "Even the nerds who didn't play football or basketball?"

"Even the nerds who smoked pot and read that weird fucking rainbow book."

"*Gravity's Rainbow?* I'm going to sound like a dick here, but that is not a reference I would have expected from you."

"Franny and I used to drink together..."

"Franny?"

"The school librarian. We still hang out. You don't know her name?"

"I don't know her as Franny, that's for sure. Wait, in high school you used to drink with..."

He trailed off as she challenged him with her eyes to say more, then held up his hands in mock surrender. Lisa went on. "Anyway, she told me that some kid had asked her to order a book about retards..."

He paused. "*Confederacy of Dunces?*"

"Whatever. But apparently he was also the only person she'd ever met who read this ridiculous, hard book called *Gravity's Rainbow*. She gave me a copy and I tried to read it, but it was bullshit. And then when the retard book came in, she let me read that first, but that one was complete shit too."

"What do you mean, 'first'? I was the first one to check it out. She called me when it came in and said she'd saved it for me."

"Nope. She gave it to me first. I took it home, tried to read it for like an hour, and brought it back the next day. Like I said — shit."

Tom's eyes narrowed and he looked as if he was about to ask something, then he changed his mind, and then changed it back. "The lipstick kiss inside the cover — was that you?'

Lisa smiled broadly, "Yup."

"I thought it was from the librarian. I thought she was the one making fun of me. But it was you."

"Are you for real? I wasn't making fun of you, you dumbass. I did it because you were cute."

"I really thought she was making fun of me."

"No. She thought you were cute too. We all did. But you lived in your own little world and if you hadn't had your little crush on her," she motioned with her head out into the store, "we would have all figured you were gay."

"GBF," he muttered.

"What's that?" Lisa asked.

He stood up. "Nothing." He looked at his watch. "All right, let's get ready to open."

***

It was later that afternoon that Kate drove past the Stewart's store and turned onto Long Place, wound her way the short distance until the road dead-ended on Rice Lane, and pulled into the driveway of the last house on the street. From the driveway of the tall Victorian, she could see across the lake to Vermont, so she could only imagine what a beautiful view Tom must have from the walkway at the top of the three-story tower that dominated the front of the house. As she stepped up onto the porch, she could hear loud, intermittent noises coming from the back yard, so she followed the wraparound porch to the back and found Tom there.

He was wearing blue jeans, which she had only seen him in two or three other times. The blue jeans, however, were not what most caught her eye. Tom was shirtless, something she had *certainly* never seen before. What was more, he was gorgeous. Stunning. Beautiful. All of the words that women use when they talk about men's bodies swam through her head. It was one thing to see a beautiful body in a calendar or a television commercial. Or even on a stage at a strip club, which she had always found more funny than arousing.

But Tom wasn't trying to look sexy. He had his back to her and he was using a sledge hammer to drive metal wedges into a huge section of a tree. It was too big to be called a log; it was just a piece of tree trunk. Without realizing she was moving, she walked closer. Close enough to hear the small, controlled expulsion of air and see the puff of frozen breath each time he brought the sledgehammer down onto a wedge. Close enough to watch the individual beads of sweat run down his neck and join together in rivulets flowing down his back.

And my god, what a back. Because he always wore such loose shirts—even when he changed out of his store uniform before rehearsals, Tom wore a baggy, long-sleeved t-shirt that he must have gotten at the big and tall store —he just looked like a chunky guy trying to hide his flab. She knew better from his hugs but could see now that there was no flab on Tom whatsoever. He was not only cut, and she felt she could have counted each individual muscle fiber if she'd had the time, time she was feeling would be a worthwhile investment, but he was also bigger than she expected. He was not lanky or lean or wiry – he was stacked.

He must have heard her steps on the porch and because she was watching him so closely she was able to see, in just a second or so, the number of steps he went through before turning around. He stopped the sledgehammer, stopped it dead in midair on its way down, and his head cocked slightly to the left. Somehow he must have recognized it was her because she saw the tension left his arms and shoulders as he turned, but in that tiny eternity between him stopping the sledgehammer and the recognition, she felt a sense of danger, of a willingness to do, and a competence at doing, violence that startled her even more than had her own reaction to seeing Tom's body for the first time.

This sense of violence and danger, she had seen this

in Billy too, though never aimed at her of course. She would have left him in a second if it ever had been. But Tom? Funny, sweet Tom. Tom who was crazy about her, as she and everybody in town knew. This was as difficult to process as the surprise of his body.

She shuddered, caught herself, wondered what the hell was going on with her, and forced herself to say, "Hi, Tom," as plainly and normally as if she was seeing him in his khakis and button-down shirt at the Market.

Tom turned around (*Don't look at his abs. Don't look at his abs. Holy crap, look at his abs*) and smiled his familiar, crooked smile. "Kate. Quel surpris." He picked up the t-shirt on the picnic table beside him and she allowed herself one last gape as he stretched his arms up over his head and pulled it on. Sadly, it was the typical, Tom, way-too-big shirt and she would have to continue to satisfy her aesthetic interests with his forearms. Even that went away when he pulled the hooded sweatshirt on.

"What's up?"

"Actually, I was just driving by, kinda bored because Billy is away on one of his secret business trips, and I thought I'd stop in to visit." She looked around. "It's funny, you've been stopping by... our place – *that should not still feel weird to say*, she thought – and I've never actually been down here to see your home." She looked around her. "It is absolutely beautiful, Tom. You sure you don't have a woman who sneaks down here to help you pick out colors?"

"Very nice," Tom said with a wicked twinkle in his eye. "Are you teaching those stereotyped gender roles to the young minds under your care?

"Oh, please. We're adults here." She hoped Tom hadn't caught the odd way her voice had caught in her throat when she'd said the word "adults."

Tom smiled and he either hadn't noticed or was playing it off as if he hadn't. She figured he must have missed it.

"So, no, I picked out the colors myself. I could say that

they just felt right, that they spoke to me. But actually, I saw a picture spread in a magazine of a house in San Francisco and I copied it wholesale."

Her eyebrows raised as she smiled. "San Francisco, you say?"

Tom loudly laughed and said, "Fine. Let's go into my non-gender-stereotyped castle and I'll give you the ten-cent tour."

"I would be honored," she said with a smile. She couldn't help but notice, as she had before, how Tom's way of joking with her was so different from Billy's. So much more gentle and with a conspiratorial sense that made her feel as if Tom was including her in the "we" and not the "they."

"Besides," Tom said, "the only refreshment I have to offer you out here is Yoo-Hoo."

"You built *that* body with Yoo-Hoo?"

It popped out before she could stop it and she could see Tom's face instantly start to redden, but he laughed and said, "Don't forget the Reese's Peanut Butter Balls cereal."

This time she was able to keep her thought (*I'll have to get some of that for Billy*) to herself and said, "Ok, so let me see the place."

The house was, as she now realized she should have expected, amazing. Her and Billy's work on his – *their, dammit* – house helped her know what to look for in the details. The floor and ceiling molding and quarter-rounds, the straight and symmetrical pattern of the hardwood floor (Tom proudly called it "real hardwood" in contrast to a lazy "floating floor" and she would have to remember to ask Billy what that meant), and the color choices Tom had made throughout the house. The colors were not identical in every room, so there was no feeling of bland sameness. The colors of each room seemed to make sense for that particular room, but there was also some sort of unifying theme that she could not quite place. She didn't believe for a second that he had found these varied color combinations in a magazine.

She groaned inwardly when she realized she was deconstructing his house the same way she would a novel and tried to make herself stop. She only succeeded in a more conscious literary analysis of Tom's home, which she feared would distract her from what he was saying about the house as they walked through it. This thought caused her to realize that Tom was hardly saying anything about the house. Neither was he setting the pace as they walked. He was allowing her to discover the house on her own and at her own speed and she wondered who else he had allowed such intimacy to. Maybe no one.

It was well known in town that Tom didn't date any one woman regularly, and wasn't known to date any women from the local area at all. The logical assumption about the reason was widely shared and she allowed herself a guilty sense of pleasure in the fact. The more she thought about it, the more honestly she assessed herself and admitted that this was not the first time she had allowed herself the secret smile about Tom's poorly concealed feelings toward her. It would have been nearly impossible not to feel flattered by it, coming from whom it did.

The rooms of the house were obviously not arranged by someone expecting company, but looking past the pieces of Tom's life lying around (an ashtray with a pipe – *a pipe?* – a half-empty glass of water, books, copies of *The New Yorker* and *The Washington Post*, no wait, it was *The Washington Times*. She had never even heard of *The Washington Times*), the house was very organized... no, not really organized. Things were where they made sense, not according to any scheme she could discern, but because they were where they made sense. She was doing it again. Occupational hazard.

Then they went into the Victorian tower, which turned out to be Tom's library. Some people who love books, genuinely *love* books, and who go on to graduate degrees in literature or library science or history find that in studying too finely the constituent pieces of those things that they treasure, they have killed the wonder they'd had for their treasures. By acquiring the necessary skills and vocabulary to put into words what it was that an author was doing to make them feel sad or joyous or ashamed or scared witless, by peeking behind the curtain and finding out how the magic tricks are done, many lose touch with that which caused them to seek out the answers in the first place. This, thought Kate, might be the entire point of graduate school – to separate out those who can look behind the curtain, who can know the secrets, and who can still keep hold of the joy at the magic.

Tom's library was made of magic. As she stepped into the tower, she saw a spiral staircase that went right up through the center of the room. Her eyes followed the beautiful, wrought iron stairs and railings all the way up to the conical roof, which had five long skylights coming together at the point, creating a brilliant star of sunlight. Other than the staircase and the walkways at the second and third levels, the tower was open all the way to the roof.

At each of the second and third level walkways – more than walkways, really, they were floors with the centers taken out to make room for the spiral staircase – she saw an overstuffed reading chair and ottoman and a small writing desk and chair. The bookshelves were the full height of each level and ran the entire way around the outside walls of the tower, broken only by three, evenly-spaced, floor-to-ceiling windows on each level. Attached to the bookshelves on each floor, including the first floor, were rolling ladders like those at bookstores. She wondered if Tom had built these himself and realized that before today the idea that Tom might have anywhere near the skill necessary to build such things would not have occurred to her. Which was dumb, really, when she rewound and re-listened to all of the comments Billy had made about Tom's ability in high school to fix motorcycles and cars. And chainsaws. And wiring and plumbing. She shook her head slightly as she wondered why she had never been more curious about Tom before today, why she had never looked past the image she had constructed of him as slightly stiff, more than slightly geeky, and goofily infatuated with her.

She had allowed herself to shape her own thoughts based on what others believed she was thinking and that was unacceptable. She was smarter and more independent than that. At least, she had been before Billy.

She had stayed intrigued by and attracted to Tom since that first meeting, but it had been easier for both of them to fall into the roles that had been defined for them once she'd started dating Billy.

***

Tom saw her shake her head ever so gently, saw her hair move in perfect, golden waves, saw the gleam of wonder in her blue eyes, and found himself oddly amused by the situation. Why wasn't he more wound up about this? About her – *her* – alone with him in his house. And acting the way she was.

She was reacting to him in a way she hadn't since their first meeting. In a way that he had previously fantasized she might someday. But, to Tom's surprise, his own reactions did not align with his reactions in past daydreams.

I should be falling all over myself, trying to keep this mood alive, he thought. Which, of course, would screw the whole mood. He wasn't nervous, which was strange, because he felt he should be. What was more – and this thought, as it formed, startled him – he wasn't aroused. Not physically, not emotionally. He wasn't... attracted. Tom kept coming back to the word, "amused."

She was still standing in one place, eyes sweeping around the library of which he was so proud. "Listen, Kate. I absolutely reek, so I need to take a shower," Tom said. "So can I...?" He was going to ask if she would like him to walk her back to her car, but she turned quickly and finished his thought in her own way.

"Can you leave me here in the library? Are you kidding?" She was absolutely beaming and some of his amusement began to melt. "You couldn't kick me out of here if you tried!"

"Right. Ok." *Think quick, Tom.* "Ok, so, if you need anything while I'm in the shower, you now know where the kitchen is."

She smiled again and said, "Actually, I think I'll save my appetite for supper. You're taking me to the new restaurant in Ti."

Amusement, gone. Check.

"I am, am I?"

"Yes, you are. Now go shower. You stink. And take your time." She swept her arm around the room. "I have exploring to do."

He smiled, turned, and left the library, heading towards the back stairs. Normally, he would have gone up the library stairs to the third floor and entered his room through the door he had built into the bookshelf. He wasn't sure why, but he didn't want her to know that it was there.

Billy. The name that should have entered his consciousness long before now finally did. With Tom's neighbors, one in particular, plus a public meal at a restaurant, there was no way Billy would miss hearing about this.

"So what?" he said aloud. They were friends having dinner together. There was nothing to hide. They saw each other a few times a week already.

And I'm sure Billy will see it exactly the same way. He laughed and went to take his shower. It occurred to him that Sunshine, his cat, was nowhere to be seen. This was unusual, as Sunshine was an utter tramp for human affection, taking it from any and all who entered the house, regardless of whether she had ever met them before or not.

While the blasting hot water beat against his shoulders and the back of his neck – *the massaging shower head might well be the single greatest invention of the 20th century, he thought* – Tom half hoped that if he took too long in the shower she might leave.

That thought startled him and he grabbed at it before

it could drift off in the steam of the shower. He slowly turned around and turned off the water. His amusement was back, but directed at himself this time.

He really did want her to leave. Not because she wasn't interesting and fun to be around and certainly not because she wasn't a pleasure to look at. But balanced against the trouble that he knew could be caused if they spent too much more time together today were only those limited positives. If the relationship among the three of them – he refused to even think the word "triangle" – wasn't so complicated, he would love to go out to dinner with Kate for the intellectual stimulation of her company. But was that all there was? If he were really as smitten as he had apparently led everyone to believe, shouldn't he be jumping at the chance to spend this time with her?

As he had been thinking about Billy's reaction, he realized that he was as much interested – concerned? – about Molly's. Tom toweled off and dressed, still looking at his feelings from as many different angles as he could.

You know what? Screw it. Tom decided that he would go out to dinner with Kate, enjoy her company, and try to figure out later what he was feeling. Right now he was feeling hungry, both for food and for interesting conversation. Tom also decided he wasn't going to let a guest, even this guest, especially this guest, make him uncomfortable in his own home, so he came out the door that opened on the third level of the library.

He could hear Kate one floor below him, humming to herself as she read. She heard him close the door and looked up, startled.

"Tom? That's you, right?"

"Yes it is. There is a door up here that leads to the third floor of the house."

"Is there one down here too, to the second floor?"

Tom walked down the stairs to where she sat in the chair, feet curled up beneath her, legs covered in his ratty old blanket. "Sure is. It's that bookshelf right beside you."

She looked up, squinted, then set her book down and got up, walking over to the bookshelf he had pointed at.

"Bull. There's no..." She stopped as she saw the door handle. "Holy cow. That is wonderful. It's a secret passage-way!"

"I am a profoundly lazy man, Kate."

She smiled. "That's a shame, because I've changed our plans."

They stayed in, because Kate had decided they would be staying in, and while Tom cooked pasta and reheated some sauce from the refrigerator, Kate looked through his collection of vinyl. She eventually chose *Kind of Blue* and after putting it on the turntable, opened the bottle of wine he had chosen. He nodded appreciatively when she didn't immediately pour it, but neither wanted to wait very long, so the bottle only had a short breather before they were clinking glasses.

"Ok," Kate asked, while he was draining the pasta. "Best movie ever?"

Tom scoffed and, because of the wine, or the lack of sexual tension he was feeling, or both, he answered openly and without filter, "That's a crap question. There's no such thing."

"Fine, smarty. Favorite movie."

"Only slightly more answerable. It completely depends on the mood I'm in."

"Oh, for god's sakes. Commit."

"Seriously. There are times when I feel glum, so I watch *The Bicycle Thief*. Or nostalgic, so I watch *The Godfather*. Spooky and I watch *Gaslight*. Creepy — *Rear Window*. Uh... If I want to be terrified, I watch *Exorcist*. I don't know. Give me a category or emotion."

"Category or emotion... Oh, best guilty pleasure movie."

"Piece of cake. *Con Air*."

She started to laugh. "Oh my god, you boys. Put. The bunny. Back. In. The box."

He was astonished and his face clearly showed it, because she burst out laughing. "Every man I've ever met... check that, every man I ever met who wasn't in grad school for Comparative Lit loves that movie."

"Ok, what about you? Wait let me guess... Branagh's *Much Ado*... No, no. His *Henry the Fifth*."

It was her turn to be astonished. "How in the world did you guess that?"

He smiled, more to himself than to her, then lied, "You told me once. At a rehearsal. Sorry for cheating."

"Ok, last movie question. Go-to movie. If you can't think of anything else to watch and you don't feel like reading. Or writing."

"I'm going to cheat again because I have three. When I can't settle on something to watch, I shuffle the three DVD cases and pick one with my eyes closed."

"Hmm..." She poured more win into her glass. "Are any of them in English?"

He laughed. "They are all in English and I hope you're not disappointed that they are all terribly conventional. *Casablanca*, *The Thin Man*, and *The Apartment*. There, I guess I do have favorite movies."

"Oh, this is fascinating. But you put them in the wrong order."

"There's no real order. I just shuffle..."

"No," she interrupted. "It's an evolution. Loner, then unconventional courting, and finally wedded bliss. *Casablanca*, then *The Apartment*, then *The Thin Man*."

"Holy crap, you did that fast. I've never put it together like that and you did it in a heartbeat."

"My parents would be thrilled to know their college

money wasn't wasted."

The pasta was perfect, despite the distractions, and the conversation while they ate was as interesting and relaxed as any they'd ever had. The first bottle of wine became a second and, by the time they were clearing the dishes, a third.

They briefly considered watching a movie, but were enjoying their conversation so much that they just moved themselves and the bottle of wine to the living room. Kate curled up on the couch with a quilt and, after starting a fire in the fireplace, Tom sat in the chair opposite her.

"I have to admit," she said with no lead-in, "that even as a Lit major and English teacher, I've never been able to read *Gravity's Rainbow*."

"That was astonishingly random and startlingly perceptive. How did you know that was my favorite book?"

She smiled mysteriously, or as close as she could approximate with her current body weight to alcohol ratio. "Wouldn't you like to know."

He was confident that the actual answer had the name "Billy" somewhere in it, but there was no harm in playing along. "Your analytical skills are intimidating."

"There's no need to be intimidated. I can be very welcoming."

"All righty then. Next topic."

"Ok," she said. "For the moment."

It didn't last much longer than a moment. Tom tried to get Kate to talk about her interests — books, movies, anything — but she focused entirely on books and movies she either knew or assumed he liked. It wasn't all flirting. They talked about *Zen and the Art of Motorcycle Maintenance* and both admitted that they hadn't understood the ending, had both hated it, until reading explanations of the change from one narrator to another.

Kate like Fellini movies; Tom didn't. Tom loved Jean-Luc Goddard; Kate didn't. They both loved Spike Lee. Tom compared Quentin Tarantino's work to Toni Morrison's, and after he explained his belief that they were both so well-studied in their fields, it was hard for them to hide their puppet strings, she decided it wasn't as crazy a comparison as she first thought.

But whether from nerves or from a desire to build an excuse or from some different reason altogether, Kate kept drinking. Tom had stopped after his first glass from the third bottle, but Kate insisted they open a fourth bottle when the third was empty and from there she became less and less subtle until, sounding frustrated and drunk, she asked, "Are we going to do this or not?"

Even while they had been deeply engaged in conversations about books and movies, about narratives and schools of literary criticism, Tom had been unable to shake the out-of-body sense of the night. As if the night itself was a scene from a play or a movie and he was as much audience as actor. He had tried to let his guard down because he'd wanted to enjoy the night without his normal layer of self-protection, but that gap between his consciousness and the moment had been there since they'd finished eating.

"Isn't what we're already doing pretty cool?"

She had been lying on her side, head propped up on one arm and now she rolled onto her back. She dropped the quilt onto the floor and put her hands behind her head, which lifted her breasts until they strained against the fabric of her shirt.

She closed her eyes and sighed. "The journey's been great, but it's time for the destination."

Tom's throat and stomach tightened. She was so beautiful and he did adore her, but he could see that what was coming next was going to irreversibly change their friendship. He almost whispered when he said, "Kate, you're drunk."

"Yup," she said, popping the "p" with her lips. "But I wasn't when I got here and I had the same idea then." She opened her eyes and looked at him. "Everybody knows how you feel about me, Tom. It's ok."

He shook his head. "Everybody certainly thinks they do. And what about you? Doesn't everybody know how you feel about me?"

"They certainly think they do, right back at you. And I thought I did too, but I was wrong."

He kept looking at her. At her eyes looking back at him. They were the wrong eyes. He knew it. Even without her relationship with Billy, this would have had to end the same way.

"Ok, Kate. Everybody knows how I feel about you. Instead of talking about it, let me show you." He got up from the chair and she smiled. He walked towards her and their eyes stayed locked together until he reached down, picked up the quilt, and covered her back up.

She propped herself up on her elbows and looked unsteadily at him. "Seriously?"

"Seriously," he said, gently.

"Fine," she said. "I'm going home."

He smiled and sat down on the couch next to her. She rolled onto her side to make room for him.

"No. No, you're not. Neither one of us could drive you home."

He put a hand on her head and smoothed her hair and the wine finally took its toll on her as she started to relax. "I adore you, you know," he said. "None of that has changed. But, Gorgeous, even if I thought you would say the same things sober…"

Tom didn't finish the sentence. He sat for a few more minutes as she drifted deeper and deeper into sleep, then kissed her on the forehead, got up, and put a second blanket on her. He turned off the lamp by the couch, knocked the fire down and closed the glass doors to the fireplace. Then he turned off the music and went into the kitchen. He put his boots and coat on, turned out the kitchen light, and started the walk up the hill to the store.

The bitter cold cleared his head some and he stopped at the bottom of the porch steps, then turned around and went back into the house. He turned the kitchen light back on, gathered up all the dirty dishes and loaded the dishwasher. Then he got the dishwasher soap out from under the sink, set it on the counter for morning, and left the house again, turning out the light as he did.

****

Lisa watched through her bedroom window as Tom left his house and headed up the hill. Part of her was angry with him for not taking advantage of what she was certain had been offered to him, disappointed for the loss of something she knew he wanted so much. But that was a small part of her. She was mostly thrilled that her understanding of Tom had held. That he was way too good for that teasing little bitch. She understood Tom better than any other person on the planet did.

But how was she to get him to understand that he was also too good for Molly? That he didn't have to waste his time mooning over somebody who was too stupid to leave a cheating, abusive husband. That there was somebody right here, right in front of him. She had been working at the store for months before Molly wormed her way back into his life. Tom and she had been growing closer and closer, but that stopped when Molly came to work at the store. Lisa was self-aware enough to realize that her own reaction to having to share Tom's attention, her own inability to control her jealousy and temper had been a factor, but she also knew that Tom's romantic vision of himself was tailor made for Molly's "poor me" bullshit.

Ok, it wasn't actually bullshit. Mike was an abusive fucker who would only get worse as it became more and more clear to him that his life had peaked at least 10 years earlier. Cissy had been a complete bitch, but her killer hadn't taken care of the town's biggest asshole

Lisa could also only handle one problem at a time and the one at hand was Kate. She picked up her cellphone and punched in a number.

WEEK 2 – FRIDAY
December 24, 1999

Tom woke up on the couch in his office; stiff, cranky, and with an astonishing headache. His entire body ached, but his head was winning the pain race by a large margin. *Oh sweet Jesus. How much wine?* He vaguely remembered talking Kate into staying. There was no way either of them could have driven with as much as they'd drunk. He remembered walking up to the store to sleep in his office. He looked at his watch and saw that it was six a.m. This was going to be an interesting morning.

Wait... He looked at his cell phone with a combination of resignation and panic, hoping not to see what he did indeed see. A call to Billy a little after two in the morning. He remembered finding himself sitting in the bathroom at one point looking at his phone. Apparently this memory was created just four hours ago.

He did a little paperwork to kill time and try to recover any additional memories and, happily, her car was gone when he finished the short walk down the hill to his house. He walked into the kitchen, put on a very quiet Keith Jarrett CD, measured out five tablespoons of coffee into his coffee press, and then put the water on the stove to boil.

"Meow!"

He looked down at the rotund, long haired, orange cat looking up at him.

"Meow!"

"Good morning, Slim. You certainly made yourself

scarce last night. How's my favorite girl?" As he picked her up and held her against his chest, she stretched her front legs over his shoulder and tucked her back legs up against her stomach. She looked like a very hairy baby. A very talkative, very hairy baby.

"Meow!"

"Now, we've been over this. You know I don't understand you." She answered, as if she knew she was supposed to.

"Well, sure, I could go with the obvious joke, but we don't have a well. We're on town water. And I don't even know a Timmy."

"Meow!"

"Feel free to keep saying it louder and slower, but that still won't help."

"Meow!"

"I know. You can't speak English... what's that? That's not what you said?... Not can't?... Oh, Kant. The philosopher. I think you're pronouncing that wrong... I know, right? Pronounce that one the wrong way in public and we'll both be in trouble."

He set her down, silently set two places at the table, and started to pull out the tools he would use to make breakfast, but she wasn't pleased with the lack of attention and expressed it. Loudly.

"This?" He held up the whisk he was going to use on his eggs. "No, goofball. They're referring to a flyswatter, not an egg whisk."

The cat looked at him, silently, as if she knew the lines to the koans.

"You're right," he said. "Let's get this place cleaned up first." Tom went to the couch, folded up the blankets, and brought them and the pillow back upstairs. As he carried them, he caught the scent of Kate's perfume on the pillow and, as overwhelmingly feminine and desirable as it was, he smiled broadly at his actions of the previous night. It wasn't often that Tom Hudson allowed himself to feel that sort of pride, but he gave himself that gift this morning. He deserved it.

As he came back down the stairs, he saw that Billy was sitting at his kitchen table, the trollop of a cat purring happily in his lap. "Setting a place for two this morning, I see."

As Tom poured the boiling water into the press, he said. "Yeah, I was expecting you. Were you already coming back to town this morning or did you come back early because Lisa called you?"

Billy chuckled as Tom waited for the coffee to be ready. Billy had more than one laugh. One of those laughs was a quiet chuckle that had such a coldness, such a hardness to it, it was chilling to hear. This wasn't *that* chuckle. This had an amused, almost gentle-sounding quality.

"That's good, Sherlock. How did you know she'd called me?"

"When I was getting a blanket for Kate, I saw Lisa's sweet little face peeking through her curtains. Her lights were still on when I walked up to the office to get some sleep."

Billy chuckled again. "Jesus Herbert Walker Christ. I don't even have a hard time believing you slept in your office. And not just because of your fucked up hair."

Tom checked the clock on the wall, then slowly and evenly pressed the plunger to the bottom of the coffee press. Then he poured a cup for himself and one for Billy. "This is not how I expected this conversation to start."

Billy laughed. "There is a presumption in there that we would be having the conversation at all. You and Kate didn't make a plan last night to keep your little rendezvous a secret?"

"Not so much," Tom said. "First off – there's nothing wrong with two friends having dinner together."

"Yeah. We'll get back to that one. Second?"

"Second. Even before I saw Lisa's sweet face peeking

through her curtains last night, I knew that if one or the other of us didn't mention this, it would look wrong." Tom smiled.

Billy laughed again. There was none of the bitterness in the laugh that had been there in the past when he and Tom talked about, or uncomfortably avoided talking about, Kate. "Don't blame Lisa. The poor girl wants to get into my pants. It's not her fault."

"How could a girl resist such a temptation?" Tom realized he was smiling. Had he not realized before this moment how much the previous tension between him and Billy had dissolved? If this situation, and Billy's reaction to it, didn't clinch it for him, nothing would.

"You need to look out for yourself. I'm her second choice."

"Please," Tom said. "Everybody knows that you and Mike Rush are neck and neck... well that's probably not the right body part, but let's stay with it, that you two are the prime targets of her... um... charms."

"Not even close, dolt. Christ, you are just as dense as you were in high school." Billy sat down on the corner of Tom's desk. "If I was ranking, I would put me ahead of Mike, just out of ego. Well, that and common sense. But, please don't try to tell me that you've never noticed the way Lisa looks at you."

"Me?" Tom was legitimately surprised and showed it. A person couldn't help being surprised now and then. This Tom believed and so, didn't see it as a weakness. But he had trained himself through the years, with good cause, not to show his surprise. It wasn't working right now and he realized he was getting soft. "Lisa can't stand me."

"Man, you are something else." Billy shook his head. "What Lisa can't stand is you and Molly hitting on each other. She is nuts about you."

Tom sighed. "Dammit, there is a difference..."

"Yeah, yeah, your famous difference between hitting on and flirting. Blah, blah, blah. I'm not buying it."

"There's nothing to buy."

"Please. You could have had Lisa any time you wanted. You may not have realized that, but you do have to know that you probably could have had Kate last night too if you'd wanted." Billy held up one finger to stop Tom when he started to protest. "Have you thought about why you ended up in your office?"

Billy paused. "Probably not, since I'm guessing I got here before you had a chance to really ponder the evening. Listen to me, and listen closely." Billy spoke slowly, enunciating every word. "You would have ended up sleeping there even if Kate was free. Which she is not, by the way, but she and I will have a little talk about that later."

Tom rubbed his eyes. "Wait. Wait, wait, wait. Too many threads. Say that again."

Billy laughed again. This was his head-thrown-back laugh that sounded like Satan himself. "Wine or scotch last night?"

"Wine. Syrah. Four bottles." Tom lethargically shook his head from side to side, then took a long drink of his coffee. "Bite me."

"Oh, wine hangovers are the worst." Billy laughed his demon-laugh again. "Kate is going to be grumpy all day, fuck you very much."

"Yeah, great. Whatever. What the hell were we talking about?"

"Wait, shit. I missed a que syrah, syrah joke."

"Thank god for small favors. Hey, when are you going to tell Kate why you go to Glens Falls. It's..."

Billy pointed at Tom. "Nice diversion. But listen, here is your homework for the day. Actually, this is a timed test, but you can take a coupla days if you need to. You're pretty fucking dense when it comes to this stuff."

Tom's head really hurt and more than anything else in the world he just wanted to lie back down and close his eyes.

"What stuff? You're killing me here."

"Yeah. It's fun to be on this side for a change." Billy pointed at him again. "Here's the deal. Like I said, I propose that you would have ended up sleeping in your office even if Kate were completely free and unencumbered. Your mission, and you have no choice but to accept it, is to answer me one simple question. Why?"

"Why?"

"Yeah. Why? What in the world would have kept you from the woman that you have led everyone in town to believe you're madly in love with?"

Tom's thoughts were starting to catch up to full speed and he realized that he was now probably too much awake to go back to sleep. Which really sucked. "Shit I already know the answer to that one. With as much wine as I drank last night..."

Billy's smile went away and his voice raised. "God damn it. Listen to me. I'm being serious. I want you to think about what I said." He got up from table, walked to the door, and opened it. Standing in the doorway, he turned back around. "I mean it. Take some time to think. Oh, and dude. Shower. You stink but awful." He started to go, but turned back around once again. "By the way, did it not occur to you that I just strolled in here through a locked door this morning?"

As Tom rechecked his memory of coming home this morning, Billy held up a house key. "You want me to put this back up in the crook of that tree?"

"How in the hell...?"

"Please. If you had any idea of the world I used to live in your hair would curl."

Tom thought, *Ditto, brother*, as Billy left, closing the door behind him.

***

Tom watched Molly. She was smiling and visiting with a customer as she was ringing up the older lady's groceries. Tom didn't recognize the lady, which meant that she was probably a new resident of the Lee House. No tourists in town on Christmas Eve.

He wondered if Molly ever wished she had left the town. If she ever wondered how different her life would be right now if she hadn't gotten pregnant during her senior year of high school. Mostly, he wondered if he was starting on a path that would destroy their friendship.

Tom had Grace take over Molly's register and brought Molly into his office. She looked a little wary as he had her sit down. He brought his chair out from behind his desk and sat facing her.

"Just a coupla things I'd like to talk about, Molly. One not so much serious and one a little more so."

"Ok."

"Well, first, take a good look at the walls to this office." She looked puzzled. "How tall are they?"

"Six feet or so? What's your point?"

"Close enough. Ok, now look w-a-y up there at the ceiling. See the big gap between the top of the walls and the ceiling?" His tone was lightening her up, even if she still wasn't following his line of thought. "Ok, try this. What is Lisa saying?"

They could both clearly hear Lisa simultaneously chatting with a customer and gossiping with Grace.

"Tom, you can hear her as well as..." *Aha.* Tom nearly laughed as the recognition of his point clearly registered in her face. "Oh my God. You can hear everything in here, can't you?"

"Yeah, pretty much." He let her think about it for a minute, then plowed right in before he could think himself out of it. "And that is a piece of information you'll probably find yourself using in the very near future. I'm promoting you to Assistant Manager, which is typical of me to try to take credit for deciding something that has already been the case. Oh, and I want you to run the Market while I'm out of town for the next couple of weeks."

A few beats passed before this new surprise replaced the last on Molly's face.

"Wait? What are you talking about?" Tom hadn't taken a full work day off, not one, in the three years since he had bought the Market. He came and went throughout the day, more so now since he and Billy had renewed their friendship, but he had never even discussed a day off before the ill-fated visit to Ed's hunting camp.

"Molly, I'm going away. Anywhere from ten days to two weeks. And you won't have any way of contacting me, so you'll essentially be on your own, running the store."

He was surprised, though he chastened himself for not giving her more credit, that she recovered so quickly. "There is a whole series of issues involved in this."

"True. And I've thought them out. I mean, tomorrow is Christmas, to start with. But it's entirely possible I've missed something, so let's go over my thoughts and then you can hit me with anything I missed."

"No, I think I'll start." That startled him. "You think running away from your feelings will solve any of your problems?"

Oh shit. Was he that transparent?

"Molly, that's not… it's not exactly what I'm doing. I just have some thinking I need to do…"

"Of course you do. That's what you do, Tom Hudson. You think. And if the thing you're thinking about is scary enough, you keep thinking until any decision has been made for you."

"Wait a minute. I don't…"

"Nonsense. You let Billy get to that girl first because you

were too busy dicking around, mooning over her instead of going after her. Now that you actually have a chance to have what you wanted, you're afraid to take it. That's just stupid." She sounded genuinely angry.

"This isn't about Kate."

"Everybody knows how you feel."

There it was again, and he couldn't help that it pissed him off as much as it did. "No, Molly. Everybody doesn't know how I feel." He kept his voice low, controlled, but couldn't stop himself from gritting his teeth as he spoke. "Everybody always fucking assumes they know how I feel, but they don't."

"So you're saying you're not in love with her."

There it was. As plain as could be. Here was his chance to either bail on the whole topic, to let things stay the way they were for God only knew how much longer, or to man up and tell her how he felt. He had taken a sharp ground ball to shallow short and couldn't decide if he should throw to first or second. So, as he had done so many other times in his life, at least when it came to love, he threw it into the right field stands.

"Ok Molly, I am kind of in love, but…"

"Well, no shit. The whole freaking town can see that."

"Ok, let me interject here for a sec and point out that that whole 'being able to hear over the walls' thing works both ways." He had noticed that the store was unnaturally quiet, especially with Lisa and Grace working at the same time.

Molly stopped instantly and they waited until Grace and Lisa both started talking furiously about utter nonsense, trying to hide that they had been listening.

In a much quieter voice, she broke the pause. "Look, we all know about what happened with Kate last night and we all know that you and Billy had it out this morning."

Tom's right eyebrow raised. "We do, do we? Would we know that from Tom, Kate, or Billy?"

"Well, Lisa said…" She trailed off.

"Does that sound *more* smart or *less* smart, now that you've said it out loud?"

Chagrined, Molly said, "Maybe less smarter than when it was inside." She smiled cautiously. "So, you didn't sleep with her, did you?" The astonished look on his face almost made her laugh. "Don't answer that. Deep down I knew you wouldn't. I'm ashamed I almost believed her."

"Yeah, moving right along," he said. "Listen. You know I trust you to run the store while I'm away and I trust you enough to tell you that I have some personal feelings I have to work through, which is why I'm going away for a little while." He paused and took a deep, cleansing breath. "But it's not Kate. I'm not in love with Kate. I'm not sure if I ever really was in love with Kate or just with some clay goddess that I built in her image."

Molly shrugged. "You thought you were in love with her, right?" Tom nodded. "And you felt you were in love with her, right?" He nodded again. "Well, then you were in love with her, idiot boy. That's what being in love is – thoughts and feelings. We don't choose to be in love. It just happens to us."

"Well, I happen to think loving someone is a choice…"

"Jesus Christ, will you listen to me. I said 'in love' as in a feeling, a thought, a passive. Loving someone, as in actively loving someone, as in action verb? Completely different. One is something that happens to us, sometimes against our will. The other is a choice we make and the actions we take based on that choice. We can be in love with more than one person at a time. It's called crushes. Same thing."

Tom thought for a minute. "You know what, I think that's the same thing I've always thought, the same way I've always felt about it. Love isn't feeling; it's action. But I never put it into words before."

"Well, you didn't put it into words just now. I did. And actually, that was kinda the first time I've ever formed it into a full thought before."

"I like it, sensei. But the problem comes when out of all

those people you have ever been in love with, the one person you want to love is someone you can't. Because of... I don't know, timing."

"Join the real world, bucko. That's called life."

Tom laughed. "Did you just call me bucko? You're like some Buddhist monk wise man channeling Howdy Doody."

"You hush." Then the light bulb went on. "Wait a minute. You're kind of in love? What the hell does that mean? And if it's not Kate... There's some other person you're in love with besides her?"

Tom's smile went away. "Yeah. And I always have been. Since elementary school."

"Elementary school? Who were you in love with in elementary school? Other than Franny, I mean."

"Oh, you know her." Tom's voice was as quiet, as gentle as he could make it. "I left her notes in her locker. I even took those godforsaken French classes because she was in them. At least the first year anyway."

Molly started to say something, then stopped and looked directly into Tom's eyes. Her face was as serious as he had ever seen it. "What are you trying to say?"

Damn it. He was mad at himself for saying this much, for having so little control. He wouldn't say more. Not now.

"I'm not trying to say anything, other than that I want you to run the store for me while I'm away. That is all I wanted to talk to you about. Can we stick to that topic, please?" *I can't believe I'm pussying out,* he thought.

"Fine." Her face was hard now. Angry. He marveled at how they could go through what felt like ten or twenty different moods in a three-minute conversation. "I already know every piece of this store. Forwards and backwards." She lowered her voice. "The only problem I foresee is Lisa. She's been here longer than I have and she'll throw a fit."

"That's not the only reason she'll throw a fit, but yeah, that is what I see as a problem also. I'm going to be talking to everyone in a couple of minutes, but I wanted to tell you first…"

"Tell me?" She had changed again. She still looked determined, but the anger was gone. There was even the smallest hint of a smile at the corners of her eyes. How the hell can women change their emotions so damn fast?

"Well, yes." He paused, tried to catch up with where she was going, then shook his head. "Molly Rush, I am a dumb, dumb man. What I meant to say is that I wanted to *ask* you if you would be amenable to helping me out in this way."

"Go ahead then."

He sighed dramatically and rubbed his face with both hands. "Molly, would you be amenable to helping out in this way? Please, kind lady."

"The 'kind lady' bit was a nice touch, but I still want a raise. At least while I'm running the place."

"Sounds like 'Milady' would be more appropriate."

"Yeah, I like that even better, but don't expect a Milord in return. A dollar an hour."

"A dollar an hour, it is. And it will be a permanent raise."

She laughed. "Done. I would have taken twenty-five cents."

Tom softly said, "Thank you. And thank you for giving me some time to think."

She squinted at him as she got up. "Use it well, mister. Because I know that I'm going to use the time wisely. And you and I are going to talk when you get back."

"Should I be afraid?"

"Probably. No, definitely."

As soon as she turned her back to him to walk out of his office, her brave face fell away. *He'll be alone on Christmas.*

***

Tom and Molly had been right about Lisa. They had waited for a slow time towards the end of the day to talk to everyone and Lisa had thrown a fit. An epic fit. Tom let her go on a few minutes, then explained again that he had chosen Molly because he felt she was the best choice, that he knew that Lisa would do a good job, just as she would have had he stayed the night at Ed's camp but that Molly would do a better job. He eventually had to send everyone else back to work and take Lisa out the back door, behind the Market.

She angrily took out a cigarette and lit it. When she mockingly offered Tom one he shocked her by taking it, lighting it, and taking a long, blissful drag.

"You smoke?"

"Only when driven to it."

"This is motherfucking bullshit and you know it." Her hands were shaking so badly that it took her multiple tries to get the cigarette back into her mouth.

"What I know is that the way you're acting now proves that you're not ready to run the store."

"I've been here longer than her," Lisa's voice, usually so strong and demanding, was now so plaintive, it tore at his heart.

"Lisa," he said, trying to keep his voice gentle and firm at the same time, "you've been here longer than *I* have. That doesn't change who own the store."

"So that's the answer? You're the boss and I just have to shut up and deal with it?" Her anger was back, which made it easier on Tom than her sadness had.

"You know what? We may get to that point in this conversation, but if I was going to go that route, do you think I would have let you carry on this argument this long? And in front of everybody else? No, what I'm trying to get across is that as the owner, I have a responsibility that I take very seriously."

When she rolled her eyes, he started losing the calm that he had been so successfully holding onto. "You know what, Lisa, go ahead and mock me. But this store is keeping twenty people in work. Twenty people, you included, who don't have to drive fifty or more miles to work and back every day. If you could find another job at all. And this store gives those people in the Lee House up the street an independence that they wouldn't have without it. And it gave this entire town some kind of hope, when every other fucking business on this street looked like it was going to close."

"You talk a good game. Really, you do. Your innocent little act, your Flirty Boss routine, even charmed me for a while."

"I have never ever tried to..."

"I know it," she practically screamed at him. "Not once. Even before she started working here." Spit flew from her mouth when she said the word, "she."

Tom stood, astonished, as Lisa wiped her mouth with her sleeve, trying to compose herself. She started to walk away, then stopped and turned back to face him.

"You've lost a good friend today. And the chance for more than a friend. I hope the bitch is worth it." She started to leave again, then turned back around one more time. "You can mail my last paycheck to me. Oh, and Tom? Get a very good lawyer."

Oh, Lisa. Tom wasn't surprised at how sad he was. Losing a friend changed the balance of life more than gaining one. He looked at his watch and realized it was almost exactly twenty-four hours ago that Kate had come into his back yard while he was minding his own business, just chopping wood. *A helluva day's work, Tom Hudson. A helluva day's work.*

It hadn't taken Tom long to pack the previous night, even though he'd be camping outside in December. His pack was always ready with enough supplies for ten days, so it only took half an hour to add his sleeping bag, tent, clothes, and crampons. There wasn't enough snow this year to worry about snowshoes, but the trip up the mountain was steep and often icy at the beginning and end of the trail.

He had put everything into the Dart before going to bed and got up before 0500 after the least restful sleep he could remember in a very long time. As he'd tossed and turned during the night, he'd been tempted to grab all his gear and hike in overnight. The fact that his brain was entertaining such a dangerous idea meant that he needed this break more than he'd realized. It had been so long since he'd been completely alone for a full 24 hours, much less several days in a row. He deeply craved the isolation.

Just before leaving, he texted the word "Hurricane" to Bob. Once Bob had heard all the other parts of the story, he would know what it meant. As isolated as he wanted to be – needed to be – Tom didn't have it in him to disappear without at least leaving the possibility of being found. You never knew.

The drive went quickly, though he was in no hurry. Not much traffic before sunrise on Christmas morning. He went up through Westport to get to Elizabethtown, then on to the trailhead. Hurricane Mountain was a popular hike, even in the winter, but Tom figured he'd likely be the only one lonely enough to be camping up there Christmas week. He was planning on pitching his tent in the trees on the south face of the mountain opposite the old fire lookout tower. He would cover the tent with branches as soon as it was up and if someone did a day hike while he was there, he would hide in the tent and meditate.

When he reached the trailhead, he left the Dart unlocked but took the stereo faceplate and all the spark plug wires with him and headed up the mountain.

***

Up with the sun, as the song went, but Bob had been up since before the sun. In fact, he and Tom had gotten out of their beds within minutes of each other and during the rounds he'd driven that morning he'd barely missed seeing Tom drive north on 9N. Since the day after the murder, Bob had been getting up well before dawn and doing rounds. Just driving.

South Moriah Road to Edgemont, left on 9N through Port Henry, almost to Westport then left on Pilfershire to go past where the dump had been when they'd been kids (the dump where they'd gotten the parts for the bikes they'd made and ridden all through their high school years), past Grover Hills and Linney Field (the site of his first kiss with Cissy. First sex with her too, though not on the same night), right on Plank Road past the old Presbyterian church (where the minister had showed movies of Arctic explorers in the basement), past where the old O'Brian house and the pharmacy used to be (both burned down, 30 years apart), past Huchro's (he couldn't count the number of pizzas, Mountain Dews, and games of pool with Billy) and the old Mineville Cemetery (where Billy always swore he'd be buried), up Fisher Hill past Moriah Shock, then left on Dalton Hill past Belfry Mountain (and the fire tower where Tom had convinced them to camp one Christmas break), and finally down to the first place his autopilot failed him that morning.

Normally, he'd turn right and head past Roe's Pond (every child in every era for as long as the pond had a name had been startled as an adult to learn it wasn't Rose Pond), out the Tracy Road and to at least as far as Newport Pond, though usually all the way to the trailhead for the trail up to Crowfoot Pond, where he would turn around and head back.

This morning he stayed stopped at the stop sign at the bottom of Dalton Hill Road for minutes. This was no mystical feeling like those Tom pretended not to have. Bob knew exactly what had his stomach tight. Turn right, head out the Tracy Road, and within a mile he'd be at Ed's house. He didn't want to drive past Ed's house, even this early in the morning, because if Ed saw him he'd be forced to stop.

Bob did turn right eventually, but turned left twenty feet later and went down Bridal Row (*company houses for newlywed miners?* He had no idea), then did the full loop of Silver Hill Road (past the house where he'd kissed his first girl), then back to Witherbee Road, through Moriah Center, Moriah Corners, and back home.

As he pulled into his driveway, he saw Ed's old Chevy pickup in his driveway.

***

Tom sat in the lotus position on the hard rock next to the fire tower on the top of the mountain. His tent was pitched and camouflaged, all his gear was unpacked and arranged, and he was taking this time to cleanse himself before eating breakfast. The razor sharp, zero-degree air made his lungs sing with each intake of breath.

He uncrossed his legs and stretched his hamstrings out by putting one leg straight out in front of him and raising it in the air from the hip, then returning that leg to its previous position and stretching the other. He felt his ischium grind into the rock of the mountain as he moved.

He had plenty of discomfort this morning – physical, intellectual, and emotional. Physical discomfort was an assurance that the body was still alive, still attuned to its own needs, still interested in its own survival. Intellectual discomfort was an assurance that the mind was still alive as well, that it still had the capacity to question preconceptions, that it could still learn and grow.

There was nothing wrong with emotional discomfort either. It meant the heart, to use the corniest possible construction, was still alive. Molly hadn't been entirely off track when she'd chided him for not pursuing Kate, but she hadn't been entirely right about his motives either.

He didn't believe in pursuing love, but it wasn't out of fear of rejection or a lack of self-worth or any of the other theories friends had expressed about him over the years. Tom just didn't feel that love pursued could ever be love fully reciprocated. If you had to prostrate yourself at the feet of another to prove your love for them, to convince them to love you, how could that relationship ever be equal? How could the prostrater not eventually feel resentful at the prostratee for not going equally as far to prove their love?

Was that path only a degree removed from a rationalization at not acting for fear of rejection? Potentially, and after two years' distance, he had no confidence that he could honestly say which path he'd taken with Kate at the beginning. The end result was obviously the same, but exploration of his thoughts and motivations was a path itself, a path of self-knowledge, and he would force himself to walk it.

Or at least he would after he ate. He was starving.

***

Billy had woken up in awkward situations before, but not often in his own bed. His first thought on waking was a hope that Kate was either still asleep or would pretend to be asleep so that he could get out of bed without talking to her.

They had slept in the same bed the night before, but Billy knew it was entirely because neither wanted to address what it would mean for one of them to sleep elsewhere. He pulled the covers off himself, being careful to keep her covered, and sat up.

He wished Tom was around. Today would be a perfect day to sit in the garage with a fire going in the woodstove. Maybe pull the Harley Knucklehead basket case out of the back of the garage so they could pretend to work on it, drink beer, and laugh at each other's less-than-truthful stories. He'd stopped in at the store the previous evening, where he'd been told by Molly that Tom had gone camping. He was probably up on some mountain right now, sitting in the lotus position and pondering the meaning of his goddam fingernails. Who the hell goes camping on Christmas?

Oh, shit.

Christmas.

He got up, dressed, and went downstairs to put on coffee and make breakfast in bed for the woman he still, despite his best efforts, deeply loved.

Tom stood in his spot beneath the fire tower, drinking green tea, and watching the first orange glow light up the horizon to the east. He smiled, remembering Pete Garza one time, well into his daily dose of Genny Light beer, complaining that the "traitorous, rebel clayfooters" in Vermont got to see the sun before he did every day. Pete would have done well in the Balkans, where it was nothing to hold a grudge for centuries.

It was so perfectly quiet. Too early for the daylight animals, too late for the night life. He'd spent the past 24 hours entirely alone and was forcing himself to not look forward, to not think of however many days in the future it would be when he would have to see people again.

He intentionally had no return date, so that he wouldn't have a countdown clock running in the back of his mind. Two days, five days, ten days... let's see how long the food lasts.

His beaten, faded paperback copy of the *Tao Te Ching* was the only book with him, and he'd spent the previous day and night meditating on his two favorite chapters, one from each of the two sections of the book. He didn't need the book anymore to remember the words of the chapters, but he carried it with him nonetheless. It was still the first copy he'd ever owned and at this point the physical manifestation of the book was more a talisman for him as it was a medium for the expression of wisdom.

Chapter Forty-Seven, thanks to George Harrison now

known pretty much universally as *The Inner Light*, was, also thanks to George Harrison, the chapter that had brought Tom to the book and eventually to Zen. He got his love for the Beatles from his mother and the first CDs Tom had ever bought were the two Past Masters releases. The first Indian music he had ever heard was the sarod in the opening of *The Inner Light* and he still remembered how hearing those notes had stopped his brain in its tracks.

He also didn't need the copy of the book to remember his notes, which were on every page of the book. Some were extensive, some were simply one word. Of Chapter Forty-Seven he had written, "Your truth is already inside you. Find it there."

His notes for Chapter Thirty-Three were longer and in part inverted the words of the verse, words which expressed internal attributes as superior to external attributes. *If you know others, you are intelligent, but if you know yourself, you are wise. If you master others, you are strong, but if you master yourself, you are genuinely powerful.*

Tom's notes spoke to his lifelong awareness of man's ability to delude himself. What if you think you know yourself, but don't? What if you think you have mastered yourself, but haven't?

When it came right down to it, Tom knew that he had to trust himself to know himself, especially after putting in the time for self-examination – of his thoughts, feelings, reactions to others. That is what led him to this mountain. Of course there had been a spark with Kate, even on that night. She was beautiful and their intellects were well matched in a way that let them joke and talk in shorthand. He didn't sleep with Kate for a number of reasons. Her level of intoxication, his loyalty to Billy, his loyalty to her. But above all, it was his love for Molly.

If he and Kate had gotten together from the beginning, it might have been different. But it also might not have. In every adult relationship he'd ever had, he'd compared the woman to Molly. And not to a perfect Molly of the imagination, but to the real girl he'd known in high school and the real woman he'd reestablished a friendship with when he'd come back. None of the others had measured up in a way that would let him move on, move on from a relationship he'd never even had.

So, where did that leave him? She was married and whatever that marriage meant to Mike, it also meant something to her because she was still in it. He knew that he couldn't actively try to sabotage it. Not only would it be disrespectful to her, but he would also be inevitably damaging the trust Molly had for him, a trust that had been built on his being a safe refuge for her. If he tried to seduce her – not that he thought he even could – he would not only no longer be her safe place, he wouldn't deserve to be.

So again, where did that leave him? He knew exactly where. It left him waiting, even hoping, but not acting. He'd been born an Aries, but in the most important facet of his life, he was without an action to take. But it was inaction by design; it was inaction on purpose. An active inaction, if he was being glib. If something ever did happen between him and Molly, he wanted both of them to be able to look back at the beginning of it with pride, not shame. He wanted their story to be one that they could tell friends and family with smiles and laughter, not a story they had to hide or shade with lies.

He also knew where this left him with dating. Finished. It wouldn't be fair to start dating someone, anyone, with the knowledge that if a serious relationship developed he would still consider it settling. That he would always be wondering if he would drop her if Molly came to him. He was done with dating and because it was through a thought process and a conscious decision, he was at peace.

Ok, time for breakfast.

***

Bob looked at the pack of cigarettes on the kitchen table, absentmindedly swirling the remains of his coffee in his cup. Not his cup. Cissy's cup.

She'd bought the New York State United Teachers mug right after being elected to the school board, which had surprised him since the NYSUT – or at least her evil caricature of it – had been her real opponent in the election. He knew it wasn't a genuine gesture, but he'd assumed that she'd use the mug as a showy way of pretending to bury the hatchet. He'd assumed wrong. She'd brought it home and used it as an ashtray.

The cigarettes and mug had stayed on the kitchen table until that morning, when he'd washed the mug and poured his coffee into it. It was only 6:00 and he was on his third cup.

Bob's methodical, tenacious mind was playing and replaying the conversation he'd had with Ed the previous morning. Ed was practically twitching, he was so eager to talk to Bob, to tell Bob that Kate had spent Tuesday night at Tom's house, that Billy had confronted Tom at the Market the next morning, that after the confrontation Tom had flipped out and fired Lisa. Now, Tom was nowhere to be found and Molly was trying to run the store by herself.

Ed was... manic was the closest Bob could come to describing him. There was a gloating piece in there, but there was also something more. Ed's gloating had been the unhappiest, least satisfied gloating he'd ever seen. As if he was getting just what he wanted, but losing something even more important. Bob's brain was gnawing on that and also on the question of where Ed had come by all of this information. This was a lot of pieces and parts all stitched together by a man who wouldn't have heard the story from any of the principals. That left a gap in Bob's knowledge of the situation. A gap that wouldn't be filled by coffee. Time for work.

***

Mike smiled as he pulled out of the parking lot at the mill. He was coming off the last night shift for a while and it was going to be a good day. Overtime plus holiday pay from yesterday meant that his next check was going to be a big one.

The pulp part of the mill, like all pulp mills, smelled like the devil's cabbage farts and people who didn't work there – and fucking tourists – hated it. To Mike and everybody else who either worked at the mill or relied on somebody who worked there, that sulphuric ass stench was the smell of mortgage payments. And Christmas presents. And to Mike today, it was the smell of the sweet, sweet bud that his friends were bringing up from Boston this morning.

Shit, he might even drive out of his way and get some flowers for Molly.

***

Tom sat, legs crossed, palms open to the sky, and thought. It had been years before he could do this without inwardly giggling at the pretentiousness, the Steven Seagalishness, of it.

It was the western man in him – that logical, everything must have a tangible explanation man in him – that told him it was probably the vibrations of the footsteps coming up the trail that first alerted him to the presence of another.

The sounds of the birds and other animals probably changed too, he thought, groaning at his mind's insistence on assigning reasons to everything.

He stood as Billy came out of the trees into the clearing. Billy's face was as grave as Tom had ever seen it.

"You have to come home. Now."

"What's going on?" Tom's voice reflected the concern

he was seeing in Billy's face.

"It's Molly." Tom waited for Billy to catch his breath. He had apparently walked up the trail faster than he was used to. "Mike beat her up."

"He hit her again? Fucking asshole!" Tom felt his jaw start to tighten, then spasm and he fought it back under control.

Billy shook his head. "No. He didn't just hit her this time. He beat her up. Bad. She's in Ti hospital."

Tom closed his eyes for a second, breathed in and out once, then stood and ran back to his tent. Billy watched as he popped his torso in, then came back out with a handful of… spark plug wires? Tom silently walked past Billy towards the trailhead. He stopped after a few steps and turned back.

"The kids. Where are the kids?"

"They're okay. They're with Erin."

Tom nodded, then disappeared down the trail at a lope that quickly left him out of sight.

Billy expected him to turn around and come back with other questions, but he didn't. He had planned to tell Tom the reason for Mike's anger, or at least hint at it. Hopefully, there would be time later, before Tom did anything stupid.

As he stood there processing, Billy realized that Tom had run down the trail wearing… what the fuck was he wearing? They looked like house slippers. In the snow. He looked around at the campsite that was to have been Tom's home the next several days and realized that at some point in time, probably some inconvenient and random point in time that would make sense only to Tom, the dumbass would feel guilty for not wiping all traces of his stay from this mountainside.

"Fucking idiot will probably come up here in the middle of a snowstorm or some shit like that," Billy grumbled as he rolled up Tom's tent and stuffed it into its bag.

"How the fuck did he fit all of this shit in here?" Billy groaned as he tried to cram all of Tom's equipment into the small backpack. He soon gave up and stuffed everything, including the backpack and the tent, into the sleeping bag, tossed it over his shoulder, and, like a sweaty, cursing Santa Claus, walked down the trail to where his truck was parked. He threw the bag into the back of the truck and headed back to town. As he drove, he dialed Bob's number on his cell phone. Amazingly, he had a signal. He wanted to let Bob know as soon as possible that Tom was on his way back.

***

Billy had heard the emergency call that morning over his scanner and had called Bob to find out what had happened. He had gotten Bob's voice mail, but Bob had eventually called back and told him the details of Molly's beating. Within minutes of Mike coming home from work, the neighbors had heard his screams of anger and her screams of pain. The neighbors had called the fight in and by the time Bob had arrived, Molly was already unconscious, lying face down in the living room, a terrifyingly large stain of blood surrounding her head. She had looked dead to him.

There had never been a gradual escalation of the violence in the way he had expected from Mike. As far as he could tell, Mike had never before moved past pushes and shoves, grabbed and squeezed arms that left bruises but never led to hospital visits. He'd watched for it and if he was honest with himself, the smallest part of him almost hoped for it. Something that would give him the cause he needed to lock Mike up and give Molly the reason she needed to leave.

As Bob had walked into that room, eyes and ears alert for Mike, a weight in his gut had told him he was too late. Surprisingly, he had found a pulse, a fairly strong one, and made sure she was breathing through a clear airway. The blood had all come from a cut over one eye, an eye that was already swollen shut. A trampled bouquet of flowers lay near Molly.

He updated Marcy on the radio, then did a sweep of

the house, where he had found Mike in the kitchen, at the table, drinking a beer. Mike, his knuckles bruised and torn, the front of his shirt spattered with blood, had looked up at Bob, smiled, and said "She fell down the stairs."

Fighting the acid burn rising in the back of his throat, Bob had asked Mike where the kids were and had learned that Molly had asked Erin to pick up the kids the previous day, apparently with the foreknowledge that her planned conversation with Mike wouldn't go well.

Mike hadn't put up any fight when Bob had told him to stand up and put his hands behind his back.

"You know what she said to me? She said we were through." Mike shook his head with disbelief. "After all I gave her, she said that she could do better than me. Merry fucking Christmas. Can you believe that shit?"

"I'm one of a hundred people who told Molly over the years that she could do better than you. So, yeah, I can believe that shit."

While Bob was snapping the second cuff closed, Mike had half turned his head and looking over his shoulder, had said, "Don't fool yourself, man. I let you cuff me."

Through gritted teeth, Bob said, "You have no idea how much I wish you would resist, you fucking chickenshit."

They both heard the approaching ambulance's siren wailing as Mike said, "Oh, don't be that way. We'll still be friends when Judge Parker lets me out of jail tonight."

The tires of the ambulance crunched the gravel of the driveway and Bob shoved Mike towards the door. "Not this time. Not even your drinking buddies will be able to get you out of this one."

Mike laughed and said, "We'll see, man. I have the over-under for me in jail at 2 hours."

Bob sent Mike to Elizabethtown with a County Deputy, then followed the ambulance to Ti Hospital.

***

The Dart practically slid into the Ticonderoga Hospital entry road on two wheels, then Tom gunned the engine as he went up the short hill and stopped in the Emergency Room parking lot. There were three State Police Tahoes parked by the ambulance entrance.

As soon as he walked through the emergency room door, he heard two Troopers talking just inside the door. He paused and drank from the fountain so he could hear them and within seconds he'd learned all he needed to know.

No visitors.

She's not pressing charges.

Mike was already out of jail.

He finished his drink and fished his phone out of his pocket, pretending to answer it. He said, "Oh shit. You're right. I completely forgot. Ok, I'll be right there," to his imaginary caller and turned around, back out of the hospital and to his car.

***

As Tom strode towards the house, he could hear the loud Guns N' Roses coming from out back. That likely meant Mike was working out. *Adrenaline. Good.* He would be easier to provoke.

For the first time, he consciously acknowledged the plan that had formed in the back of his mind. It was a simple plan – he was going to beat the living shit out of Mike Rush. But there was a crucial first step in the plan that was not only necessary to keep him out of jail, he also needed it so he could look at himself in the mirror tomorrow morning and, more importantly, to be able to look Molly straight in the eye in the future.

Mike had to swing first.

Mike had to connect first.

Tom needed that bruise, both for himself and for Molly. It would help with the Troopers, too. Sure, it was a rationalization, but it was enough for him.

Tom walked around the house, towards the back porch where Mike worked out, but stopped walking when he heard the voices. Two, no, three voices, one of which was Mike's. This complicated things. At least two extras, and if the other boys insisted on joining in the fun, Tom might have his hands full. Mike's friends might not prove to be the most reliable witnesses either.

Faced with the decision of acting or waiting, the coolness that Tom had forced over himself began to slip and the mental image he had created of Molly lying in the hospital bed pushed its way back into his mind. He set his jaw and walked the rest of the way to the back of the house and through the screen door to the porch.

Quickly surveying the scene – Mike bench pressing; short, heavy-set guy with a pony-tail spotting for him; tall, lanky guy with a goatee doing curls, and doing them with piss-poor form. Scattered beer bottles and an ashtray with three very small pipes on a table by the far wall – Tom walked over to the boom box and turned the music off.

All three heads turned to Tom. All three faces looked confused, but Mike's changed first as a look of disbelief was quickly followed by amusement.

Mike put the weight bar on the bench's hooks and sat up. "You can't be serious."

Tom stood still without saying anything, trying to project a nervous anger instead of the calm that had washed over him as he had walked into the room. It was on. He could tell by Mike's body language that goading him would be possible, though there was no way yet to tell if the pot would make that easier or harder. He was still trying to get a read on the other two. Tom didn't recognize either of them.

"Did you come over here for some of what she got, GBF?" He drew out each letter of the nickname.

Quietly, Tom said, "Do you even know how to hit a man, Mikey?" That got the "ooooo"s that he was hoping for from the other two. At least they were helping with the goading.

"You know what, asshole? I was going to talk you into leaving, but now I'm going to enjoy beating your ass."

"You talk this much when you're hitting women, Mikey?" That did the trick. Mike roared as he surged up from the weight bench and practically flew at Tom. Everything began to move very slowly for Tom as he watched Mike move towards him, the tall guy pick up a dumbbell and also start towards him, and the short guy stay in place.

Wait on it. Wait on it. As he saw Mike's arm cock back – *this is going to hurt tomorrow* – Tom stood up on the balls of his feet and bent his knees slightly. He had never tried this particular move before, but it was too late now for doubts. He caught much of the force of the punch with his shoulder, but let the fist, still carrying some steam, take him squarely on the cheek, above the point of the chin but below the orbital bone around his eye.

Fuck. That's going to hurt.

The sparkles of light he saw told him that he would have plenty of bruise to show off.

Mike stopped after he threw the punch waiting for Tom to fall. He blinked slowly a few times, still waiting for Tom to fall. Tom staggered a little, then narrowed his eyes and looked at Mike.

"You only get the one." Mike was still waiting for Tom to fall. He should have gone down from that shot. Tom made a slight motion, as if shrugging his right shoulder, and suddenly Mike's head felt as though it was exploding. His vision crackled with white arcs of light and when he brought his hands up to his face, he could feel the blood gushing from his broken nose.

The tall guy with the dumbbell was right behind Mike

now – the short guy was trying to get something out of his pocket, but doing it slowly – so Tom put everything he had into another open-handed blow to Mike's face – *that felt like a broken jaw* – and sent him reeling back into the tall guy. Tom followed Mike as he fell backwards and half lifted, half pushed him into the tall guy's chest, sending them both to the floor in the corner of the porch. He turned to double check the short guy and saw him still fumbling to get something out of his pocket.

Tom dropped to the floor, scooped up the dumbbell the tall guy had dropped on his way down, and sent it flying into the short guy's midsection. Tom could hear the ribs cracking from across the room as a small automatic – *looks like a .22 or a .25*, his mind flashed – clattered to the floor.

"Tom! Stop." Tom was bent halfway down towards the pistol when he recognized the voice. He looked over his shoulder to see Bob standing in the doorway, Billy right behind him. Bob had his service pistol drawn and Billy was tucking something back into his waistband in the small of his back. *Perfect*, he groaned to himself.

Tom held his hands out at his sides, palms facing forward, as he stood up. "Bob, this isn't what it…"

Bob laughed. Tom couldn't remember the last time he had seen a smile on Bob's face. "Put your hands down, you goddam idiot. I just don't want your prints on the gun." He looked from the short guy, who was still lying on the floor with his arms wrapped around his sides, to Mike, who was on his hands and knees throwing up, to the tall guy, who was sitting in the corner with a stupid look on his face, and finally back to Tom. Bob whistled and shook his head. "So, that's what Delta Force training looks like?"

Tom's jaw dropped, but he stopped himself from saying anything. The look on Billy's face, he assumed, was probably a mirror image of his own. The questions he was asking himself must have flickered across his face, because Bob laughed again. "You know, we actually talk shop at all of those boondoggle seminars I go to. One of the guys I talk to when we get together told me that if I ever thought it wise, I should drop the name 'Ugly Joe' on you."

Tom smiled. "Colonel Ugly Joe."

"Yeah, well Ugly Joe also gave me his permission to deputize you if I ever needed to." When Tom started to open his mouth to speak, Bob interrupted. "Posse Comitatus doesn't apply to civilians, Tom. Of which you are one now. Inactive Reserve."

"Point taken. But you don't have to ever mention this to the Colonel, do you? I picked up some of this stuff outside of the Army and he would kick my ass for going in unarmed."

Bob said, "Well, we'll have to see how much it's worth to you when the time comes."

Billy hadn't said a word yet and didn't while they waited for the ambulance. Bob had Tom give his statement to Bob's Deputy, Timmy, who had arrived before the ambulance. In his statement, Tom explained that he had come to the house with the intention of convincing Mike to seek help for his anger issues. Unfortunately, Mike and his friends had decided to attack Tom, who had defended himself. Tom was choosing not to press charges at this time. If he had to guess, Tom figured Mike would go the same route.

After the ambulance had taken Mike to the hospital – Bob anticipated Tom's question and assured him that Mike would be going to Burlington Hospital and nowhere near Molly in Ticonderoga – Tom and Billy walked back around to the front of the house.

Billy still hadn't spoken. "How much did you see?" Tom asked.

"We followed you to the house, dumbass. I can't believe you didn't see Bob's Tahoe behind you."

"That's not good. I can't either."

"I guess you must have slept through the 'Watch out for big assed cop trucks following you' class."

Tom shrugged. "You know how you feel when you get

on the bike for the first ride of the spring? After not riding all winter?"

"Gotcha. But I have a question, dude. Bob and I both saw the midget going for his piece, but you ignored him."

"I saw him."

"But you went for the other two first. You couldn't have known he was going to fumble for the gun so bad."

"It just felt right. That's all I got." Tom stopped walking. "So wait a minute. You two watched me walk into a room with three guys, three weightlifting guys, and you didn't jump in to help? Or to stop me?" He started walking again. "Nice."

"Don't look at me. I started to go in, but Bob stopped me." Tom looked at him incredulously. "No, I swear. He turns to me and he says, 'This is gonna be good.' No shit. That's exactly what he said."

"The Colonel's gotten a big mouth in his civilian life."

"I'm just glad you turned that goddam music off. Why is it that every weightlifter of a certain age insists on working out to the music of that skinny-assed motherfucker?"

Tom stopped again. "You listen to Guns N' Roses when you're working out."

"This is what I'm saying."

"*What* is what you're saying?"

"I'm saying you need to get to the hospital so Molly hears this fucked up story from you before she hears it from anybody else."

"Oh shit. I didn't think it that far through."

***

Tom's hopes sank when he looked through the window to Molly's hospital room and saw exactly what he had hoped he wouldn't – a State Trooper was standing at the foot of Molly's bed, just closing his little notebook and putting it away. The Trooper nodded to Molly and walked to the door. When he saw Tom standing outside the room, he did a quick, almost comical double-take.

"I hope the other guy looks worse," he said.

Tom was confused for a second until the Trooper pointed at the left side of Tom's face. When Tom instinctively reached a hand up to touch his cheek, the shock of the touch almost brought tears to his eyes. *Well, that explains the head-ache,* he thought. He had forgotten about the punch he had taken. That whole let-Mike-have-the-first-punch thing might not have been such a great idea after all.

"He looks much worse. Can I go in and see her?" Tom asked.

"Her guest list is pretty limited, pal. And from the looks of you..." The Trooper's aggression seemed to come out of nowhere.

"My name is Tom Hudson," Tom said calmly and flatly, making sure there was no impatience in his voice that could be misinterpreted. "I hope I'm on the list."

The Trooper's face softened some, but remained wary. "I.D?"

"My wallet is in my back pocket." When the Trooper nodded, Tom pulled his wallet out and showed his driver's license. The man immediately relaxed.

"Well, it looks like you from one side, anyway. I thought you might be her husband." *Aha.* "Your name is first on the list."

"If you don't mind me asking, how much did you tell her?" Tom knew he was stalling, but he couldn't help it.

"Tell her about what? She was telling me what happened for my report."

"Report? Is she pressing charges?"

"She sure is. Said the more she thought about it, the

more pissed off she got." He smiled. "That is the best possible response, as far as I'm concerned."

Tom's relief showed on his entire body. "Me too. So you didn't tell her about me and Mike?"

"Mike Rush? Her husband?"

"Yeah, her husband."

"Her husband was the 'other guy'?" The Trooper scowled and looked Tom up and down. "I see his name on the blotter at least once a month and as far as I know, he doesn't lose fights."

Tom shrugged. "I got a lucky shot in." The Trooper shook his head and turned, walking down the hall towards the nurse's station. Tom watched him for a moment, then slowly opened the door and walked into Molly's room. Her eyes were closed and her breathing was regular. *Good. She's sleeping.*

As he approached the bed, trying to find a position where she would only be able to see the right side of his face, her eyes slowly opened.

"Well, aren't you sneak..." she began, then gasped as her eyes opened wide. "Oh my god Tom, what happened?"

He had never felt more stupid in all his life. The words started pouring out of his mouth with very little thought behind them. "Molly, I am so sorry. They wouldn't let me in to see you before so I didn't know you were pressing charges."

"Oh no." The look of horror on her face tore at his heart.

"Molly, I'm such an idiot. I wasn't thinking, I didn't think..."

He stopped when he realized her look had changed to one of concern. "Tom, are you ok? Are you hurt?"

"Hurt? No, but..."

"Did you even see a doctor yet?"

"No, listen Molly, I'm not hurt. Well, ok, it does hurt, but," he said, pointing at his cheek, "this is it."

Now she looked baffled. "You went to see Mike?"

"Yeah, I did. And I feel so stupid..."

"And that's the only place he hit you? He didn't hit you again after he knocked you down?"

Tom tried, he tried so hard, to bite down on the macho disdain creeping into his face. He realized that it was probably making him look like he was in worse pain than he was. Although now that everybody kept mentioning it, it really did hurt. A lot.

"No, Molly he... he didn't hit me again. I didn't let him."

"You didn't..."

"Listen Molly, this is important. I went to talk to Mike..." He stopped himself. He could smoothly lie to Bob and Billy, not that they believed him, he knew he could lie on the witness stand if he had to, and he knew from experience that he could lie to a prisoner during an interrogation. But he would not lie to this woman. Not to her. He filed the possible repercussions of that away for later.

She saw the turmoil in his face and waited. "No. I was angry and I went to make him pay for what he did to you. It was stupid and wrong and I hope you can forgive me."

"I don't understand. What are you talking about?"

"I'm screwing this all up, but it feels like that's all I've done all day. I'm just sorry. And I wanted you to hear it from me first."

A thought, the only reasonable thought, flashed into her mind. "Oh my god. You shot him."

"What? No, I beat him up. I hurt him pretty bad. I shouldn't have. It was wrong. And if it changes our... our friendship, I don't know what I'll do."

Her eyes narrowed. "You did what?"

"I beat him up, Molly. Pretty bad."

"By yourself?"

He knew that the macho smirk had gotten away from

him this time, but he bit it off as quickly as he realized it. He ran his hands through his hair, then rubbed his eyes, trying to fight down the pleasure that filled him. And that's exactly what it was, a primeval pleasure he hadn't felt in years. He hoped he just looked tired.

"Yes, Molly. By myself. I was in the Army, remember?"

"You said you were a *clerk* in the Army. What kind of scary-ass clerk were you?"

He was trying to stay serious, but she wasn't helping. And she certainly wasn't reacting the way he expected. "Molly, that's beside the point right now. I just want you to know that I'm sorry and... Well, that's all I guess. I'm sorry."

She laughed and shook her head, grimacing at the pain of the movement. "Ow. You are such a dumbass."

"I know, I know."

"No, you don't know. You come riding in on a white horse like a knight in shining armor and beat the shit out of the dragon and then apologize and expect me to be angry with you? You don't know much, mister."

Tom was confused, but this sounded promising. "But shouldn't you be mad or something? You're supposed to say that violence isn't the answer or... or... who am I to think that I can solve your problems for you. Something like that."

"You're my friend. That's what friends do. Well, they don't always beat people up for their friends." She pointed at him with one finger. "And I don't want you to do it for me anymore." She paused. "But it means a lot to me that in your testosterone-soaked little Neanderthal pea brain you thought you were doing the right thing for me. Hell, I didn't even know you had a testosterone-soaked Neanderthal pea brain."

She paused. "Thank you. You don't mind being my boss and my... my friend at the same time, do you? Or have you fired me for missing work today?"

"I think I can be both at the same time. And I'll just dock your pay to cover today."

She laughed, then winced as the laugh made her stitches tighten around her eye. She laughed harder as she saw the anger in Tom's eyes flash as he thought again about the man who had done this to her.

"I meant what I said about not doing it again."

"I know."

"No, I *meant* what I said. You don't know how dangerous he can be." She stopped because that little macho, smart-assed smirk that he had been trying to hide, poorly trying to hide, was back and she was a little surprised at how hot she found it. "Look, you obviously can take care of yourself. Take care of yourself in a way that I don't think any of us knew or you wouldn't even be here right now. But Mike has friends. Bad friends. They come up from Boston and I'm pretty sure they're drug dealers."

She looked thoughtful for a second. "It just pisses me off." He gave her a puzzled look. "That it got to a point where you had to get involved in this at all. That I let it go on so long." Tom didn't say anything, assuming she needed to vent some of her anger and frustration. "This sucks. If this was a book, I'd be stronger."

"Huh?" was all he had.

"If this was a story in a book, at least one by a woman, I would be stronger. Nora Roberts would make me stronger."

"Well, ok, but this isn't a book. Besides, if this was a movie, you would be a pathetic weakling who can't live without a man to take care of you."

She laughed. "Unless I was on Lifetime."

Tom laughed with her. "If this was a Lifetime movie, I guess Markie Post would play you."

Molly said sarcastically, "Thanks a lot."

"Hey, she's beautiful."

She smiled and raised her eyebrows. "Is that why she would play me?"

Tom stuttered for a second, then laughed again. "This is definitely real, because in a book or movie somebody would walk through that door right now to save me."

They both turned as the door opened and Billy walked into the room. Together, in stereo, they said, "Creepy."

Billy stopped and looked behind himself, then looked back at them with bewilderment. "Jesus Christ. Thanks a lot. Maybe the two of you should get some mirrors and see who looks creepy."

He turned as if to leave, then stopped and turned back around. "Um, you guys are supposed to say no, no, no, don't go away Billy."

Molly said, "Ok. No, no, no, Billy. Don't go away."

Billy smiled smugly. "Well, ok, since you asked so nicely. Anyway, Tom, you should be the one asking me to stay. I have word for you." He hesitated. "So, um, how far have you gotten on your side of the story?"

Tom said, "I'm pretty much done." He turned and smiled at Molly. "And I'm not even in trouble."

Molly scowled. "Bullshit, you're not. I'm just biding my time until I'm not plugged into half a dozen wires and tubes."

Billy looked disgusted. "Jesus Christ on a bike, Lucy and Ricky. So anyway, you told her the whole story?"

"Yes, I told her the whole story. There wasn't that much to tell."

"Ok, so no secrets?"

"Damn it, Billy. No, there are no secrets. She knows the whole thing."

"Okay then, I've got news for you about the other two guys you took out." He stopped as soon as he saw the reaction from both of their faces.

Tom stuttered, "Oh, that part of the story," at the same time Molly was saying, "Tom Hudson, how many men did you beat up today?"

Billy shook his head. "So, for future reference, when you say 'No secrets,' what percentage does that actually cover?"

Tom was looking back and forth between Molly and Billy, completely at a loss. "I forgot that part?"

Molly squinted at him. "You forgot how many men you beat up?"

"No, no, no. I just… I mean…" He looked at Billy, pleading with his eyes. "Dude, a little help?"

Billy laughed his evil laugh. "Not a chance."

Tom pointed at Billy in mock outrage. "I'll remember this."

Molly said, "Not based on what you've shown in the past five minutes, you won't."

"Anyway," Billy interrupted, "the tall guy was clean. Just some retard friend of Mike's. The short, tubby dude with the pistol was another story." Billy ignored Molly's gasp at the word "pistol."

"When Bob looked up his driver's license, he found that pony-tail-boy was named Scott Baldwin and that he had two outstanding warrants in Massachusetts. One for failure to appear at a possession with intent to distribute hearing and one for – say it with me – assault with a deadly weapon."

Tom cocked his head to the side for a second, while both friends watched him as he thought. "Sounds like you were right about the drug dealers from Boston."

Her voice was shaking as she said, "Oh, this is bad. I'm not talking about small-time, here. I think Mike was starting to get involved with the big people."

Billy had picked up enough to understand the context. "You may need to go back into the woods for little bit, my friend."

Tom was shaking his head. "Molly. You should have told me about this before."

"Well, who knew you would put yourself in danger..."

"No," he said gently. "That's not what I'm talking about. You should have said something about Mike's connections. I could have taken care of him a long time ago."

"That's complicated. Before two days ago, I wasn't sure I wanted him taken care of. And I never had any proof of any of it. He always tried to keep that part of his life separated from me and the kids."

"Then how..."

"I'm apparently smarter than I look. Phone conversations, drunken boastings, his separate checkbook – those kinds of things plus a little bit of research. So there was nothing anybody could do. And now, you're in danger."

Tom smiled tightly. "Not really, actually. Lucky coincidence, but I have some friends in Boston..."

Billy cut in. "Tom, this isn't something some cops in Boston can fix for you. This is serious and it is dangerous. I used to..."

Tom put a hand up, which was good because Billy had no idea what the next words out of his mouth might have been. "Guys, I have friends, well former friends, who used to, um, work with me in the Army. They're still in the business, but on the private side of things. Let's call them personal protection entrepreneurs."

He ignored the skeptical looks on both their faces. "When I got out, they had already started a company and they wanted me to take over their training program and maybe run a team for their more challenging projects. I thought about it, but my bar was just a little bit higher than theirs in picking clients. Anyway, I'm going to send word out tonight that Mike Rush was, uh, hurting his wife, that one of the guys in their circles knew about it and let it go on, and that he got in my way when I went to fix things." He smiled and nodded. "Trust me. It'll be ok."

Billy looked like he wanted to say something, he even looked like he was about to start saying something a couple of times, but he finally just shook his head and walked out, leaving Tom and Molly alone.

As they looked at each other, each hoping the other would speak first, Billy popped his head back. "Molly, have you told Tom yet why it was that Mike got mad at you? That might be a good place to start. Yeah, definitely a good place to start. All righty, see you kids later. I gotta go home and wrap my head around this fucked up day." He left again.

Tom cocked his head to one side, looking curiously at Molly. "You just said something a second ago. Something about deciding something two days ago."

"That was a lot of somethings."

"Mm hmm."

"Ok." She steeled herself. "I came back home right after opening the store yesterday. I left the kids with Erin the night before. When Mike got home from work, I told him I was leaving him."

"And then he hit you."

She shook her head. "No, not based on just that. I've told him I was leaving a million times before. This time I finally had an answer for his normal, smart assed response."

Tom didn't say anything, just waited.

"Every time I leave him, he asks me if I think I can do better. And every single time he has asked me that in the past, I haven't had an answer. Well, yesterday I answered."

Tom's voice was almost a whisper "What did you say?"

"I said to him that I was in love with you, that I had been in love with you for a long time, that I wasn't sure if you felt the same way about me, but I thought you did. But even if you didn't, not being with the man I love is better than being with the man I hate. And then he hit me." She had been looking down at her hand on the side of the bed, focusing on the IV in the back of it. Now she looked up at him, waiting for him to respond.

When he didn't say anything, she took a deep breath.

"Even if I misunderstood you in the store, I'm still glad I said it." She waited again.

He cleared his head with a shake and said, "No, no, I'm sorry. I'm just… stunned I guess. And I'm trying to decide if it's tacky to beat up your husband and ask you to marry me on the same day."

She laughed, mostly from relief. "Yes, it is tacky. And I suppose, at some point, if you make it worth my while, I might consider gracing your life in that way."

He carefully leaned in to kiss her forehead, but she put a hand on his cheek as he descended and met his lips with her own. Both of them ignored the pain.

WEEK 5 – MONDAY
January 10, 2000

Tom looked carefully behind him as he walked through the back storage area of the store, then over his shoulder again as he passed through the back door. When he was sure nobody was following him, he let the door close behind him. As he started to reach for the small drop box attached to the wall beside the door, as he anticipated the sweet, sweet relief that he knew was within, his hand stopped on its path, almost of its own accord.

There was something wrong. He couldn't place what it was that didn't feel right. Maybe the lid of the drop box wasn't closed as tight as it should be. It could have been something else entirely. He'd learned to trust his senses, understanding that his mind could register things before his conscious, logical brain could identify or categorize them.

Behind him, he heard the door begin to open. First making sure he wasn't being flanked from outside, he turned to face the door. It opened a foot or so, then from behind it a shapely hand appeared, slowly waving a pack of Lucky Strikes. The hand was followed, lower down the door, by an even more shapely leg encased in tight jeans, then, higher up the door, by the most mischievous smile a man could ever dream of seeing.

"Did you lose something, sailor?"

Oh, shit... "What? What are those? I mean, I know they're... I mean... Those are Billy's!"

"Seriously, ninja boy? That's how you react to pressure?"

"Molly, and you know I say this with love, I am so much more afraid of you than of any man I've ever fought."

"You want them?" She waggled the pack again.

He looked down and kicked at the ground with one foot. Pouting, he said, "No."

She looked back over her shoulder, then closed the door. "Ok, here's the deal. You can have one last one, but only if you promise not to tell on me."

She shook two out of the pack and handed him one. He was without words.

"I haven't had a smoke in years because I was afraid the douchebag would catch me."

"Um, if you haven't had one in years, this might not be the right brand to start back up with."

"Just light me up, tough guy."

As he lit her cigarette, then tried not to laugh at the stunned look on her face when the angry, unfiltered smoke hit her lungs, he quietly appreciated the banter. Over the past two weeks, they had both tentatively felt their way around the new relationship and this joking was one of the first times it hadn't felt forced. He understood that a new norm would take time, especially with the evidence of the violence visited on Molly still so apparent every time he saw the bruises on her face and the bandage covering the stitches over her eye.

She smoked less than half of the cigarette, then threw it on the ground, spitting pieces of tobacco out after it. "Jesus Christ!"

Tom started to put his out, but she stopped him.

"No, stay out here and enjoy your quiet time. I respect your need for sanctuary."

He smiled. "Thanks, Molly. I won't be too long. I can't believe how windy it is out here."

"I know," she said. "I just saw Lisa fly past on a bicycle."

He laughed and covered his mouth in mock shock. "Oh, damn."

"Oh, and hey, dipshit. It's the year 2000."

He looked back at her, baffled. "Well, that was gratuitous exposition. I know what year it is."

"Really? Because the last check you wrote said January 9, 1999."

"Shit. God, I hate the new year. I almost wish Y2K had taken us down so I wouldn't have to remember the date."

She chuckled and turned, opening the door.

"Hey, beautiful?"

"Yeah?"

"I don't hate this particular New Year. I love you."

"You promise?"

"I promise." He started to make a joke, but saw that she had turned serious. "What is it?"

"I can't help thinking about..." she started. "Are you sure you have your feelings for Kate figured out? I love you so much, but I won't ever be the other woman. The one you settled for."

He smiled with a gentleness that came from confidence in his answer. He had asked himself that very question when he was alone on the mountain. The answer had been easy.

"Molly, if things had gone differently with Kate, she would have been the one I settled for. I know how ridiculous this is going to sound, but since the Ninth Grade, every woman in my life who wasn't you has been the other woman. The one I was settling for. And I knew it every time."

She caught her breath and said, "I don't think you really do know just how ridiculous that sounds. But I'll take it." Then she went back into the store.

Tom didn't finish his cigarette, but waited a few more minutes to enjoy the cold, January air. He laughed at himself.

It had only taken him 21 years to tell her he loved her. Baby steps.

As he walked back to the front of the store, he knew there was going to be a harder thing to talk about. There would be no secrets between them and that included his money. As soon as she started looking more deeply at the books for the store, she would find out that they didn't actually turn a profit. The store wasn't deeply in the red, but he intended to lay out all of his finances to Molly and she would see that he didn't actually need the store to turn a profit. That because of his investment income and the liquidity he had built into his portfolio, he could keep prices artificially low and salaries artificially high.

As he walked through the aisles, he enjoyed the vibe of the store. Before the previous week, it had been a fun place to work, but it had always had an edge from the knowledge that Lisa could pick any time of any day to lose her temper.

Not fair. She wasn't picking the time any more than she was choosing to get angry. But that uncertainty – hers and everyone else's – had colored the environment so thoroughly that it wasn't until she was gone did everyone in the store realize how oppressive that mood had been. Ok, oppressive was probably too strong, but the sun did seem to shine brighter without everyone walking on eggshells.

Molly was waiting in his office, sitting in his chair, feet up on the desk. He knew she'd been stocking shelves, so she must have run in here just ahead of him. God, he loved her.

To be able to love the one person you'd wanted to love nearly your entire life. To see her looking at you in a way you never believed would or could happen. It felt so terrifyingly fragile. Tom kept waiting for the universe to wake up and see what had happened when it wasn't paying attention, to immediately spring into action to correct this imbalance.

"Hey," she said softly, looking straight into his eyes. "This is real."

"Am I that transparent?"

"Not necessarily. I was saying it as much for me as I was for you."

"Wow."

"Yeah. Wow."

***

"The leaves keep tremblin' on the tree, tremblin' on the tree..." The voice choked on the last words. The old, black phone lay on the floor where he had thrown it after ripping its cord from the wall. The handset was snapped in two.

The interior of the trailer, every room, was a catastrophe. The kitchen, bedroom, bathroom, even the screening room – all were destroyed. His cherished projector lay crumpled against one wall.

Ed sat in his recliner, head in hands, rocking rhythmically. Like a metronome.

He'd slept there, in the recliner, because he hadn't wanted to sleep in his bed after the pain of the previous night. She had come to him, had come to his own home, and he had completely misinterpreted her motives.

She'd never been to his house before and he'd always understood why. Last night, when he'd opened his front door and she'd been standing there, he'd allowed himself to believe that it was because she was finally ready to be his. Really, openly, his.

Or he, openly hers. They both knew who had the power in the relationship. Which one owned the other.

But he was more than willing to be openly hers. To show everybody that he could feel, could love, just as well as Tom and Billy and even Bob. No matter how openly contemptuous Cissy had been of their marriage, Bob had always ennobled it. He was a testament to bad love, but love nonetheless.

Ed was the man without love.

He had always been the man without love, but for one, beautiful year – one short, beautiful year – he'd had love. As soon as she'd started to speak, he'd know his love had ended. Ed had never believed he was anybody's first choice, much less hers, but over the year he'd done so many things for her that he knew, he just knew, that he was earning her love.

And last night she had come to him. He'd heard the car pull into his driveway, lost his breath when he'd looked through his window, and had been waiting for her at the door.

Anger owned her face. Her eyes, her mouth. She glowed with anger. As soon as the door was open, she'd grabbed him, kissed him as an act of violence. She grabbed his shirt in both hands and as his strength melted before her dominance, she'd pushed him back through the trailer to his bedroom. His clothes had come off with no words, just her grunts and bites. And then she'd slapped him.

She slapped him hard across the face and he had just looked at her. It wasn't that it hadn't hurt. It had hurt plenty. If a man, or any other woman, had hit him half as hard, they'd be picking teeth out the opposite wall.

She slapped him again and he still couldn't react. So she punched him. She was athletic, had always been a fighter, and she hit as hard as many men. His head didn't snap back because his neck was far too muscled for that, but he was stunned for a second.

It was in that moment that they both recognized how unequal they were. She owned him. The same phrase entered both their minds simultaneously. He was her bitch.

She dropped her hands and slowly said, "Why can't you be him?" Then she turned and walked back down the hall and out of the trailer. He remembered standing there, blinking, processing. Then he remembered the anger. Then he remembered nothing.

And now, in the harsh, cold light of morning, Ed was again the man without love.

The man who was above love and beneath it at the same time. They wouldn't put it in those terms, but that was how everyone saw Ed. He knew it. They all looked at him and none of them understood that he wanted love as much as any human being does, but that he was such a… specific… person, he couldn't fall in love with every perky, fucking blond who sashayed her ass into town.

That fucking bitch!

He hated her. Hated her, hated her, hated her. He didn't know how, but this was her fault.

He stood over the broken phone, looking down at it. That didn't make sense. He'd been sitting in his chair only a second ago. He looked up and saw the sun settling over the trees outside his living room window, but just as quickly as he questioned what had happened, he accepted that it was now almost evening.

He looked back down at the phone, watched it for minutes. Logic told him that he was the only one in the house, and despite her strength, the only one who had been in the house who had the raw power to snap the handset of the old telephone.

Why had he done that? It didn't make any sense. He loved that phone.

Billy had given him that phone. That's what he needed. He needed to talk to Billy. Billy would know what to do. Billy had always been his friend.

There was a small thought in the back of his head, almost like an itch, that Billy might not want to talk to him, but that was crazy. They were friends.

***

Around noon, Molly had reminded Tom that she had been planning to leave early to see her grandmother at the assisted living apartments in Ti. They danced around for a few exchanges before she asked him if he would come with her and he jumped at the chance. She surprised him by agreeing when he asked her if she wanted to drive the Dart.

He looked at her as they drove through Crown Point. The line of her jaw, the freckles on her nose and cheeks. A face without freckles is like a night without stars, the Irishman in him thought.

She turned suddenly and asked, "What?"

Startled and busted, he said, "What do you mean?"

"You were looking at me."

It should have felt like the moment of truth, but he knew that the moment of truth had passed him by long, long ago. This was merely the moment of out loud.

He looked straight at her, nodded, and said "I was going to give you my old answer. The one I always used to have to give you. The one where I say I was just thinking, or staring off into space, or looking at an island through your window."

"And this time?" Molly asked.

"This time, I'm going to say I was looking at you. Looking at you because you're beautiful and I can't not look at you. I'm going to say I was looking at the way the sun makes your eyes twinkle. I'm going to say that I was looking at the freckles on your cheeks and the adorable upturn your nose makes on the end and the soft point of your chin and how all of these together make you look like a beautiful, fairy princess. And you know what else? From now on, when you ask me 'What?' that's how I'm going to answer. Because I can." Tom folded his arms across his chest, nodded once emphatically, and looked straight ahead.

"Fair enough," Molly said, in a voice that cracked the smallest amount.

***

Tom could see Grandma Byrne sizing him up as they walked into the room. He knew that if any of the heroic men and women he had served with could have seen him now, they would have pissed their pants in delight at the fear in his eyes.

"So, you beat up my grandson-in-law?" she asked in her strong, Celtic voice before he had fully crossed the threshold into the room.

Shit. Ok, so we're cutting straight to the chase. Tom noticed that Molly was showing no inclination to lend a hand. He filed this away for a future discussion. "Well, Mrs. Byrne, it is complicated. He…"

"Don't be a pussy. Did you beat him up?"

Roger that. "Yes, ma'am. I did indeed."

She smiled brilliantly. Beautifully. Molly's genes were clear in the sparkle of her eyes. "About fucking time somebody did. What size is your neck?"

The comment, followed rapid fire by the non-sequitorious question, completely threw Tom and he simply stood there, unable to respond.

Grandma Byrne turned to Molly and said, with no small amount of pity in her voice, "He's pretty enough, but he doesn't seem real bright." She turned back to Tom. "I'll say it slower, cutie. What size is your neck?"

Sometimes, when you're dreaming, you go along with the unreality of the situation you are in, knowing that it makes no sense but also knowing that this information will be of no help to you in the dream. Tom decided that this situation might just as well be handled in much the same way. "It is about 18 inches, ma'am."

Both he and Grandma Byrne ignored Molly's throaty "Mmm…" noise. "Katherine Hepburn said she loved Spencer Tracy's neck because it was 17 inches and that is the minimum size a man's neck ought to be. I am inclined to agree."

She looked past them to the door. "Now, your timing sucks but before you leave, and I'm pretty sure you're going to want to because I don't figure either of you want to watch me get my sponge bath..." They both looked behind them and saw the nurse standing in the doorway. "Before you leave, I will warn you to treat this person with respect and kindness."

Tom stepped towards her and said, "I promise."

Grandma Byrne shook her head and said to him, "No dumbass, I was talking to her." She turned to Molly and said, "Like I said. Pretty, but not real bright. Now kiss me, you fools, and go away."

***

Billy and Kate sat in the garage, watching the last of the day's light flicker out. The front doors were open and a fire in the woodstove kept the worst of the cold at bay. They were facing each other but not looking at each other. They'd tried to talk about it. Had spent a week trying to talk about it, but hadn't even really made a start. School was back in session, which gave her another place to be and them an excuse not to talk. Tom had been up that morning, early, before school started or the store opened, and had visited with Billy for half an hour or so, but Kate had stayed in the house until he left. She wasn't sure why.

She wanted to be in love with Billy, but was starting to wonder how much of that was just stubbornness. She knew she'd done the same thing before. Multiple times before. Kate didn't see herself as a quitter, but did that leave her in dead relationships? She didn't know.

The sound of the motorcycle made them look up and they shared an uncertain look as they saw that it was Ed and he was turning the big bike into their driveway. They looked at each other in confusion, then watched him cut off the engine, drop the kickstand, and get off the bike.

The icy roads notwithstanding, it was far too cold to be riding a motorcycle without heavy gear. Ed was wearing jeans and an unbuttoned flannel shirt over a t-shirt. He wasn't wearing a helmet either – Ed always wore a helmet – and his expression was oddly blank. Then he looked over at Billy and smiled a huge, genuine smile. Kate had never seen Ed smile like that before. Had she ever seen him smile, period?

Kate knew what had happened at the hunting camp, so the sight of Ed coming here at all was disconcerting, but that smile made it surreal.

Ed held a hand up as he walked towards the table, closing it as if on something in the air just in front of him. Then, still walking towards them, he held out his index finger, bouncing it up and down.

"There's something… Something, I just can't… It's right there, Billy. And I can't…"

"Ed?"

He snapped his fingers and locked his eyes on Billy's. "It was your speech, man. Your valedictorian speech when you guys graduated." He was pointing his finger at Billy now. "You looked back at them, all of them up on that stage, and you told them to try to capture that moment in their memories. Because they would never all be together in one place again. You said… you said that even if every one of them got back together, it still wouldn't be all of them because they would be different people than the ones they were on that stage in that moment. And that was it, man. That was it."

His voice had become wistful, almost tender, but then the intensity in both his look and his voice ratcheted up. "But you know what? You know what? They. Didn't. Fucking. Listen."

Ed turned back around and walked back to his bike. He sat on it and fumbled around on the handlebars for something.

"Where's my helmet?" he asked, confused. He looked back at Billy and said, "Listen Billy. It's Kate, She's the one causing all this. She's the one."

The he started his bike, walked it backwards out of the driveway, put it in gear, and rode away.

Billy and Kate looked at each other, unsure of how to evaluate what had just happened.

"Bill, am I in danger?"

"I honestly don't know." He shook his head and asked, "Did he make eye contact with you?"

"No," she said, relieved that he had noticed. "I don't even think he saw me here."

Tom looked at his watch when the phone rang. Seven in the morning. *Somebody is a go-getter.*

"Tom Hudson?" Formal, but friendly. *This could be interesting.*

"Speaking."

"Mr. Hudson, my name is Dean Hughes and I have been retained to represent Ms. Lisa Ford."

"Aha. I was wondering what was taking so long. Is your process server having trouble finding the place, Mr. Hughes? We are the only grocery store in town, so it seems like they might not be trying very hard." As Tom spoke, he was searching Google for Dean Hughes and quickly found his firm's web page, noting that they were based in Albany.

Hughes' friendly tone didn't change. "Actually, Mr. Hudson, we're hoping to avoid taking this disagreement down so formal a path, despite the fact that we have every confidence that we have a very compelling case."

"Wrongful termination, I'm assuming. Maybe some sexual harassment, for added spice?" Tom kept his tone light. Even a little playful. *There's no such thing as a royal flush in legal cases, and despite the fact that it made Tom feel slightly misogynistic, he had to accept that it was especially so when you have an attractive woman suing a man. But he was pretty comfortable that he was holding four of a kind. Let's see what his opponents cards were. Or at least which cards he was willing to show.*

"It's good to hear we're on the same page," Hughes said.

Tom smiled. "For the purposes of the recording I assume you are making, Mr. Hughes, please don't interpret my previous comment as anything other than a guess at what claims Ms. Ford might be making. And before you protest, I stipulate that New York is a one-party-consent state."

"Well, of course that is exactly what I inferred as your meaning." He ignored the recording issue altogether.

"Good. So, I have your web page up. Is the State Street address the best address to mail the videos to?"

The pause was nearly imperceptible. This guy was good. "Videos. I hope you're not implying consent on the part of Ms. Ford for her treatment, Mr. Hudson."

"Oh sweet lord, that's not what I was suggesting at all." Tom barely stopped himself from making a joke about him not being the one consenting to what Lisa wanted. *You're being taped, dumbass.*

"No, Mr. Hughes, I mean the videos of Ms. Ford loading merchandise from the store into her personal vehicle."

"Then you're implying theft, Mr. Hudson?"

"I'll also include the video of her transferring money from a co-worker's cash register to her own purse during that co-worker's break period." He paused to see if Hughes had a comment. When none came, he continued, "I hadn't decided yet whether or not I was going to report these to the police, but obviously they would become public record in a lawsuit."

Tom heard Hughes chuckle on the other end of the line. "The State Street address will be fine, Mr. Hudson."

"I'll get copies of the tapes in the mail today."

"Thank you for your time."

"Have a great day, Mr. Hughes." Hughes didn't respond before hanging up his phone.

"Good talk," Tom said aloud as he hung up. Then he stood up to go find Molly. She had been asking him to teach her some "bad ass ninja shit," which sounded like an excellent excuse to make out in the back of the store.

****

"Tell me the truth. Was Billy actually valedictorian of his high school class?"

Tom tried to ignore the edge in Kate's tone. The rehearsal was going badly. Tom hadn't been to rehearsal the previous week and the kids had been far too happy for Kate's liking to see him back. They had also been far too genuine in expressing how much they'd missed him and, as the story of his confrontation with Mike and friends was now known to everyone in town, had been far too impressed with his unexpected level of badass.

The boys looked at him differently, the girls certainly looked at him differently, and Kate openly vacillated between needing to be near Tom and wanting to be anywhere else. Her question had come out of nowhere during a break.

"Yes, Billy was indeed valedictorian. And an unappreciated one."

"Oh, he told me his parents hadn't believed he'd be able to do it. But seriously, how many people were in his class? Fifty?"

"It was sixty-nine and it was more than his parents who were surprised. Did he tell you the whole story?"

"How much of a story could there be?"

Tom hesitated. If Billy hadn't told her, then he didn't want her to know. Or maybe he just didn't want to be the one to tell her stories like that one. Tom made a judgment call.

"The year Billy graduated, the guidance counselor had this brainstorm. He brought the top three students into his office once their final grades had been set by all their teachers. Nobody had calculated their overall GPAs yet and he thought it would be cool if he did it while they were in the same room and they'd all learn at the same time who was valedictorian."

Kate's edge softened some. "That's a horrible idea. It's... it's borderline cruel."

"He just hadn't thought it through. He was actually a really nice guy. Anyway, he knew that the gap between the three of them and the rest of the class was going to be significant enough so that he was safe with just them in the room. And all three of them, all four of them actually if you include Mr. Grote, pretty much had the same expectation. Randy Miller was going to be first, Kristin Crosby was going to be second, and Billy was going to be third. Kristin, coincidentally, was Billy's girlfriend at the time."

"Really? A bad idea made much, much worse."

"Pretty much. So Mr. Grote calculates all three and Billy has the highest GPA. And before any of the kids can say anything, Grote says, 'Well, that can't be right. Let me do that again.'"

Kate put a hand over her mouth. "Oh my god."

"Yup. So he recalculates, it comes out the same, and he turns to Billy and says, 'Wow. You really are the valedictorian.' And he shook his hand."

Kate's hand had stayed over her face and she repeated, "Oh my god."

"That's not even the best part. Randy, entirely genuinely, congratulated Billy. As an aside, I still hate that guy. He was the best looking guy in school, he played football and basketball, he was seriously smart, and he was one of the nicest people I've ever met. Seriously. He was just awful."

"The best part?" Kate had dropped her hand but she was still clearly unsettled.

"Oh yeah, so Kristin... The girlfriend, remember? She walks out of the guidance counselor's office with Billy, then stops him in the hall and tells him that she simply cannot congratulate him because he doesn't deserve to be valedictorian as much as she does. Because he doesn't work as hard as she does. Apparently Randy would have been acceptable to her as valedictorian, because who didn't love that guy, but not Billy."

She had come home from rehearsal the night before and gone straight to bed. Billy had been reading on the back porch and she hadn't said a word to him. She dropped into sleep with a thousand thoughts circling and colliding like dust specks in a ray of sunlight. No, it was more like an electron cloud, because they had all orbited around a central nucleus and that nucleus was Tom. A decision was forming as she drifted and when she woke – Billy's side of the bed was undisturbed – the decision was solidified.

Kate got out of bed, dressed quickly, and packed a small suitcase. She steeled herself for the conversation that was to follow. If she didn't have to gather her laptop and corrected homework for school tomorrow, she might have been tempted to just walk out with her suitcase. To leave without saying a word. But no, this was better. She knew that she would cede the moral high ground to Billy if she left without telling him why. And to where.

The bizarre visit from Ed had been the clincher. Since that visit, she'd felt a stronger and stronger sense of unease. She honestly felt she might be in danger. Danger, mortality – these were feelings that were foreign to Kate. But she didn't push them away. Instead she considered them.

Life is short, dammit. And when you come to that realization, she'd decided, you owed it to yourself to be with the right person for you. Your other half.

Billy sat at the kitchen table, in the very seat his father had always sat on Sunday mornings and had shared coffee and gossip with Billy's mother. Billy was drinking coffee and he had Kate's cup ready for her. He watched her as she came down the stairs, taking in the clothes, shoes, and suitcase.

"I was hoping that wasn't what you were doing."

"I have to go, Billy. If we're being honest, we both know I stayed too long."

"So this is go, go. Not 'some time to think' or a pretend break that just lengthens until the inevitable." He nodded. "I respect the honesty."

"It's human nature to try to avoid uncomfortable situations, but it would be wrong to pretend to you that this is something other than what it is." She paused. "This is goodbye."

"Do you have a place to go?"

His genuine concern surprised her. They'd drifted so far apart lately that she expected him to be relieved that she was the one pulling the band-aid off. Maybe he still was and this was just the decency that she'd seen early on, the decency that not everyone else saw and that attracted her to him for longer than the physical attraction alone would have lasted. That made what she was going to say next all the worse, but she still had to say it.

"Tom. I'm going to Tom."

That surprised him, though it shouldn't have. "At some point, Kate, that man is going to get good and tired of being your fire extinguisher."

"My what?"

"Your fire extinguisher. Break glass in case of emergency. Go pull him out when things are shitty, when you think nobody else is there for you, assuming he'll always be there, no matter what."

"That's not what..."

"Do you ever wonder what the fire extinguisher feels like? Day to day, watching you go through your life, wondering what it would be like to be with you when it's not an emergency?"

"That's not what Tom and I are to each other. Are you just trying to hurt me?"

"No, I'm sticking up for my best friend. I'm trying to explain how it must have felt to him before he and Molly got together, when you would go to him whenever we had a fight. I'm trying to explain how he must have wondered if he was ever on your mind when you were happy instead of when you were sad or angry. Or just bored."

"That's not what this is." She had to stay the course. "I'm not going to Tom's to find a place to hide. I'm going *to* Tom."

"What? So, he's... Wait a minute. He doesn't even know you're coming, does he?"

His analytical speed was another thing she saw that few others did. "Not exactly, but..."

He interrupted, but gently. "Kate, he's with Molly now. If you won't stop and think for us... And I wish you would..."

"That's a little condescending, Bill."

His voice rose slightly. "It's not condescending, it's desperate. I'm desperate. If you leave me, right here and now, and go spend some time away, then change your mind, we can recover from that. If you try to go to Tom, then come back, I don't think we can."

"You still think there's a chance for us?" She was surprised, almost incredulous.

"Of course I do."

"You still want there to be an us?"

"Jesus, Kate. How can you not see that?"

"Wait, you said if I try to go to Tom, then come back. You don't think he and I would make it?"

"No, you don't understand. You wouldn't get a chance to make it or not. It has nothing to do with you. He's in love with Molly. He's been in love with Molly since we were kids."

She walked to the table and sat down, then realized she'd made a mistake when she saw the false hope in his eyes. He really did still want to make this work. But she couldn't weaken.

"He may think he's in love with her, but she's not the one. The one for him."

He sighed. "That again?"

Kate said, "You really don't think that there is one perfect person for everybody, do you? The one person you're meant to be with." Billy shook his head, but didn't say anything. She could see how tightly he was controlling himself, but she needed to make sure that everything that needed to be said was said. That it was said in this moment. She needed him to understand.

She had the thread now and couldn't let it go. "I wasn't sure I believed you. That you really don't think there is a perfect other half for each of us. But now I do. I do believe you and that's why we can't be together."

Billy shook his head. "You're not serious. You can't be."

"No," Kate insisted. "I'm serious. You're not like anybody else I've ever known. You intrigue me, you challenge my pre-conceptions, you absolutely fascinate me. But that doesn't really sound like love, does it?"

"I'm not going to philosophize with you about what is and isn't love," Billy said. "We each have to make our own definition. All I can know is what love feels like to me. And I have to assume that's how it feels to everybody else. To you." He took a breath and said, slowly, "I love you. When I think about whatever love is for me, you're it."

"No, Bill. Love is the bond between the two people who are meant to be together. Plato's two halves of one. What if he is my real other half? What if he is the one for me?"

Billy looked more disappointed than anything else. Not surprised any more. "So, out of curiosity, essentially, you are willing to destroy our relationship. And try to destroy Tom and Molly's relationship. Just in case."

"Not 'just in case,' but if it's meant to be…"

"Oh bullshit." He still wasn't raising his voice, but he had to accept that his battle was lost. "You're bored with me and want to move on, that's all. Leave out the Prometheus and Bob bullshit about other halves. You want to move on and you have your eye on Tom."

"There's more to it than that."

"Kate, please. First off, if that other half nonsense was even true, it would describe Tom and Molly. To a T. But hey, I've been on the other side of this conversation a few times. Granted, I was always more honest with myself than you are, but now I really do understand."

He saw a look of triumph in her eyes and knew that whatever was coming next would hurt him in ways he hadn't been hurt in years. Would hurt him in ways that might not heal.

"Really? Honest? Really? What about you little trips down to Glens Falls? I know you go to the hospital down there. I assume you have a little nurse who treats your ills."

That was it. That was the break that could not be healed. "You assume? Meaning that's what you've assumed for a while? Maybe all along? If that's what you thought, how could you not call me on it? Were you just saving it up for when you needed it?"

"Billy, look…"

As he interrupted, he marveled that she seemed to genuinely believe her own load of shit. And that's exactly what it was. "No. You've been living with me, telling me you love me, listening to me tell you I love you, and all the while thinking I had a piece on the side? I can't even wrap my mind around being able to do that."

He shook his head. "Ok, here's the deal," he said, with a calm, cold voice. "I'm going out. I won't be back until tomorrow morning. I want you to use the time wisely. Get every last bit of your belongings out of my house." His emphasis on whose house is was could not have been clearer. "I don't want to see a trace of you left in my house when I get back."

Kate was shaken. She wasn't sure what she had expected, but this was not it. "That certainly was an abrupt change in tone."

Billy shrugged. "Kate, if it's over, I need it to be over. For me. Over the years, I've learned to recognize hopeless situations and know when to cut my losses. It's why I'm still alive."

He walked towards the door, taking his leather jacket off the back of the chair on his way. Billy put the jacket on and, as he walked out the door, without looking back said over his shoulder, "Goodbye, Kate."

As Billy headed to his truck – he wished the roads were good enough for his bike because today was definitely a bike day – he saw Ed's truck turn the corner from Joyce Road and head up the hill towards his house. The truck turned into his driveway and stopped. Ed got out slowly, economically.

"We need to talk."

He looked stable, like every Ed he'd ever seen prior to the visit two days ago. So normal that it was natural Billy would question his own memory of the previous visit.

"Dude, I'm sorry. I feel real shitty about it, but I'm going to have to rain check you."

"You got stuff. I understand." Ed seemed sincere. And, again, stable.

Billy shook his head. "Still. We should talk. But man, I got no talking in me today."

Ed looked off to the side and ran his tongue around the inside of his mouth. Deciding. He looked at Billy and he started to say something, but Billy interrupted the words that would have changed everything that was to follow.

"Ed, Kate just left me. In fact, she's leaving right now."

"Leaving you?"

"Yeah, it's over. She's... she's moving on."

Ed started to say something else, then stopped himself

and got back in his truck. He backed out of the driveway, then headed back down the hill towards Joyce Road. Billy's senses told him that Ed wasn't as stable as he seemed, wasn't the same old predictable asshole, but he didn't have the spare brain cycles to process it. He was in his truck and away before Kate came out to her car, heading up the hill and out towards the Tracey Road and the Northway. He'd be spending the night in Glens Falls tonight.

Kate had seen Ed's truck pull in and then leave and she waited for Billy to leave too before she came outside. She had no intention of packing her belongings up now. She had things to do.

Well, one thing to do. Maybe the most important thing she'd ever done.

She called Tom on his cell as she was driving away, telling a wary sounding Tom that something important was happening, something she could only tell him in person. He agreed to meet her at his house. The last thing she needed was Daisy Mae hovering around for this moment.

Kate had a smile on her face the entire drive to Port Henry. It was a sincere smile, a smile of anticipation, but in the corners of her eyes lay a small sense of uncertainty. Billy's words, his entire reaction, kept forcing its way back to the front of her mind. No matter how she tried to concentrate on Tom; on the warmth of his smile, the way his humor made her feel, the nearness of his body as they had sat on the couch that night at his house, no matter how much she tried to focus on all this, the hurt in Billy's eyes – a hurt that was all too apparent, despite his show of toughness – kept returning to her. It had surprised her, the depth of it.

She pulled into Tom's driveway, parked her car, and walked towards his door. Before she could reach the front steps, the door opened and Tom came out. He looked a little unsure, but he didn't say anything. His head slightly cocked to one side, – *God, he's adorable*, she thought – he looked at her questioningly.

"Tom. I left Billy"

His forehead crinkled. "What do you mean?"

"Just what I said. Billy and I are through."

He still just stood there. "Did something happen?" Despite his unease, the warmth of genuine concern in his voice melted her and she lost any doubts she was still holding onto.

"I woke up, is what happened. I finally figured out how blind I've been. And I realized how much better I could do than Billy."

"Better?"

"Yes, Tom, better. Do you remember what you said to me when you tucked me in on your couch?"

He looked startled, even panicked for a split second. "I remember, Kate. Do you?'

"Are you joking? I can still hear it. What your voice sounded like, the look on your face. I asked you to lie down with me and you called me 'Gorgeous.' You said, 'Gorgeous, if I thought you would say the same thing to me sober, I would lie down with you right now.' That's what you said and I'm here to call you on it.

Tom frowned sadly. "No. No, it's not. I said, "Gorgeous, *even* if I thought you would say the same thing sober...' and then I stopped. You filled in the rest."

"Then what was the rest? What was it?" She could feel her face reddening. No one had ever reacted to her like this before.

"Kate, I don't love you. Not like that." Tom's voice was sincere, but flat. Careful. But as he continued, it grew more passionate. "Go back to Billy. He does love you. More than he's ever loved anybody else, as far as I can tell."

Of course. He's being loyal. I should have expected that. "No, Tom, Billy understands. I told him I was coming here and why. He won't bother us."

"You're still not listening. I said I don't love you." He spoke so quietly, but what to him was gentle sounded to her like pity and it shook her to her very soul.

"I know all about your difference between being in love and loving somebody." He started to talk, but she cut him off. "No, let me finish. I know you're in love with me and if you give this a chance, you'll love me. I know it and you do too."

Tom frowned again and started to shake his head, but stopped himself. The pity was unmistakable to her. "Kate, I don't love you and I'm not in love with you. You are a wonderful person and you must know how much I treasure your friendship…"

"Friendship? Do you know what I'm offering you? Do you really understand?" She looked at Tom fiercely. "She wasn't your first choice. I was."

She waited for Tom to respond, but he said nothing. He had nothing left in him to say. To say more would be cruel. She saw that in him and slowly walked back to her car, all the while thinking that he would call out to her, tell her he hadn't been thinking clearly. He would come to her. He would take her in his arms.

She reached the car, opened the door, hesitated, then sat down in the driver's seat and closed the door behind her. She saw him through the windshield, still standing in the same place. They locked eyes and looked at each other for a moment, then Tom turned to walk back up the hill to the store. To Molly.

Kate started her car, backed out of the driveway, drove out to the main road, and turned left, south on 9 N. She would spend the night at a motel in Ticonderoga and get her things in the morning, Billy's warning be damned.

She didn't notice the pickup truck pull out behind her as she passed it on Greely Street. It had followed her all the way from Mineville.

Billy's trips to Glen Falls were hit or miss – sometimes they were great and sometimes they were heartbreakingly unsatisfying. Yesterday had been a good one. To make sure Kate didn't call and ruin his mood, even with an unlikely apology, he'd turned his phone off as soon as he'd gotten to the hospital. He was up early, had breakfast at the McDonald's – because fuck it, why not – and headed back north with his phone still off.

He allowing himself a small smile as he pulled into the driveway. *Well, she didn't burn the house down while I was gone.* He went into the house – she had, however, left it unlocked – and started the coffee pot. A quick scan of the house showed that she hadn't come back for any of her things.

He wasn't surprised and figured they could awkwardly arrange a time for him to be away from the house at some point this week. God only knew where she was staying or how much space she'd have for her astonishing number of books.

He chuckled dryly as he thought that Tom would probably have, for the smallest second, considered letting her stay with him just out of kindness. He didn't consider for a minute that she'd been successful at coming between Tom and Molly.

When the coffee was ready, Billy sat at his father's seat at the kitchen table and turned his phone on. Might as well get it over with. He heard the police siren at the same time he heard the phone start to vibrate. He wasn't sure where to look because as each successive voicemail and text notification came in, the phone would pause for a split second before beginning to vibrate again. It was still vibrating when Bob's Tahoe slid into his driveway.

Bob leapt from the vehicle as it was coming to a stop and in a surprisingly fluid motion pulled his weapon from its holster and ran towards Billy's house. He didn't knock and Billy half expected him to kick the door in, but Bob instead opened the door and ran into the house.

Billy knew he didn't have time to get to a weapon and didn't think he'd be able to make it to the back door, so he steadied himself and prepared to see where this went.

Bob's face was bright red and he huffed, "Are you alone?"

Billy's eyes narrowed. "Yes..." He saw that Bob wasn't aiming his weapon at him, wasn't really locked onto him as a target, but he stayed wary.

"Ed. Have you seen Ed today?"

"No, I haven't seen him since yesterday morning. What the fuck's going on?"

"Trust me for a second here. How long have you been home?"

"Like ten minutes. I stayed in Glens Falls last night." Shit, he should have held back that detail. Was he going to need an alibi?

More sirens. His head snapped as he saw one State Police car, then another, each coming towards his house from a different direction, skid to stops in front of his driveway, blocking it.

Two State Troopers came running towards, then into the house.

Bob turned to them as they came through the door. "He's been home ten minutes, nobody else is downstairs, I haven't swept the upstairs yet."

They nodded and headed up the stairs. Billy heard, "Clear," four times – two bedrooms, laundry, and bathroom –

then they came back down.

"Mr. Ridge," one of the Troopers started, but Bob interrupted him.

"He doesn't know yet."

"Fuck," the Trooper muttered.

Bob answered, "I got this," then turned to Billy, holstering his pistol.

Billy stood up and said, "Ok, enough. What the fuck is going on?"

"Let's go out to the back porch." Bob pointed for him to go first. Billy took a deep breath and went out to the porch, sitting on the couch. Bob sat opposite him in the armchair.

"Listen, I have one or two more questions I have to ask..." He held up a hand to stop Billy's interruption. "Man, I know but I have to. We have to do this right. For later. Now, you already told me you haven't seen Ed since yesterday morning. What about Tom?"

"Monday. Monday morning. He came up for a little bit in the morning."

"Ok, what about Kate?" Billy heard his tone change and knew that the question about Tom had been just to set a baseline. "When was the last time you saw Kate."

"Bob..." Billy paused and Bob let him have the time. "The last time I saw her was yesterday morning. She told me she was leaving me, so I drove down to Glens Falls and spent the night there. Now, before I say another word, you need to tell me what happened." Billy was holding it together as best he could, but he could tell from Bob's demeanor that an alibi wasn't what Bob – and the State Troopers – had come here for.

"Last question. Swear to god. And then I'll tell you everything. Ed. You said you saw him yesterday morning. What did he say? How was he acting?"

And then he knew. "Jesus, no. No. Fuck. Fuck!" Bob waited, not pushing. He just waited.

Billy gathered himself, just to get to the end of this. "He came here yesterday morning. As I was leaving, he stopped by to talk to me and I told him what had happened with Kate. He left before I did but... I don't know... I don't know where he went."

Bob said, "Ok," then went straight into the words he'd give anything not to have to say to his friend. "Kate's dead. And Ed's credit card was used to jimmy open the window."

Billy asked, flatly, "What window?"

"She was at the motel in Ti. We talked to Tom and best as we can tell, she left here and went straight to see him. It, well, it didn't go like she'd hoped it would and it looks like she went straight from his place to Ti, spent some time at the Wagon Wheel, then checked into the motel. Ed left his credit card behind, which looked like it was planted at first, but his fingerprints were all over the place."

"How bad?"

Bob reached across the coffee table between then and put a hand on Billy's knee.

"It looks like he killed Cissy too. That bad."

Could he have stopped her? Billy knew that those thoughts would do him no good, would do nobody any good, but he also knew that for the rest of his life he would wonder what he could have done to save her. Not *if* he could have done something, but *what* he could have done. What he should have done.

In every movie and television show, Billy knew what the next question would be, knew that it was such a cliché, but he couldn't make himself not ask. "Was it quick? Was she dead before he did... you know?"

"It looks like it was fast. There hasn't been an autopsy yet, but the FBI crime scene guys say that all of the... the awful stuff happened post mortem."

"That only partly makes sense," Billy said, quietly.

"Why do you say that?"

"Logic says it's not an isolated building, there's no way to know how many other people are staying there. I'm assuming she didn't even know she was staying there until she got there, so there's no way to prepare."

"Yeah, we had all that. But why only partly makes sense?"

"Have you seen him the last week?" Bob nodded knowingly. "He's lost it. And he was so pissed at her. He hated her. He blamed Kate for me and Tom not getting along, then blamed her when we were good again."

"Yeah, when I told Tom this morning, he explained..." Bob trailed off.

"Oh fuck, do you think him and Molly are in danger?"

"No, we got State Troopers at her house. And Tom's going to stay there with her until we get Ed."

Billy smiled humorlessly. "Good luck with that. If he's comfortable Molly is safe, you know he's going to be out there looking for Ed. And you're smart enough to know I will too."

Bob shook his head. "I wish you wouldn't, but I do know damn well that the only way to stop you is to arrest you and I just don't have the energy. But listen to me, Billy, there are three counties' worth of local cops, more State Troopers than we had for Garrow, plus the FBI, all running around an area that they don't know that well. Don't get shot by the good guys. Well, hell, don't get shot by the bad guy either."

"The bad guy." Billy shook his head. "Ed's the bad guy."

"I know." He stood up and started to say something about getting back to work, but Billy remembered something from their conversation.

"Wait. You said when you saw Tom this morning, he explained something. But you didn't say what it was." He saw from Bob's face that he'd been hoping Billy had missed that comment.

"Ed wrote something on the wall of the hotel room. He wrote 'Take that, Yoko.' Apparently it was something he had said to Tom about Kate at Cissy's crime scene that night."

"What did he write it with?"

"Don't make me say it. You know the answer."

"Ok."

Bob left the room, talked to the State Troopers who were still standing in Billy's kitchen, then left the house.

Billy went back into the kitchen and got out two more coffee cups for the Troopers, then took his cellphone back to the back porch. Nearly every call and text was from Bob or Tom. At least the first several. As he scanned the phone, it was still getting calls and texts, madly vibrating in his hand. He left it on the table, picked up the landline phone, and dialed Tom's cell.

Tom answered the call with, "Come down here. To Molly's."

"Yeah," Billy said gratefully. "Thanks, man."

***

The State Troopers stayed at Billy's house in the unlikely event that Ed would show up. There were more of them outside Molly's house. The kids were watching the television in the living room and Tom, Molly, and Billy sat around Molly's dining room table, nursing cups of coffee gone cold.

As soon as he'd arrived he'd felt a distance between Tom and Molly and he was concerned he was the cause of it, so concerned that he decided to leave, even though he'd only been there half an hour.

Molly stopped him. "Don't try to leave. You're spending the night here tonight."

"Molls, it's ok. I think I'll just head home. Besides, it feels like I'm adding stress to you guys and there's already plenty of that to go around."

She and Tom exchanged looks, his questioning, hers hurt.

Tom said, "Hey, Bill. Let's go out back for some fresh air." They all knew that fresh air was a euphemism for air that was anything but fresh, but none of them smiled.

As they went out the back door, Tom said, "I hope you're carrying, because I haven't had a chance to hide any here yet."

Billy pulled out a pack of menthol lights and shrugged. "This is all I have, man."

"I'll take it." They both lit up and stood quietly for a minute. Tom pulled the cigarette out of his mouth and looked at it. "Wow. That tastes really good."

"So," Tom started after another minute of silence, "I didn't stay here last night. We're not doing sleepovers yet –or at least we weren't – but I was back here this morning and this is where Bob found me and told us what had happened."

"Yeah, he told me."

"Well, he apparently didn't tell you that I hadn't had a chance to tell Molly yet why Kate came to see me."

"Ah."

"Yeah."

Billy had finished his first cigarette already and knocked another out of the pack, lighting it from the glowing tip of the first. "But you said you hadn't told her *yet*. You were going to tell her."

"Oh god, yes. I was actually hoping she'd ask me what was up when I got back to the store yesterday. That way, I wouldn't have to figure out the right time. When she didn't ask, I decided to tell her this morning. Just never got the chance."

They both stopped as the back door opened with a creak and Molly stepped out. She looked at Tom, said, "That's all I needed to hear," and walked to him, putting her arms around him. They hugged for a second, then she detached and turned back to Billy. She held her hand out and said, "Hit me."

He looked at Tom, questioning, but looked back at her when she cleared her throat.

"Do you think I need his permission? In my own house?"

"No ma'am," Billy responded and handed her a cigarette, then lit it for her.

She inhaled deeply, openly enjoying the taste and hit of the smoke, then exhaled with an equal amount of pleasure. "Oh sweet Jesus, that's good. That's what a cigarette is supposed to taste like. Not that shit Tom smokes."

Billy smiled for the first time that day, then caught himself the way people catch themselves smiling at a funeral and tell themselves they shouldn't be.

Molly put a hand on his arm. "I'm sorry, Billy. I'm so sorry." He could feel himself starting to fold and she must have also, because she dropped her cigarette and put her arms around him, laying her head against his chest. He dropped his also and clung to her.

Billy was over a foot taller than Molly and a hundred pounds heavier, but she held them both up. He didn't cry. He couldn't. Not yet. But he felt destroyed in a way he had never before and the flow of friendship, of support, of love from Molly was keeping him standing.

After long minutes, he realized that she was shivering and lifted his head up. Tom wasn't with them and as they walked back in the house, Billy's nose told him that Tom had put more coffee on and was cooking bacon and eggs.

He looked at the two of them and asked, "What do other people do? People who don't have friends like you guys?"

Tom looked back at him from the stove and said, "You'll never have to know, man."

They sat and ate in silence, each locked in his or her own thoughts, but each thinking the same thing. Molly knew she would have to be the first one to say it out loud.

"You two are going after him, aren't you?"

Tom and Billy looked at each other, almost sadly and Tom said, "We have to. He's our responsibility."

Billy said, "Nobody knows these woods like us."

"Except Ed. Ed still hunts and neither of you do anymore."

Tom didn't want to say it, so Billy did. "True. But killing two unsuspecting civilians is different than hunting a Special Forces operator."

She looked at Tom. "I do think you should go after him. I know what you can do now, or at least I know some of what you can do now, and because of that…" She turned to look at Billy. "Because of that, I think you two are the best chance of bringing Ed back alive." She emphasized the last word.

Billy interrupted Tom before he could do more than open his mouth. "Yes. We are bringing him back alive."

"We are," Tom said. "He's still Ed. But he's not in the woods."

They both looked at him and Molly asked, "What do you mean? Why wouldn't he hide in the woods?"

"He would. It's big enough and there are like a million camps to break into. But he didn't." He asked Billy, "Do you remember the mirror above the fireplace in the hunting camp?"

Billy paused, then said, "I see where you're going, but he could have gotten that length of cable anywhere. Or he could have had it for years. That shit was everywhere when we were kids."

Tom said to Molly, "Ed had a mirror over his fireplace and the frame was made from that thick steel cable they used in the mines. Plus, he had a huge chunk of magnetite sitting on the mantle. He was taunting us with clues."

"Clues to what?" she asked. "It's not like he knew it was going to go down this way."

"No, but I think he knew it was going to end at some point. He wants it to be Billy and me that go after him."

"Where are we going in? All the old entrances we used as kids are either capped or under 50 feet of water."

"Not exactly. You remember the three holes up on Hog's Alley where we used to go in? At some point, somebody brought a winch up there and pulled the metal gate right off one of them. There's a tree growing in front of it, but if you squeeze behind the tree, you can get in.

"How the hell would you have discovered that?"

"Ed did. Last year he told me that he goes up to visit the place a few times a year. Now that I'm saying it out loud, I'm realizing he's probably the one who pulled the gate off."

"Jesus Christ, I haven't even thought about those mine excursions in years. And he still wanders around up there?"

"Narnia, man. I think we're only now realizing how disconnected from reality Ed's life has been. And I think he's desperate to recapture the best time in his life – when we were all best friends in high school."

"You can use that," Molly said, and they both looked at her. "You can use it and maybe nobody gets hurt."

Bob came a few hours after they'd gone and Molly told him everything.

Tom's watch vibrated gently, with no noise, and he woke. Billy felt him wake and sat up too. Despite the reasons, they both felt a visceral joy at reactivating senses that had been dulled over the past several years. Each had worked to maintain as much of his edge as possible, but both knew that you couldn't fake the real thing.

It was 4:00 AM and they were waking from their second ninety-minute sleep cycle. They had both been accustomed in the past to working several days without long stretches of sleep, but Billy had never studied the science of sleep cycles in the way that Tom had. Billy had made the expected jokes during Tom's explanation of monophasic and polyphasic sleep, but they both knew that as soon as they got out of the mines, he would immediately research the topic.

As soon as they got out of the mines...

Ed had left the previous day's newspaper inside the mine entrance, so there could be little question about where he was hiding. It was possible he'd placed the paper there to throw off followers, but they both knew that Ed just didn't think like that. Neither of them could see Ed setting a false trail to escape their pursuit. He would want a confrontation. He would want the opportunity to explain everything he'd done, to try to get them to understand. They were both counting on Ed's need to be understood.

At first, they'd tried to go without lights. They would turn on their lights for a few seconds, make mental pictures of the thirty or forty feet immediately ahead, then turn off their lights and try to walk that memory map.

It didn't work. It might have, if each had been alone or if they'd trained to work together like this, but the constant back of forth between light and complete darkness meant that their eyes couldn't adapt to either. This led to an attempted lecture by Tom on rods and cones, but luckily for Bill, he'd remembered enough from high school biology to shut that shit down.

Other than the night vision issues, once the lights were out they invariably each took the same path and so they kept running into each other. Eventually, they'd decided that Ed already had such an advantage, the tactic was losing them more than it was gaining them, so now they were each carrying a glowstick to tell each other's position and whichever of them was in the lead was keeping a flashlight lit for navigation. Ed's advantages kept multiplying.

Tom pulled the glowstick out of the pocket where it had been covered while he slept. Billy had already done the same.

Tom asked, "You know what I don't get? The connection with that Bederman book. How would Ed have even known that you and Kate had talked about it?"

"You're assuming he chose something that he knew – of at least hoped – one of us would figure out. Ok, yeah, I'm operating under the same assumption. The whole time he's been leaving clues for us, but different clues for each of us. You didn't know about Bederman; I didn't know about the Yoko Ono comment."

Billy shook his head and continued. "I don't know how he could have known about the book. Hell, I didn't remember it until Kate reminded..." He stopped and looked away and Tom stayed silent.

"Ok," Billy said, clearing his throat. 'Up and at 'em. We should be close to that huge cavern."

"The Cathedral," Tom said.

"That's right. I forgot you called it that. Ok, it's your

turn on point."

They walked slowly, alert. There was no way to know how often Ed had been coming in here, so it was impossible to tell how much work he'd put into making this his very own fortress. The work he'd done on the hunting camp suggested that he'd spent most of his time over the past year there, but it also showed how much work he could do when he had a specific goal in mind.

The pitch grew steeper for a while and they picked their way carefully, alert to their footing. The air was damper than Tom remembered it being when they were kids and as they got deeper, he realized he was hearing water lapping far in the distance. As they'd been doing since leaving the surface the previous day, they stayed to the left at every fork for no other reason than that's what they'd done as kids. Any time a fork dead ended they backtracked and took the next possible left. As kids, they knew that this ensured they'd always be able to get out and this seemed to both Billy and Tom to be the tactic Ed would most likely take now. They were both convinced he wanted to be found. Wanted to be found by them.

Tom reached a dead end and as he turned around to let Billy know they'd be backtracking again, he saw two glowing lights behind him. For a split second his mind churned. If he'd been by himself it would have been easy to throw his flashlight in one direction and his body in another, but that would make Billy the only viable target. He instead hissed at Billy to "Move!" and swung the flashlight beam directly at the glow, hoping to blind Ed. For a split second, Ed's face was illuminated. Tom's hand was reaching for his pistol when he simultaneously saw the muzzle flash and heard the gunshot. He felt the slug hit him in the side, felt himself being spun around in a circle.

Tom dropped the light and hit the ground, rolling over to cover the glowstick in his pocket. He lay as still as he could, controlling his breath while knowing that pain would be with him soon enough. It was, but through it he was able to hear scrambling and more shots, then both hear and feel a deep rumbling that shook the ground under and the walls around him. Dust filled the air and he fought a cough that was forming in his throat.

Tom had been shot before and he knew what shock felt like, but as he lay there in the black he also knew that the speed with which he was losing focus also meant that he was bleeding more seriously than he ever had before. In a few minutes, he would be unconscious and then bleed out while Billy looked for him. If Billy was still alive. As consciousness slipped from him he made a choice and rolled over onto his back, exposing his glow light. He sensed the figure come towards him, then bend over his body. As his vision tightened to a tunnel, then to a narrower tunnel, and finally to a pinpoint, he heard a voice say, "Shit."

***

Tom's face felt wet. For the shortest space of time, that's all he felt. His face was wet. That feeling was nearly instantly replaced with pain and he gasped. The air he sucked in was as much dust as air and he started coughing, making the pain that defined his midsection that much worse.

"Easy, buddy. Easy."

Tom realized that there was light, light coming both from a lantern on the ground near him and a brighter glow coming from the cave itself. Ed's face appeared in his line of sight and he realized how limited his peripheral vision was. He moved his hands to his wound and found Ed's hands already there.

"It's not good, man," Ed said. "I fucked you up pretty bad."

Tom tried to say Ed's name, but his throat was so dry that hardly any noise came out.

"Don't talk." Ed held a canteen up to Tom's mouth, but

only let him sip the water he so desperately wanted to gulp.

"I have a lot to say. A lot. And I don't want to run out of time." He looked back over his shoulder towards the glowing light. "I knew the risk of shooting you, man, but shit. This is way worse than I wanted. Billy…" He gritted his teeth. "I think that fucker got away without a scratch. As usual." Then he smiled. "Unless the cave-in got him."

"Ed," Tom rasped.

Ed gently put a finger to Tom's lips. "No talking. Ok, where to start. Cissy, I guess."

He gave Tom another drink of water, then went on. "I have to skip a bunch because I thought I'd have more time. It looks like neither one of us may have much, so jumping ahead…"

Then he laughed. "Jesus, what an awesome Bond villain scene this was going to be. I know, wish in one hand… Anyway, so that whore Cissy rejected me every goddam time I hit on her. I mean, I'm not that great looking, but Jesus Christ, was I seriously the only guy she wouldn't bang? I think I've pretty much reconstructed her last night and honestly, there's a lot of coincidence involved. I know that she went to Plattsburgh to meet some guy she'd connected with online. And apparently, Cissy's charms – and age – weren't what they used to be. They certainly weren't what this kid was expecting. So, she drove back home and it looks like she and Bob had a fight."

Ed shifted his hands and the movement made Tom gasp again.

"I know. I know," he said, then gave Tom another sip of water.

"Thanks," Tom said and Ed's face completely lost its confidence. He struggled to compose himself, then went on with his story.

"From what she told me when she got to the school, I even think Bob may have hit her. Jesus Christ, I hope so. Bitch deserved it and more." He laughed, then started talking fast again. "Okay, my bad. I guess she did eventually get the 'and more.' So anyway, she called me when she left Bob. And I wasn't alone when she called." He smiled with an odd pride. "I had completely moved on like a year ago and now she's calling me. How awesome is that? I had finally found somebody and here she comes trying to ruin it. Well, we showed her."

Tom's fog of pain wasn't so deep that he could miss the reference to "we," but he said nothing.

"We decided to have her meet me at the school. What a perfect place to teach her a lesson. Her base of power. How pathetic... She thought she was so special, so important... because of the school board?

"I do have to admit, the whole thing got a little out of hand. A lot out of hand. I'm usually more... subtle. Making things disappear." He stopped, as if he'd been caught saying something he shouldn't. "We can come back to that."

He looked around. "God, I love it in here." He looked intensely into Tom's eyes. "This is my favorite place in the world. The four of us in here, just exploring, always with the chance that we wouldn't get out... Those were the best times of my life."

"Kate.." Tom was able to get the word out with some effort.

Ed's face contorted with anger. "Stupid. So fucking stupid. I was just going to scare her. Swear to god. My mind had cleared a lot and all I was gonna do was tell her to stay the fuck away from you and Molly. But then *she* showed up and it all got out of hand. Again."

Tom was still alert enough to recognize that the "she" who showed up wasn't Kate. He decided to wait, to conserve his energy and see how far Ed would go without prompting.

"I told you, man. I like to hide things. Make them disappear. She likes to make a big splash." Ed laughed ruefully. "A big splash. Very funny." He shook his head. "She never did figure this place out. I hoped she would. I left hints for her."

He stopped and looked at Tom for a moment. "You... You figured out the hints and she didn't. I guess I wasn't as important to her as I thought I was. But yeah, of course you would. You know, you and me never stayed as tight as we should have, man."

"I've thought that too," Tom said, trying not to sound too weak. He was stalling. For what, he wasn't sure, but as long as he could hold on, there was some small chance. He had lost too much blood and he knew the next time he lost consciousness would likely be the last.

"I believe you. That's what makes this next part so hard." Ed drew in a deep breath and held it. He was stalling too.

That was it, then. Tom knew that he had no strength to fight back, that he would have to take whatever came and hope that he would take it with dignity. We all die, Tom knew. But we don't all get to die trying to catch a killer in an old mine. He was surprised to find himself smiling at that thought. *How many people get to die with a cool story like this one? They'll talk about this forever.*

"Ok, Ed. At least I won't be alone when I die."

"Die? Oh, I gotcha. Well, when you do die, Tom, you will die alone. Man, we all die alone. We're all alone. Always. Every one of us. We're born alone, we die alone, and all of those times in between are just attempts to fool ourselves into believing we're not alone then too. People with homes, people with families, they don't think they're going to die alone. They all have this Walton's Mountain picture in their heads, surrounded by loved ones on their deathbed. But listen, you and me, we know better. Even when we're with friends and family we're still alone; we're just surrounded by other people who don't realize they're alone too."

Ed exhaled and said, "Whoa. Soapbox. Sorry." Tom braced himself as Ed removed the pressure from Tom's gunshot wound. Then Ed gathered up Tom's hands and placed them over the wound. He felt the large piece of cloth that Ed had been using to hold pressure, felt how stiff it was with his blood, how it didn't seem to be seeping new blood, and realized that the wound might be mostly coagulated, that if he had gotten help, he might have made it.

"Ok, bud," Ed said as he stood. "I know you don't have a lot of strength left, but hold pressure as much as you can. This will be over soon. I'm sure of it."

Ed wasn't making sense but, the current situation being what it was, Tom guessed that Ed not making sense made perfect sense. He watched as Ed pulled his pistol out of the holster tied to his leg. Tom smiled again when he heard Ed pull back the hammer on his .44-40 Colt Peacemaker. *What an awesome gun to be killed with. The story was going to be even cooler.*

"So, like I said, this is the really hard part. As weird as it is, I think you could forgive me for everything but this."

They both froze when they heard Molly shout, "Tom!" Ed stared at Tom and put a finger to his lips, but he hadn't needed to. There was no way Tom was going to call back to Molly and draw her into this.

"Shit!" Ed swore. "Ok, listen, I wanted to do this more gently but... Goddammit!" He looked back over his shoulder.

Tom pulled one hand from his side, pointed at Ed, and hissed, "Not her!"

Ed looked confused for a second, then said, "What? No, you goddam idiot. I would never hurt Molly. Fuck man, I go to my grave ashamed that I never did anything to Mike. Listen, we're out of time. I dragged you up here so they could find you after I tell you." He wiped his forehead with the back of his gun hand.

Molly shouted again and this time her voice was joined by Bob's. Then they heard Billy call, "Tom! Ed!"

Ed's eyes were locked onto Tom's "Your mother... She was my first. I... I went to your house, you weren't home, I lost control... It doesn't matter, but you need to know that she never would have left you."

Tom was stunned into silence. He couldn't make thoughts, much less sounds.

Ed waved his pistol back into the mines. "She's in here. She's been in here the whole time. I came back to leave you a trail but I ran out of time. I'm so sorry." Then he put the barrel of the pistol in his mouth and pulled the trigger.

***

Molly's face. Each time he'd opened his eyes, Molly's face was the first thing he saw. It was no different this time, but he felt he would be able to keep them open for a little while now.

"You want some ice, baby?" she said quietly. He nodded and opened his mouth and she put a single ice chip on his tongue. Oh sweet Jesus did that feel good. He opened his mouth again and stuck his tongue out for more. She laughed and gave him another and he heard Bob laugh on the other side of him. He turned his head and nodded as Bob came into his field of view. He felt more energy than he probably ought to, so he tried to shift himself a little on the bed.

Big mistake. The pain shot from his abdomen down to his toes and up to his eyes. The sparks were pretty, though.

"Hey, dummy. Sit still."

He looked back at Molly and half smiled, half grimaced. "Did the doctors shoot me again when they got me here?" he croaked, then begged for more ice with his mouth open like a baby bird.

"Don't be a wuss," she said, as she gave him more ice.

"I got shot!"

"Do you want a kiss or not?"

"Yes, please," he said, his voice growing stronger as the ice hydrated his mouth. He puckered up and she kissed him. It was good to be alive. It was *amazing* to be alive.

Molly eventually pulled away, then looked at Bob sheepishly. Bob just smiled.

Tom asked Bob, "Ed?"

"You don't remember?"

"The last thing I remember, I think, is seeing him put that cannon in his mouth and pull the trigger. But the light was bad and I was about bled dry."

"He's dead. We came running to you after we heard the shot," Bob said, then scowled in Molly's direction, "the wrong one in the lead. Once we pulled you out and had you in my truck, Molly and I drove you down to the firehouse and Billy went back in to wait by the body. For the State Troopers."

Tom looked around. "Where is Billy?"

"You've been in and out of consciousness all day, but once they patched you up and got some blood in you, you were out of the woods, so Molly finally convinced Billy to go home and get some sleep."

"Ed shot me, then I think he went after Billy. Wait, he said something about a cave-in."

Bob nodded. "It looks like Ed had picked that spot by design, because Billy said there was a trip wire that set off the cave-in. But Billy was able to track his way around it and get back to the surface. He was coming out just as we were getting there."

"He always did have the best sense of direction out of the four of us."

Bob leaned over the bed and squeezed Tom's shoulder. He stood there for a second, about to talk, then nodded and started to leave the room.

"Wait!" Tom said as his memories returned in a flood. "Shit, there's somebody else and I think I know who it is."

Molly's mouth dropped open. "What do you mean somebody else?"

Bob turned back around. "I've been thinking the same thing, but all I have to go on is the hunting camp."

"The bed, I know, Tom said. "But in the mines Ed all but

told me that he's been with somebody for close to a year now, that she had a hand in both murders. Bob, I think it's Lisa."

"What?" Molly and Bob said simultaneously.

"It's that goddam Bederman book. Ed never would have known about it, much less read it, and Lisa is still friends with Franny..." He paused to explain, but he could see that they both knew exactly who he was referring to. Of course they did.

"I think Lisa was stalking Kate, even to the point of finding out what books she was reading."

Molly held up her hands and said, "Slow down, slow down, slow down. So, Ed and Lisa were together? For a year? Without anybody knowing?" She leaned back in her chair. "That would work... Both are loners. I'm trying to tie all of this together into a story that makes sense. Lisa knew or assumed Ed could or would kill somebody, so she seduced him, strung him along, and got him to kill Cissy and then Kate."

She got up from her chair and walked towards the window with her chin in her hand. To Tom, she looked like the most gorgeous possible version of Columbo.

"Ok, it all strings together in a way that could work, with the quotes from the library book as a way to throw people off track because nobody would expect either of them to read a book like that. I think we all believe Lisa is cold enough to do whatever it took to convince Ed she loved him and we all believe that attention from somebody like Lisa would completely flip Ed."

She shook her head. "But the missing piece is the first piece. Why?"

"It's Tom," Billy said, as he half walked, half staggered into the room. He was pale and shaking. "She's in love with Tom. She's gonna kill him. And I think she followed me here."

Billy swayed, then dropped to his knees. "Hey, listen." he said. "I've been shot." Then he pitched forward onto the floor, unconscious.

For Molly, the next five minutes passed instantly. She got to Billy first, followed closely by Bob. Bob called out for the nurses and helped them get Billy on a gurney and sent to surgery, then he was out into the hall, stationing State Troopers at the door and directing the rest to search the hospital for Lisa.

At the end of this burst of chaos, she had started to turn back to Tom, when she heard him weakly say, "Hey Molls. A little help?"

He was half on the floor, half on the bed, bleeding from his arm where the I.V. had been pulled out, and he was looking as sheepish as a man could in his condition.

"I tried to help, but I think I may have passed out somewhere along the way."

"Jesus fuck," she said, feeling such a strong upwelling of love for this dumbass of a man that she could barely fight the urge to laugh. Or cry. Or both.

She and a nurse got him back on the bed and the nurse reset his I.V. Tom had clearly depleted his energy reserves and was soon out. She checked the window and was relieved to see two State Troopers outside. She then stepped outside the door and spoke to the Trooper on watch, asking that he let her know if he found out anything about Billy. Finally, she sat in the chair next to Tom's bed and looked at her watch. It was 7:00 p.m. It had been thirty-six hours since she'd last slept, but she couldn't sleep now. Not with Lisa out there.

***

Molly sat up quickly, disoriented. She shook her head to clear it and looked at her watch. The watch face showed a little after 1:00 and from the darkness and quiet she knew it was early morning, not afternoon. She'd slept six hours. A quick look out the window showed the guard detail still out there, though in their Smokey the Bear hats it was impossible to tell if they were the same two men.

She leaned over Tom, resting her elbows on the side of the bed. She stayed there a few minutes, listening to him breathe, then she put her mouth and nose right up to his and breathed in the air he was breathing out. Sharing breath and life.

After a while, she stood up. She looked out the window again and thought about the past month, who she'd been before and who she was now. The beaten wife. The employee with a crush on her boss. The woman who had revealed her best kept secret and in a single day been both punished and rewarded for it. Then the woman who had found a so-unexpected love after years of giving up hope that she had spent every waking moment waiting for it to be taken away.

Well, now she was no longer in that place. She told herself that she wasn't going to be amazed, that this was not too good to be true. This man, this love, was hers, rightfully hers. And she was going to nurture it, strengthen it, and keep it. In leaving Mike, in surviving leaving Mike, she had found a core in herself. A hard core, but not a cold one. She had a strength that came from love, not from hate, and she was going to use that strength to protect Tom and their love.

And it wasn't only Tom. She had a new life, a life that could include her family and her friends in a way that her life hadn't since high school. She walked out of the room and asked the State Troopers stationed at the door if they'd heard anything about Billy and Lisa.

The younger of the two, the man, turned to his partner with a questioning look. She was clearly his superior and he was uncertain about how much he could share. "Joe, can you go get me a coffee? Just black."

He started to question the request, then thought better of it and walked down the hall towards the vending machines.

The State Trooper, Pam, introduced herself and told Molly that Billy had gotten out of surgery around midnight.

He was expected to recover, though one of the bullets had shattered his elbow and he would likely need additional work on it.

"One of the bullets?" Molly asked.

Pam nodded. "Apparently he was over in the Walmart parking lot sleeping in his truck when she opened up on him. He might be the luckiest man I've ever seen. To be still alive, I mean, not about getting shot in his sleep."

"In his truck. In this cold. He was supposed to go home. Is every man I know a complete idiot?"

Pam smiled. "Find me one that's not and he's probably not worth a damn."

"You're right. My husband is the only man I know who isn't this kind of idiot. So, what about Lisa?"

"No idea. We swept the entire hospital multiple times and there's no sign of her. These friends of yours are two of the bravest men I've come across in a long time, but unfortunately for us they're not going to be able to help on this manhunt. Thank god we've got Bob... Chief Marty, I mean. He's not exactly the man we thought we were dealing with when this all started."

"Tell me about it. He's not the man we thought he was when all of this started either. And we've known each other since we are all born in this hospital. Is he out?"

"He's actually still in here. We talked him into at least getting a little rest before we start the search in earnest at daylight."

The young Trooper sensed it was safe to come back, and he did with a cup of coffee for Pam. She nodded and he handed it to her.

Molly decided to check on Billy after Pam told her he was in intensive care. She knew they wouldn't let her in, but she could at least check with the nurses to see how he was doing. She already knew they were going to say that he was sedated, that he was resting, and that they'd know more in the morning, but the walk would do her good. She looked in on Tom before leaving. He was sleeping in the same position she'd left him.

The I.C. nurses followed their script to the letter, so Molly decided to walk outside to get a few minutes of air, then she'd try to get some more sleep in Tom's room. The recliner in there was pretty comfortable. But oh dear lord, did she wish she had one of Billy's smokes.

She walked down to the Emergency Room entrance and walked out through the same door she'd rushed in the previous day with Tom. The same entrance she now knew that Tom had been coming in when he'd heard about her beating.

Curiosity drew her to Billy's truck. There was police tape around it, but there were no Troopers nearby, which surprised her. She ducked under the tape, walked around to the driver's side, then gasped as she saw the number of bullet holes in the window and door. How in the world had he survived?

A noise in the bed of the truck startled her out of her thoughts and she looked up in time to see Lisa standing up, aiming a pistol directly at her.

"Don't yell, Molly. Don't do it," Lisa hissed. "Just stand there."

Molly stood completely still and stayed silent. As long as Lisa was out here, she wasn't close enough to hurt Tom. And if Lisa shot at her here, even shot her, the State Troopers and Bob would be close enough to catch her. Hopefully Lisa was also thinking as clearly.

From the look on her face though, Lisa wasn't thinking clearly at all. Her eyes were red – from crying? – and her breath was ragged. She was still athletic though. She put one hand on the side of the truck and hopped out with ease, the muzzle of the gun hardly changing its aim at Molly.

Should she push or cajole? Screw it – she was too tired for anything subtle. "Go ahead and shoot. You'll still never get close enough to hurt him."

Lisa blinked in surprise. "Hurt him?" She recovered and laughed a harsh laugh. "I could never hurt him, you stupid bitch. I've been getting rid of people who hurt him."

"What are you talking about? Who would hurt Tom?"

"All of them. All of you. The whole bunch of you have brought him nothing but pain."

He thoughts were racing, but she knew she had to keep talking. "Okay. I can see Kate and I guess me and maybe even Ed, but Cissy?"

"Cissy was the worst one. She flat out told me she was going to try to get him into bed. And if he'd said no, she was going to accuse him of rape. Fucking whore told that plan to the wrong girl."

What? Molly couldn't think about that piece of information at the moment. She knew Lisa wouldn't talk much more. She had to find a way to rattle Lisa. "What about Billy? Why did you kill him?"

Lisa did stop, but only for a second and in that second the gun never moved. "I didn't know he was in the truck. I was just going to look in the truck for Tom's phone, but when I checked the door handle to see if it was locked, the goddam idiot sat up and surprised me. The gun went off and then he started screaming like a woman and I just reacted." She shook her head. "Whatever. I'm done talking. I should have killed you first anyway."

Lisa stepped towards Molly and Molly prepared herself for something, anything. Maybe Lisa would miss. She had shot what looked like an entire clip at Billy and he'd survived.

Molly kept waiting, but Lisa was coming closer and in that moment Molly thought about the game she and Tom had played in the store. If Lisa was stupid enough to get too close...

Molly put her hands up, in surrender, not above her head but with her palms forward at about head height. Lisa stepped even closer, face beaming in triumph, and placed the barrel of the gun against Molly's chest, centered between her breasts. As soon as Molly felt the pressure of the barrel, she executed the movement Tom had taught in the back of the store. And she executed it to perfection.

Spinning her body clockwise, she grabbed Lisa's wrist with her left hand. As she spun, she used that grip to pull Lisa's arm into her torso under her own arm, until in one smooth motion she had her back pressed against Lisa's shoulder with Lisa's right arm trapped under her left arm, the gun facing away from them.

The surprise caused Lisa to flinch and the gun went off, the bullet ricocheting off the surface of the parking lot ten feet ahead of them. It was so loud and the bright orange flame from the barrel left white sparks in Molly's eyes as she blinked.

Lisa was in shock at the new turn and her finger stayed locked, holding the trigger back, panic preventing her from firing again. Before Lisa could recover, Molly remembered the second half of the maneuver and moved her right hand to the gun at the same time she reversed her body, turning counterclockwise. The pressure of Molly trapping her arm and pulling it in one direction combined with Molly's hand grabbing and pushing the gun in the opposite direction popped the gun as easily out of Lisa's hand as it had the toy gun out of Tom's.

It was hard to say which of the women was more surprised as they stood facing each other, Molly now holding the gun.

Lisa finally recovered herself and sneered at Molly. "Do you even..."

The gunshot interrupted her and she staggered back several steps, her face frozen in shock. She looked down to see the red stain spread across the chest of her sweater, spreading from the hole in the center of her chest, then looked back at Molly. Molly walked forward and fired three more quick shots into Lisa's chest, then watched as she collapsed to the ground.

Molly carefully set the gun down on the blacktop and whispered, "You're damn right I do." She heard heavy, running feet coming out of the hospital behind her and started hyperventilating as quickly as she could make herself.

Bob was first to reach her and as she turned to him and buried herself in his shoulder, she sobbed, "It just went off. It just went off. And she kept coming at me. She just kept coming."

The door to the hospital room opened and both Billy and Tom turned from their conversation to watch Molly walk in. Billy had been moved from Intensive Care earlier that morning and he was sitting on the side of Tom's bed, refining his story of waking up to the noise of Lisa trying to open his truck door and surviving the ensuing hail of gunfire with six bullet wounds. There was no screaming in his version.

She had fired an entire 15-round magazine into his truck but her panic and his speed at scrambling into the back seat had left him with five grazes, a shattered elbow, and less blood loss than Tom's single gunshot wound had caused.

Lisa had died the previous night on the operating table.

Molly said, "I have good news and bad news. The good news is that Tom is being released in an hour or so. The bad news is that Billy is also being released in an hour or so." It was a good line, a funny line, but the three of them just smiled wearily.

"Billy," she said, "I'm hoping you'll agree to stay with us at least tonight."

Billy looked at Tom. "Well, we know where you're staying tonight."

Tom said, "I just go where I'm told."

"Smart boy." He smiled at Molly. "You are the sweetest thing, Molly, but I need to be home." Billy was the only one of the three of them who lived in his childhood home, much as he had changed it, and he didn't think they understood what a comfort it was to him. He felt confident that when Tom and Molly inevitably moved in together, they'd live in Tom's house and he wondered if Tom would understand that even though she was leaving the house that contained all the worst memories of her life with Mike, she would also be leaving her home and the place of the best memories of her life with her kids.

When he got home, he would be facing something similar. No matter the end of the relationship, the house would still be his and Kate's and he didn't know if that would ever change. He'd never let anyone else in as deeply as she'd gotten and she had taken a huge chunk of him with her when she'd been ripped out of him.

"I'm going to meander a little, kids," he said to them and winked. "Maybe get my flirt on with the ICU nurses."

Tom said to Molly, "Since you knew my discharge schedule before I did, I assume the nurses and doctors haven't hesitated to share other details with you. What's the prognosis, beautiful?"

"Well," she said, drawing the word out, "It appears you will be confined to bed another few days and probably won't be walking for a week or so."

"You know what I need? I need you to stop looking so cheerful at the prospect of me being bedridden."

She went on as if she hadn't heard him. "Now, I anticipate some stubbornness with that schedule and that is fine, but you should know that I have given some thought about your salary situation while you're unable to work."

"What?"

"It seems our benefit plan…"

"We have an excellent benefit plan!"

"As I was saying, the section of our benefit plan relating to paid sick time only covers hourly workers."

He started to say something, then stopped himself. "Is that true?"

"It is."

"But everybody is hourly."

"Ah, everybody except you. You're the only one in the store not accruing paid time off for illness."

"I've known for quite some time that you are smarter than I am, but the actual size of the gap has only recently become clear."

"Well, I have a plan."

Tom said, "Go on, he says, with fear in his voice."

"If you were to marry an hourly employee, we…"

"We?"

"We, the management. As you are probably aware, I am now the Assistant Manager."

"Oh. Please continue."

"If you were to marry an hourly employee, we, the management, could perhaps allow that employee to transfer some of her accrued sick time to you, just to get you through this rough patch."

"A rough patch in which I was shot."

"The policies don't really call out specific illnesses or injuries, so as far as we are concerned…"

"We, the management?"

"Exactly. As far as we, the management, are concerned, your injury is really no different than the common cold."

"Really?"

"Really."

"Then, I accept."

She cocked her head. "Accept?"

"Your proposal. I accept your marriage proposal."

"Oh, I didn't necessarily mean me. Really, any of our employees…"

"Do you want a kiss or not?" he asked.

"I suppose so."

They stood facing each other, two outwardly different men. One in a heavy, black, leather coat with one arm out of the sleeve and in a sling, the other in his blue, nylon, uniform jacket. They stood, not speaking, in the circle of light under the streetlight outside the Rexall. The aging neon sign flickered above their heads. Billy finally broke the silence.

"You're different. You have to know that you've changed, that this whole… thing has changed you, but do you realize how much everybody else sees it?"

"I guess so."

"Everybody has that defining moment in their lives. A moment when they can go one of two directions and the direction they choose defines them for the rest of their lives."

Bob smiled. "Did you read that somewhere?"

Billy snorted and smiled his best wicked, charismatic smile. "Yeah, probably in a Louis L'Amour book. But it fits. When a man's defining moment hits him, he can take it and grow from it or he can let it crush him."

He stopped to light the cigarette he had gotten out. "You could have rolled up into a ball for the rest of your life on this one. And honestly, nobody would have blamed you. Well, they would have blamed you, but it was what they were expecting you to do. When you didn't do it after the murder, they were surprised. But when you didn't do it after everything came out about the… the…"

"Affairs. The affairs."

"Yeah, those. Well, people are still not quite sure what to make of you."

"What about yours? What was the defining moment in your life?"

Billy paused, looked over Bob's shoulder, not focusing. The war monument in the old cemetery across the street, with its small granite marker and flagpole, caught his eye.

Bob brought him back by saying, "Because it changed you too. Something happened that sharpened the edge you always had, but somehow made you more human at the same time. You're a better man than you were when you left, if you don't mind me saying so."

"Yeah, something happened. But it was something bad. Look, you're a cop. I could tell you because I trust you as a friend. But I trust your honesty as a cop too. Maybe even more. If I told you, you'd be stuck with the choice of either doing your duty or trying to ignore something I don't think you're equipped to ignore. If you let me go, if you ignored it, it would weigh on you until you felt you had to do something about it and then we would be enemies. And I can't be your enemy."

Bob's smiled broadly and said, "You don't remember us ever having this conversation before, do you?"

"No?"

"When we were kids, I think it was our junior year, you said something that I thought was the most flattering thing you could have ever said to me."

"I was kidding about you having a nice ass." They both smiled at the attempt.

"We were at your house some weekend and we were listening to that Springsteen song. The one where's he's a deputy and his brother gets in trouble."

"Yeah, I remember the song. His brother kills a guy, but he lets his brother go at the end of it."

"That's the one. You said to me that if you ever did something like that, you'd bet I'd let you go, but that I'd try to take you in if you ever came back."

"I remember the conversation, too now. I think I also said that if you did try to bring me in, you'd get hurt."

Bob smiled and nodded.

Then, a look of understanding came to Billy's eyes as he finally caught on to just how much Bob had changed. Or was it that he had always underestimated Bob, like everybody else in town had? He was starting to get tired of realizing how much he'd underestimated people back home in the sticks. Tom. Kate. Ed. Certainly Lisa. Now Bob. This kind of judgment would have gotten him killed in the old days.

"So, what are you saying?"

"That I know. Or at least I'm pretty sure about the two cops in California."

"How long?"

"Yesterday. I knew there was something, I knew generally where you were, and I had a pretty good idea of the time frame. Since you got back, when you've talked about where you were and when... those timelines haven't always matched up."

"Even with that much to work from, that's pretty tough information to find out. We've been underpaying you. By a lot. I don't know of another cop who would have gotten there, especially since nearly everybody who can connect me to it is either dead or thinks I am. What now?"

"Well, that's why I wanted to see you tonight. I need to tell you something and knowing this just makes it easier, in a weird way."

"You do know that when we had that conversation the implication was that I wouldn't leave town?"

"I know that. That's the part I wanted to talk to you about."

"I think you're all talked out, dude. I'm pretty sure I get your point."

"I don't think you do."

"Oh, I do. But remember what I said about how that decisive moment can either make you a man or crush you? Well, mine did me good. I'm not the same punk ass kid who listened to the Boss with you twenty years ago."

"I've known that since you came back. That's what makes this easier."

"Easier? Jesus, I would have hoped it would be harder. Anyway, here's the deal. I'll be gone within two hours. I'll leave a note on my kitchen table addressed to you explaining how to dispose of what things I leave behind."

Bob shook his head. "No, Billy. You're not going anywhere."

Billy's eyes steeled and Bob saw something in Billy those cops in California must have seen. "You're not even going to give me the option?" The steel left his eyes and he shrugged. "I meant it when I said I couldn't be your enemy. I won't put up a fight. Not against you."

Bob said, "I'm leaving town. I've already got another job lined up and they're expecting me by the end of the week."

Billy shook his head back and forth. He felt like a hitter who keeps guessing fastball on curves.

"You're going to think I'm messing with you, but I'm moving to Alaska. Anchorage City PD."

"I absolutely think you're messing with me."

"No, seriously. I've made a lot of friends over the years at conferences and I've had a standing offer for years from the Chief in Anchorage to move up there and try my hand at being a city cop."

"This is not what I was expecting."

"What ever is? I'm recommending that the town promotes Timmy and hires somebody from outside to be the new deputy. New blood, new ideas would be good, but Timmy deserves the top spot. I'll need you to make sure that happens."

"Sure, but you can live with knowing about me? About what I did?"

"From what I've been able to find out and what I've been able to guess about the rest, you didn't do any of it. You were involved, sure, and you bear responsibility for that. But from what I've seen, you know that and I can't see any gain in stopping the penance you appear to be paying. There's nowhere near enough evidence to convict you anyway and what I have found out tells me you'd probably be found dead in a cell long before any trial took place."

"All true. But are you sure you can leave this place? Your home? You've always lived here. I mean, if one of us has to go…"

Bob held up a hand to stop him. "No, you're wrong. You're not better equipped to be the one to leave. It's funny, but in the short time you've been back, you dropped roots deeper than mine grew in thirty-five years of living here. And I'll be back to visit."

"Well, I'm glad you're not going to be my enemy."

"You're right to be glad of that. Because I would have taken you in if that's what I decided to do. Even if you put up a fight."

Billy laughed. "It would have been an epic contest."

Bob smiled. "Epic."

The bell on the door of the Rexall startled both men, as Sue Clarke closed it and locked it behind her for the night.

"You boys have been standing out here in the cold an awful long time. Everything ok?"

Bob put his hand on Billy's shoulder and said, "It's getting there."

EPILOGUE
Spring

It was a beautiful morning. The cold was going, though not yet gone. A few trees had begun to bud and the world smelled of life. Molly walked into the confessional at the arranged time, kneeled, and when the small door slid open on the other side of the screen, began.

"Bless me, Father, for I have sinned…"

***

On that same morning, at the same time, two men sat on the bench, both absently tossing chunks of bread to the squawking ducks clustered around them. It was early and the mornings were still cool enough for a fog to form on the surface of the Hudson as it wound its way through the small city. The old man was the first resident at the assisted living home to rise every morning and when the young man, the son, visited, he was always there to meet his father as soon as the old man was ready for a walk.

Billy loved the ride down to Glens Falls on his bike. Starting before the sun was up, down 9N and 9, the throb of the v-twin under him, torqueing up over Tongue Mountain. He had pulled into the parking lot well before official visiting hours started, just as he always did, and waved at the night orderly, who was just finishing his shift.

"Is he having breakfast, Bobby?"

"Like clockwork, man."

"Thanks, dude." Billy went through the halls of the home, enjoying the sleepiness of the place.

His father looked up as Billy approached his table. "Good morning," the old man said.

"Morning," Billy replied, testing the waters.

"I know you, don't I?" the old man asked.

"Yup."

"You're my brother Steve, ain't you?"

"No, Dad. I'm your son. I'm Billy."

"You sure? You look a lot like Steve."

"I know, Dad. But I'm Billy."

William Ridge, Sr., cocked his head to the side a little. "Nah, you're too goddam big to be Billy. My Billy's a little shaver, about this high." He held his hand out at waist height.

"You want to go for a walk, Dad?"

"You know I do."

The walks were shorter now, with much more time spent sitting on this bench, their bench, but if the walks had changed in length, they had not changed in frequency.

Billy looked over at him, at his father, with wet eyes. "You know what sucks, Dad? She's been gone so long, her pillow doesn't smell like her anymore."

His father looked back at him and the increasingly rare clarity in the man's eyes almost tore Billy's soul in two. "At least you can remember what her face looks like, Bill."

Billy moved closer, putting his arm around his father, and his father laid his head over onto Billy's shoulder. They stayed like that a very long time.

***

On the same morning, at the same time that Molly was making her confession, at the same time the son was sitting with his father feeding ducks, another son was standing at the entrance to the mines. The gap had been covered with a new gate and Tom spent a moment unlocking the padlock with the key that only he and a few others had. He was wearing hiking gear, had a small backpack over one shoulder, and had a light strapped to his head.

Today was the day he would bring his mother home.

ACKNOWLEDGEMENTS

I've had three teachers over the years, two in high school and one in college, who had profound impacts on my writing, particularly on the confidence that what I write might be interesting to somebody other than myself. Everything I write is, in one way or another, written for Mary Ann, Kathryn, and Rich.

In *As Good as it Gets*, Jack Nicholson's character says, "You make me want to be a better man." That's how I feel about my kids. That's what they give me. They are three very different people, but with a common, regularly demonstrated belief that the way to take power away from the darkness is to laugh at it.

So, every night at dinner, Barb makes us heathens start with telling the family one thing we're grateful for. It's annoying and I'm immeasurably grateful to have as a partner somebody who makes me stop, think, and verbalize. Somebody who takes me out of my comfort zone.

When Barb and I met in 2009, everything was ordered in my life. I had a system (and a spotless apartment, FYI). I also had a few thousand words and a bunch of notes to a book I had been "writing" since 1991. We moved in together the next year and she brought Sunshine with her. My first real pet. A chonky, loud, demanding, heart-thieving monster of a cat. Addie, the kinda, sorta shepherd/husky/rando mix followed along soon after. As did massive tumbleweeds of hair.

Eleven years later, Sunshine and Addie have moved on, taking pieces of us when they left, but smaller pieces than the ones they added to us while they were here.

Not to worry thought, because chaos still reigns. In addition to my daughter and one of my sons now living with us (the other son is in the Army, returning from Iraq as I write this), we have four cats and a German Shepherd. And the tumbleweeds multiply.

The point is that, in this chaos to which Barb was a primary contributor, I somehow finished this book, writing more in one three-year stretch than I had the previous twenty. The chaos that I had so carefully built walls to keep out apparently somehow allowed or motivated or energized or somethinged me to actually write, without the air quotes.

So, simply, thank you honey.

On to copyediting. Apparently, I'm terrible. Quinn and Barb both made critical contributions, especially with earlier drafts, but this book wouldn't be in the shape it is without Mike Tyson's (not that one) astonishing attention for detail. Having had him as a friend, correcting me, since 1991, I shouldn't have been surprised. In fact, he hasn't looked at this section yet, so I'm certain to get an email about excessive comma usage. Seriously, Mike, thank, you. Also, please note that any errors remaining in the book are likely due to my ignoring his advice.

Last thing. In the disclaimer, I noted that "Any resemblance to actual persons, bla, bla, bla." And I'm serious. That's not you in the book. Me neither. But there is one exception. It is obvious to anyone who ever met her that the Sunshine in the book is as true to life as our real Sunshine who as I could make her.

ABOUT THE AUTHOR

Rob Simpson

Rob Simpson has worked for the National Security Agency, both in uniform and as a civilian, for almost 35 years and in all that time he has never, not once, been as cool as that sentence sounds. As proof of that, he is currently the Librarian at NSA's National Cryptologic Museum.

None of the opinions or attitudes represented in this book should be construed as being those of NSA, the Department of Defense, or the United States government.